CALL ME ISHTAR

OTHER TITLES IN THE LIBRARY OF MODERN JEWISH LITERATURE

Anna in Chains. Merrill Joan Gerber

At the Center. Norma Rosen

Bloodshed and Three Novellas. Cynthia Ozick

The Cannibal Galaxy. Cynthia Ozick

The Empire of Kalman the Cripple. Yehuda Elberg

Focus. Arthur Miller

God's Ear. Rhoda Lerman

The Island Within. Ludwig Lewisohn

The Jewish War. Tova Reich

John and Anzia: An American Romance. Norma Rosen

Lazar Malkin Enters Heaven. Steve Stern

Leah's Journey. Gloria Goldreich

Levitation: Five Fictions. Cynthia Ozick

My Own Ground. Hugh Nissenson

O My America! Johanna Kaplan

The Pagan Rabbi and Other Stories. Cynthia Ozick

Plague of Dreamers. Steve Stern

The Rose Rabbi. Daniel Stern

Ship of the Hunted. Yehuda Elberg

Shira. S. Y. Agnon

The Stolen Jew. Jay Neugeboren

The Suicide Academy. Daniel Stern

While the Messiah Tarries. Melvin Jules Bukiet

CALL ME ISHTAR

Rhoda Lerman

 Syracuse University Press

Copyright © 1973 by Rhoda Lerman

All Rights Reserved

First Syracuse University Press Edition 1998

98 99 00 01 02 03   6 5 4 3 2 1

First published by Doubleday & Company in 1973.

The paper used in this publication meets the minimum requirements of American National Standard for Information Sciences—Permanence of Paper for Printed Library Materials, ANSI Z39.48-1984. ∞

Library of Congress Cataloging-in-Publication Data

Lerman, Rhoda.
    Call me Ishtar / Rhoda Lerman. — 1st Syracuse University Press ed.
       p.   cm. — (The Library of Modern Jewish Literature)
    ISBN 0-8156-0533-1 (pbk. : alk. paper)
    1. Ishtar (Assyro-Babylonian Deity)—Fiction. 2. Suburban life—United States—Fiction.   3. Housewives—United States—Fiction.
4. Women—United States—Fiction.   I. Title.   II. Series.
PS3562.E68C35 1998
813'.54—dc21   98-3287

Manufactured in the United States of America

For Julie Coopersmith

APPLICATION FOR EMPLOYMENT

NAME: Ishtar

OCCUPATION: Mother Goddess

MARITAL STATUS: Mother/Harlot/Maiden/Wife

PRESENT ADDRESS: In transit. (Temporary address; Syracuse, New York)

AGE: [symbols] ($E=MC^2$) ($F=MA$) ?

CHILDREN: same as above

EDUCATIONAL DATA: self-taught

SOCIAL/COMMUNITY ACTIVITIES: Laying of cornerstones, setting of foundations, sacred prostitution (organizer, etc., etc...)

SPECIAL HONORS: Star of David, Star of Solomon, Star of Bethlehem, Eastern Star (Grand Worthy Matron)

RECORD OF EMPLOYMENT: (Please record employment dates in chronological order)

TITLE: Queen of Heaven

PLACE OF EMPLOYMENT: Galaxy

DATES: 4,800,000,000 - 9000 B.C.

MAJOR RESPONSIBILITIES: Fashioning stars, worlds, suns, people (everything, etc.) Prime moving

REASON FOR TERMINATION: Project completed

SALARY: Original Title

TITLE: Angel of Death

PLACE OF EMPLOYMENT: Heaven

DATES: April 9000 B.C.

MAJOR RESPONSIBILITIES: General conflagration, boils, etc...

REASON FOR TERMINATION: Reorganization of Personnel

SALARY: Peace/Quiet/Rest - Sabbatical

TITLE: Queen of Heaven

PLACE OF EMPLOYMENT: above

DATES: 9000 B.C. - 4501 B.C.

MAJOR RESPONSIBILITIES: Birth, love, death, disease, seasons, etc.

REASON FOR TERMINATION: Company failed to maintain initial commitment

SALARY: Adoration/Worship/Respect

TITLE: Angel of Death

PLACE OF EMPLOYMENT: above

DATES: April 4501 B.C.

MAJOR RESPONSIBILITIES: Flood engineer, Passover, Killing of 1st born, plagues

REASON FOR TERMINATION: Cut-back in territory and personnel

SALARY: Peace/Quiet

TITLE: Queen of Heaven

PLACE OF EMPLOYMENT: Heaven

DATES: 4501 B.C. - 1350 B.C.

MAJOR RESPONSIBILITIES: Birth, love, death augury, disease, changing of seasons, alphabets

REASON FOR TERMINATION: Personality differences (Moses & Monotheism)

SALARY: Adoration, cakes and incense

TITLE: Whore of Babylon (unemployed)

PLACE: wilderness

MAJOR RESPONSIBILITIES: Birth, love, disease, changing of seasons

REASON FOR TERMINATION: Still working

SALARY: Scorn and Calumny

DO NOT WRITE BELOW. THIS SPACE FOR OFFICIAL USE ONLY

To Whom It May Concern:
   What am I doing here? It is very simple. Your world is a mess.
   A mess.
   Your laws are inhuman. Your religion is without love. Your love is without religion and both, undirected, are useless. Your pastrami is stringy, and I am bored by your degeneracy.
   But what's a mother to do? I'm here to bring it all back together again. I'll come and straighten things out for you. I will choose an image here to do my work. To do your work. I shall spray your dusty corners with Lysol so you will find knowledge, stitch up those parts of your souls which have lost each other so that man knows what is womanly in him and woman knows what is manly in her. You hate, screw, war, starve and die without knowing me. The closets of your souls are empty of power and love. I do not like to come down here and work. There are no men here for me and I become, as a fish beyond the sea, hungry. And when I am overworked and hungry, I am mean. And when I am mean, I am destructive So watch it. You are going to have to show me some respect this time, or you will all be impotent and once more the world will come grinding to an end and that end, as in your own grinding, which I have witnessed often, uncomfortably, will have no ecstasy.
   Excuse me. I begin my threats again. I must remember, this time, that if I want you to become more divine, I must be more humane.
   Somehow, I will distribute the wonders of my baking to you, to heal and balance and restore to you the powers that once were yours in the antique. I have always been the connection between heaven and earth, between man and woman, between

thought and act, between everything. If your philosophers insist the world is a dichotomy, tell them that two plus two don't make four unless something brings them together. The connection has been lost. But I'm back. Don't worry. I am going to give you the secrets this time. You are not ready, but then you may never be and whatever will I do with them then? I must warn you I am jealous and selfish. However, I am really all that you have. I am one and my name is one and there shall be no one before me. I will forgive you anything, though, if you will love me. Cordially yours,

    I remain,
    Your Mother/Harlot/Maiden/Wife
    (The Queen of Heaven)
P.S. Call me Ishtar

*And She spread it before me and it was written
Within and without this roll of a book.*
A roll of a book was therein, and there was written lamentations, mourning and woe.
"Moreover," She said unto me, "Son of Man, eat that thou findest; eat this roll and go speak unto the House of Israel."
So I opened my mouth and She caused me to eat that roll. And She said unto me, "Son of Man, cause thy belly to eat. Fill thy bowels with this roll that I give thee."
Then did I eat it; and it was in my mouth as honey for sweetness.

"She was spreading herself like the night over the universe and found no god to lie with."
                                                           Anaïs Nin

1

I am civilized. I am discontent. I have a hungry cunt. Truly. You've seen me. A sad face through the window of a rosewood metal Plymouth station wagon crossing the Robert Moses Power Access Highway. My home is rosewood also. You may have seen my home featured in a GE ad for up to date products in color with my red, white and blue dashiki dress and my long striped hair and the seven members of my rock and roll band which we manage for fun and possible profit. They are not rosewood. They are olive and sallow and one, the leader, in the dark, sitting up in bed, in shadow profile, looks like a lizard. His straight North Italy profile suddenly slips into a thick neck so that his chin, although square, becomes saurian. I am mad for him but I suspect him of being unclean. Robert is my husband. The band sleeps late on Sundays, until four or five. I have nothing else to do on Sundays so I go with Robert to his factory, limited, in Canada.

Robert's line is polyesters. He reduces them into functional fibers. I have been in his small factory on Sundays only. I and he and all his workers, everyone, must wash their hands before entering the loom room. Robert was once a very religious man, an Orthodox Jew. Now he is only very ethical. He wears suits of olive whipcord with vests and has his rules of order, which are formidable, scratched into the tablets of his checkbooks. The factory is in Canada although we live in upstate New York. That is why we cross the Power Highway over the Falls. And on this scenic tour across the power dam and atomic energy plants, I watch out the window of the station wagon into other station wagons and sports cars to see if my destiny has arrived yet or has passed me by.

Is it too much to hope that you've read Norman Brown? It would help.

Robert has made enough money turning luminous threads of polyesters, moondrift, wrapped, ectoplasmic, around man-sized wooden bobbins into carpet fibers, yarn for men's socks, ladies' stockings, paper pulp and golf balls. He crimps, twists, stretches, cuts and shrinks the silken cords on the torture racks he himself designs. When his machines are dormant on Sundays I comb my fingers through the silken cords lying taut, waiting for their new shapes. The threads are beautiful. Do you know the legend of the white mare of Ireland? Her foals were extraordinary horses, but an indiscreet act by the farmer who owned them would cause them to gallop off to the sea, and the white mare herself would come only to the true king. If the true king made love to her, he would then be initiated into the kingship of the entire land. I have seen her in dreams, the same luminous threads of her long tail burning in the moonlight as she runs along the black sea. Of course, this is no reason to turn off the polyester machines. But it is why I go to the factory only on Sundays. I don't like his machines. Robert, watching me at his looms, drifting my fingers through his fairy threads and considering me mad, will finally, like Rumpelstiltskin, stomp his size fourteen Hush-puppy into the concrete floor and yell through the echoing loom room. "God damn it, Ishtar, you'll ruin the tension!" But I have already guessed his secret name. It is Moses.

On some Sundays I stop in time before he becomes angry and then the drive home across the chasm is pleasant. On other Sundays I make knots while he sorts through orders, invoices and machinery designs in his glassed cubicle just beyond the looms. Sometimes, if my child, who is seven years old now, hasn't come with us, on the way home Robert will touch me into orgasm with one hand while he drives. I try to arrange my climax for the moment we cross the dam. The customs officers, trained to watch for suspicious nervous twitches, are forever suspecting us of contraband and rifling through the pubic bundles of crimped and sliced fiber samples in the rear of the station wagon. I manage to contain my trembling until we are distinctly above the chasm and the power dam is in sight. It is rather a game with us and it is why Robert invites me along even though I tie knots in his looms. When he is really angry he won't play the game at all. Often I tie knots. Then I pass leisurely and unmolested through customs and I am home quickly to my son. Whom I adore.

It is, of course, my power which Robert Moses can not touch, that enormous chasm down there over which he has built his bridges and his trap doors and his harnesses for my energies, around, over and above, but never within, for he has neither touched nor loosed nor used my power. It is dammed now, functioning, limited as his factory, to my motherhood. It is still waiting. Knowing this, he explodes into tempestuous rages or sinks into sullen dank caves of withdrawal. I prefer the rages. I can not predict either. So I stare out the window sadly, hoping I will be found and touched with grace. Opened finally and alive. But each year, as I wait, I am destroyed. Huge rocks detach and roll from my superb cliffs. I turn on the air conditioning and roll up the windows to protect my complexion from the dirt of the highway and preserve myself as we cross the Niagara. I wait for my destiny as my sides cave in. I hate it of course.

Once, recently, I wrote a check from his checkbook in red ink. The rule is thou shalt not write in red ink. Thou shalt write in blue ink and then thou shalt take whatever monies are needed. I don't wish to be humorous about this for Robert is very serious about the rules. I wrote in red ink because the red pen was closest and Robert Moses became ugly and loomed large in our bedroom when he discovered what I had done. He is very handsome and not at all vain about himself but very particular about the colors of his checkbook and he is very good in bed, quite nice to me, waiting always for me because he is in such good control of most things, so when his checkbook turns up red-inked, he becomes understandably angry. I try not to laugh. I do not cry often either. I choose to ignore his large looming and go to my red and orange den with my black labrador, who lays his great wolf head in my lap. I read Martin Buber to forget Moses. He writes that within every stone is a divine spark waiting to be discovered, that man alone can let loose. I do not know if I am Man or Stone. I think I am more. That is why I look out the station wagon window. And I cry loosely over the book. I do not cry over the checkbook or the fact that soon I will climb into our angry king-size bed. I cry because perhaps I should cry over the checkbook and the bed and because I ought to concern myself with red inks and blue inks. Then he would make love to me and I would be forgiven. It is so easy to love the dog whose head lies heavy in my lap and whose sad brown eyes watch me cry. I wipe my eyes with my fingers and dry them in his fur and go to the bedroom to reseal the covenant. You know how I feel.

But then you have heard me singing "My Johnny Lies Over the Ocean" under the water in my bathtub, soaking and humming water songs and listening to my own pulsating echoes and to hear me, you know that I am joyous also. I make my son laugh. At times I can make Robert laugh.

Other times I can not. Years ago, I heard Robert telling a tight group of men at a cocktail party for carpet dealers and manufacturers, some wearing white wool socks and Robert Hall clothes, some in Barney's sharkskin, the most interesting story I had ever heard about his business. "The men in the backroom," he told them, "opened a bale of polyester rejects from Akron—tires—and there was a Chinaman's head in the middle of the bale." We had a terrible hissing fight in the cloakroom because he wouldn't repeat the story for me.

"I just want to know if there was blood on the polyester or just the head by itself."

"Drop it. It's not a story for you. You don't have to know everything." His lips shrunk like prune fingers too long in the tub and in the blacklights of the bar the fake front sugarcube tooth from his football accident gleamed wildly and menacingly.

I laughed lightly. "Aah, once a queen, always a queen." It is a line I use often to soften him and he laughs at me for then I am not serious. But this time I had stepped too deeply into his territory and he walked away with his easy sexy roll that betrays me, always. He is not my destiny, I told someone's sheared beaver. I've known that for a long time. But he might be my destiny if I'm not careful. And if he's not careful, perhaps I'll be his destiny. We are both very careful. But I am lucky. He is only smart. I had two drinks that night and spent time in the parking lot tongue kissing a dark faced sharkskin-suited retired colonel who sold oriental rugs by mail order. It is why I don't drink. Scotch opens my sluiceways. I have a self-developed allergy to alcohol. One eye aches and my nose runs. I borrow Robert's generous handkerchief. When I am due for an affair, my allergy disappears. It is a protective device.

We all have protective devices. Robert, for instance, has never seen death. He has managed by disengaging himself at the proper times. Often, as with his own parents, well in advance. Perhaps it makes him feel immortal. I don't know. He remarked when his grandmother died in an old-age home, "I'm sorry I didn't get to know her." He has never mentioned her since. I of course have seen death. My father died after he had a tooth pulled and he called me to his bed to get my mother quickly as his heart strangled. And my grandmother, who I am in so many ways, is at my shoulder always. Mrs. Morin has seen her there as has Mrs. Broga and Mrs. Tice. Mrs. Morin has also seen my grandfather in spirit. She brought him to me when I sat in her small upstairs sewing room and she rocked in her chair and clutched her throat. "An architect who can't talk. Do you know him?" My grandfather, who lost the race between the Chrysler Building and the Bank of Manhattan to build the tallest building in the world, hemorrhaged for six months into vegetation and wrote painful notes on scratch pads that looked something like I LOVE YOU but may have been something about his bed sores. It is not really Robert's fault that he has not seen death. It is not his fault that he has not been at home when each of my dogs has been struck down one by one on our country road. Perhaps it is well. I don't know what he would do in the face of death. In the face of birth, I looked up at him from my cribbed recovery bed and thought he was my father returned, until he began to retch and vomit while the nurse pushed on my stomach and removed the excess bloods from my vagina. I became a mother. He did not become a father. You understand.

I have only seen Robert cry once. We were new lovers and I threatened to leave because of his great anger. I never left. I have never since threatened and he has never since cried. I don't think he would any longer. I have no desire to leave. I just think there is something more. I have a cousin who would like to die. She is young and lovely. A handsome Greek offered to kill her and she went happily to his student apartment in Paris but he only made rude love to her. Perhaps this is why the severed slant-eyed head . . . I have it down to a simple hieroglyphic . . . two slant lines and a question mark for a nose . . . that I sketch at the bottom of each calendar month, on Robert's King Size Catalogue and all over the telephone books . . . annoys Robert. He may not care to recognize the power of death.

Having participated in birth and death so intimately, I am acutely aware of my own ripeness. Is it too much to hope that you have read Brown's *Life Against Death*? He is wrong, of course, about some things. But still he leaves me with a hungry cunt. That is crude although men discuss their needs as lightly as I request a Kleenex. However, if you have even a cursory knowledge of Freud you will recognize that I am

civilized, discontent and hungry. I want to be resurrected. My way. I am growing old before I grow perverse. I wish to return to polymorphous sex, anyway, all over.
 No hand across the border. No single soul. No one place. I want my back scratched and my hair smoothed with a coarse masculine paw. Raw. No Corn Huskers Lotion for me, nor do I weep for a Tammuz long gone. No Vaseline. I have a wonderful cat named Blue, who, if he were six feet tall, I would run away with. His brother, Green, and he lie on my bed all day and lick each other. They are orange tigers. So is their mother, Tuesday. If Blue were six foot and could support me, I'm sure I would leave. He walks beautifully also, with four feet and a marvelous upright tail which tickles my underchin as he crosses, proprietarily, my chest. Blue and Green hunt all night and leap from odd places, meeting in mid-air. Blue is a cat and I am a woman. We don't mess with each other.

2

Once upon a time when the Great Goddess, Ishtar, loved and ruled the earth and all of humankind were women and a simple chemical additive could cause reproduction of more women, an error was made. It did not indeed seem at the time a great error. It was rather a chromosomal deficiency. One of the children born was a mutant, tiny horns, too many aggressive parts in its soul, not enough intuitive parts and an odd roseate stump between its legs. Its infant features, however, were soft and pure in the image of the Great Goddess. The infant was brought to Ishtar.

Ishtar looked upon its face and spoke. "Send it away to the sea. It is necessary that it should not live."

The mother cried.

Ishtar spoke. "I see the world plunged into greed, grief, war and destruction. I see the end of civilization and the burning of our libraries. The infant is to be sent to the sea."

Wrapped in a reed basket, the infant was floated down river toward the sea. At a bend in the river, the basket was caught by bullrushes and a wolf mother dragged the infant to its lair in the wilderness far beyond the walls.

The mutant grew. At first the wolf mother suckled the infant and then lay with it. Its limbs grew thicker and hairier. The other cubs nipped at its uprightness and wouldn't play with it for its deformities. The mutant ate raw flesh and fondled other beasts as he grew. Shepherd girls, returning from the pastures, reported that it had leaped upon them in odd, heavy ways. It was last seen running across the steppe after a pack of wolves.

Slowly the women forgot about the mutant. With Ishtar's guidance they continued about their business of creating civilization as had been decreed.

Many years later, the mutant appeared at the city gates, large, bestial and clumsy.

"I can perform funny tricks with my strange stump," he called to a gentle long-necked poetess writing under the shade of a fig tree. "I want to come into the city," he called to a stately group of matrons of Law passing along the avenue in their robes. They ignored him. "Let me in or I'll break your wall down."

The mutant huffed and puffed and kicked at a cornerstone. The poetess laid a finger to her lips. "Hush, I am composing alphabets."

"Let me in. I belong in the city."

"Nay," answered the gentle poetess, "you have eaten raw flesh. You belong with the beasts."

"I'll tend your flocks and sharpen your nubs and bring you delicate grains from afar and repair your city walls and install your air conditioners and do funny tricks with my strange stump if you will let me in."

The matrons, listening, nodded to the poetess. The poetess opened the gates. In return for his labors and funny tricks, the matrons promised to civilize him.

They have never succeeded.

Eventually the walls were kicked in.

To Whom It May Concern:
In your Bible, such as it is, the Story of Job must be placed first. Then the story of Noah. Then the Genesis. First record the fire, then record the flood and then record the new beginning of your age. The entire story of Job takes place in a cave where he and his few friends hang from ropes, since there is nothing solid for their feet. They discuss why I did this thing and whether I did it because of wickedness. I, raging outside, burning animals, uprooting mountains, drying up seas, have missed a few men. Job is brave enough to go outside of the cave and ask why. He is afraid I will swallow him. But I don't. I tell him of the wonders that have issued from my womb and that it is not his place to question and he is lucky to be alive, that he is no more wicked than anyone else and I did not intend him to witness the conflagration or to live through another one. I had overlooked him. I had overlooked groups here and there. They hid in the caves and tried to keep records. The world around them was gone. Job is antique. You don't think really that the language of that poem could be inspired by a case of boils?

This was the major destruction of my heavenly body, when I reordered the universe and created new forms by the nuclear power of my fires. Job, torn and wounded after he left the cave, did not interest me amorously and I simply used the old method to reproduce. It's much easier. I sincerely hope this will clear the matter up for you. Please advise if there are further questions.

Love,
Ishtar

Void, you know.

It was the beginning again. I've forgotten most of the details and your Bible with its silly comments about cubits and gopher wood is no help. I believe I have already explained to you that Chaos is predetermined. The earth was without form. There was no light. There was no darkness either. It was spring of the world year and I had swept away all that was unholy, unruly, imperfect and noisy. How oft is the candle of the wicked put out? And how oft cometh their destruction upon them? The earth shall rise up against you . . . that kind of number I had done.

This last age I had worked too big. The preponderous beasts and low-browed men had ceased to be amusing. I had not created a proper balance between beast and vegetation. Half of the pea-brained dinosaurs had died of constipation. The smell was ungodly. But the people did nothing for it. They gloried in my ecstasies and forgot me. The men were aggressive and mean. The women, tricky and devious. No washing of hands, no dedication of first fruits, no playing of Ishtar instruments, no baking cakes to me, no dedication of sexual act. I couldn't remember the last time a man had poured his semen in my holy groves to nourish my trees. Selfish.

Well, below, the waters shimmered in my terrible red light. Here and there floated old forms of animals and men. The waters were murky with the churning and burning and shit. Soon I would have a good mulch for the new plantings. In the meantime, I had washed my hair, put lotion on my parched skin and lay down to rest before regenerating everything. Just as I closed my eyes, I heard a noise from below.

Void is void. There should be no noise. I thundereth marvelously from my golden couch. "That's all she wrote!" The noise stopped, then picked up once again. Tiny feet on wood. I cursed and descended, changing into a great raven with terrible jaws of death and destruction. I was ready to tear eyes and throats. I lifted the darkness from the face of the earth and, swooping low, saw four little red eyes wide with appropriate terror. Coming closer, I could see their small furry unusual bodies huddled on that utterly ridiculous boat. I have no idea what gopher wood is. I knew it was Noah's boat and I had been foolish enough to teach him shape-changing. You will remember that his people were closer in time and spirit to me and could affect some of my powers. They were directly related to the Tuatha de Danaan of early Ireland. The animals, whatever category they were, scurried away as soon as I saw them. I had to descend into the murky depths, the molten glass waters, etc., etc. I could see nothing. I changed to a dove so as not to frighten them away again. I remembered the light. "Let there be light," I called. Sun, stars and moon I remembered, but still I could see nothing of Noah and his stupid dull wife. I'm certain this was her idea to outsmart me.

"It's all over," I shouted from Chaos. "Come out, come out, wherever you are."

I blew the winds to the corners of the earth. Nothing. "Why do you persist? There's nothing here for you. You will be archaic. I have no time to turn over rocks and mountains seeking you." Anyway there were no rocks and mountains.

I heard their footsteps again, larger, heavier. I did the "let there be dry land" bit and caught them on a hilltop. I went to touch them with my rod of destruction but Noah looked up at me with those sad little eyes and twitching whiskers and grew his ears, as I watched, hovering, a good six inches into the air, then hopped down the hill with his wife. I held back laughter. Where next I saw them they had changed again, extending tails, adding legs, shortening fur and I each time changed into a new shape to run after them. "Let there be grass," I called out marvelously so they would be confused. I was also. I did not know what grass was yet. I changed shape into a wolf-like creature. But suddenly, as I found them, they were different, high, long-legged beasts leaping on hillocks far from me, gracefully. I wanted to leap with them.

"Noah," I called, "why are you running from me? I shall consume your bones. Your seed shall not knit. What will you eat?" Oh! Grass.

As I neared them, they spotted themselves, added leather, subtracted tails, multiplied joints, added spikes. I was fascinated. I changed into a still larger creature with legs like cedar trees and an indestructible skin—not to be outdone. I tried to stomp them. Stomp. Stomp. I lengthened my nose. As soon as I was ready to stomp them, snatch them, sever them, electrocute them, they would change. I had to laugh at their deplorable fantasies. Soon, jaws open, tusks at the ready, I was almost upon them but the new shape was so utterly graceful I could not tear them. Truly something in the nuclear blast as I shifted poles this time must have extended the edge of Noah's consciousness. He was far more imaginative than he had been before, with a good sense of aesthetics. Usually I burn up so much oxygen, aside from the radiation which completely overturns the genetic character of the age, the minds simply disintegrate and the few remaining creatures become low-level cave dwellers. I try not to miss anyone but they do have ways to hide. I was sorry I ever taught shape-changing to this Noah. I was tired. I went back up to my couch in Chaos, yawned and stretched. There was still time since there was no time yet and I would destroy them later. I watched Noah in his new shape. His loins were skillfully sleek and lean. They shone with perspiration as he raced. His ankles were thin and his parts were voluptuous. "Hey, Noah," I called from Chaos. "Let us be fruitful and multiply."

He stopped and communicated with his wife. Damn.

"Here." I plucked a feather and dropped it toward them as a sign of peace. "Tell her to go back to the ship and sweep up whatever is unholy with this feather. Tell her to sweep up everything into a wooden spoon." They argued. Jewish women, you know, still do this on Passover, sweeping up the unholy food before the Night of Watching . . . . feather and spoon. "Send your dull and stupid wife to the ship or I'll take away the sun. I've got a bottle of strawberry wine, Noah," I called charmingly. "Meet me on the mountaintop." He turned his wife into a large marsupial with a pocket in her belly and she hopped away unhappily. "You watch," I warned her, "and I'll turn you to salt."

I brought down my seven cakes which man must eat before he knows the Goddess and stretched out on the top of Ararat. Noah was naturally unsure of himself in my presence, but we drank and giggled until our heads were confused. We laughed a great deal and played with the clay around us, nipping off pieces. I teased him into shaping something foolish and ridiculous and if it made me laugh, I would breathe life into it.

"What shall we make, Ishtar?" Noah now addressed me familiarly, for he had known me by this time. I used his semen to plant flowers which he bundled into my hair.

"Hay while the sun shines." I made honeyplants, caperplants, grains.

"I can't think of anything." Noah braided my hair and blew on my neck.

I twisted bluebells into his buttonholes. Sorry about the buttonholes.

I found it difficult to think also. "Big," I said foolishly. "Big and blue with, with . . . Oh God, I can just imagine it how stupid it will be . . . with tiny eyes."

He nipped off a large hunk of clay and rolled it. I am really ashamed that I, Progenitress of Heroes and Mother of the Gods etc., etc., could have done what we did. I who lay cornerstones and set seasons. I . . .

We made a whale.

Our sides split with laughter. The wine we emptied into each other's throats and with his shoulder, Noah slid the whale off the mountaintop into the sea. The splash was wonderful.

"Do you want another, Ishtar?"

"I guess so." I conceded. We made pairs of things, huge,

tiny, capricious things. We were screwing around and we were soused. Totally soused. Noah was good and imaginative.
"We must be serious."
We passed the wine. I lengthened the course of the sun. The earth was warm beneath us. I nipped clay. Noah nipped clay and as children we modeled in pairs. We changed form often ourselves.
I a cow.
He a bull.
"Let's do it now, Ishtar."
I a ewe.
He a ram.
"Now?" I asked. "Can you still?"
I a mare.
He a stallion.
I a lioness.
He a lion.
"Again?" We spoke together.
"Ah, Noah, I am wasted. No more." I sighed prettily.
"We could try."
"There are enough," I said, pointing to our models, which we lay on a new scarp of schist, later to be called Precambrian. We had a zoo of creatures. I lengthened the shadows over them and they grew and I looked upon them with the Eye of Life and they lived. "I've had enough and you have no more. Advance when you are winning; retreat when you are losing."
"We could try, Ishtar."
"Try and try again is the worst form of hubris, Noah. Shall we dance?"
We danced to "By the Time I get to Phoenix." We danced very slowly in the sunlight across the scarp and where our shadows fell, forms sprang up in pairs and danced as we did, slowly circling with us, softly not to disturb. I smiled upon them and they disappeared by twos into the new forests and the new seas and the new plains and into those places

where they would find comfort with each other for the night. It was one Creation I relish whenever I remember it.

The present position of the neutron star that survives the supernova is Right Ascension 08^h33^m7, declination $-45°00'$ (epoch 1950). In 9000 B.C. the supernova would have passed overhead at latitude 48° South; at other times, the most northerly latitude at which object would have passed overhead was 37° South. Hence, the Southern Hemisphere would be the Prime area to search for possible evidence. However, Northern Hemisphere records from Europe or the Orient, where the supernova may have been seen near the horizon, might also exist.

Hi. This is what everyone watched for on Pass Over. Sometimes I came peacefully with milk and honey, manna and dew. And sometimes I came burning and ending things. That little Easter sunrise service you have was pure gratitude.

Besides the archaeological interest involved in deciphering any records of the Vela X supernova, the event may have biological import. It has been suggested that cosmic rays and X rays from supernovae have had genetic impact on the flow of evolution. It would certainly have been a spectacular event in the experience of anyone who witnessed it. Does anyone recall what gopher wood was?

"Listen, love, so we can remember, I'll do one that looks like you," I offered.

"And I want one that looks like you." We agreed then to reproduce. Among other reasons, it is why I feel kindness when I look upon my people.

We were wasted. Noah looked down upon himself hanging limply, what had been so voluptuous. When he recovered from his drunkenness and found himself in the arms of a kangaroo, he remembered what he had done with the Angel of Death . . . and castrated himself.

Well, blame it on the kangaroo. I didn't ask for it. I think he, if I recall correctly—these things have a way of kaleidoscoping—tossed it into the sea where the whale was. It gave rise to all sorts of myths and silly stories, ending with Pinocchio becoming a real man through my intervention. Which has always been my task. Nobody cut off his *nose* in those days. But the stories are always changed for the children's sake. It's about time you grew up and demanded the real skinny dip.

Ishtar closed her eyes, curled her tiny clawed feet under her thighs and slept. A great blue-green serpent slid over her shoulder and slept.

In the newly formed desert beyond Egypt, Moses smashed her Golden Calf. The terrified people cried to bake cakes to their Queen of Heaven and pray to her image but Moses screamed, "Thou shalt not; thou shalt not. For that is the Law." And El spoke, "Thou shalt worship no one before Me." But they had worshiped and loved the Great Mother, Ishtar, before him and they cried to her. They wandered in the empty desert under empty skies while Moses, nightly, carrying his snake banner and shouting, "Thou shalt not" over his shoulder, disappeared into a palm grove four miles beyond a new and nameless river, followed a thin beckoning hand, and lay with Ishtar. He whispered huskily to her long curls, touching her divine breasts. "Queen of Heaven, send the Fiery Cloud to Canaan."

She lay weak and pale. "My Star has fallen, Moses. It is astray, turning itself against time. It no longer lights the skies of night. The womb of the heavens is covered and hidden. The universe is barren. The people tremble."

"Rest, my Queen."

"But Venus falls from the sky. She burns smoke and death. The people no longer pray to The Star, Venus. It is the end. Help me, Moses. Tell my people I am with them still."

"It is my time, Queen of Heaven. Your astrology is done for. Spread your legs."

"Moses, your El is merely a small time weather god with an unruly temper. Choosing him is a great error. I warn you, Moses."

"We will refashion him in our image. Man matters. Your Time is ended. Please spread your legs. It will be dawn soon and tomorrow we rewrite Genesis."

"Be gentle, this time, Moses. I am now weak."

"You? With your filthy perversions and your insatiable passions. The Whore of Babylon is weak?"

"My Star has fallen, Moses. My people no longer look to The Star. My people have lost the connection between Heaven and Earth."

"Spread your legs, Ishtar. I will be gentle if you send The Cloud to Canaan."

"Just watch the horns, Moses Mutant, watch the horns."

An erect army of stone phalli thrust into a menstrual sky. The sun plunged, red purple, into its dying womb. The sea hissed distantly at the edges of a wind driven Breton peninsula. Moist black clots of night clouds drifted around the carved glans and over the sacred earth mound.

This was Carnac.

Beneath her mound, Ishtar sat in her Star room and rubbed an apple against her cheek in thought. At her back a stone slab carved at its base with five snakes, dancing tails intertwined eternally, covered the wall. Five polished stone axes, cutting side up, were stuck in the earth. Ishtar sliced the apple neatly on a stone axe and, with her forefinger, traced the star on each half of the apple. She bent to the hearth's light and filled the five points with drops of deadly nightshade, sealed the apple and held it to an eight foot star painted above the hearth. The red and purpled paints were mildewed, the gold leaf figures of her warriors and demons distorted beneath the grime of centuries and the uneven firelight. Ishtar held the apple to each point on the star, heavenward point last.

At daybreak, cold, she dressed herself as a country woman, plaited her hair into fat henna braids, painted her face with age and went from Carnac over the Seven Mountains to the cottage of the seven dwarfs. She knocked at the door.

Snow White opened the top half of the door. "I cannot let anyone in. The seven dwarfs have forbidden me. I am quite busy tidying their beds."

"Are you a prisoner, then, here?"

"Oh, no! They are very kind to me."

"Aah, that too may be a prison. I offer you from my basket a lovely apple. An apple of wisdom." Ishtar held out the apple.

"I am forbidden. I cannot speak to you."

"Tell, Child," Ishtar leered at Snow White. "Do you sleep with *all* those ugly little men?"

"Please go away, old Mother."

"It's all the same to me," answered Ishtar, half turning. "I shall rid myself of my lovely apples soon. Aaah." Ishtar turned back. "I shall *give* you one."

Snow White stretched out her hand greedily to take the apple. She slammed the half door closed before Ishtar could speak the directions for eating an apple of wisdom. Inside there was a choking noise and a tumbling of furniture. Ishtar gazed at the closed shutter with a dreadful look and laughed bitterly.

"Foolish child. There must be ritual in all this."

A prince woke Snow White from her drugged sleep. He took her home to his castle and told the entire kingdom she would be his new Queen and the old Queen would die. A soldier rode ahead of the wedding party commanding the people to kneel for the new Queen as she passed through the street. Ishtar, hearing, uttered a curse. At first she would not go to the wedding but she had no peace. Jealous and despairing, her stomach acid with anger, Ishtar entered the banquet hall of the castle that had once been hers.

The new Queen giggled over a tumbler of ale. "Keep your wisdom, Old Mother."

The prince motioned to a page. Iron slippers had been put upon the fire and they were brought in with hot tongs and set before Ishtar. She was forced to put on the hot shoes and dance until she dropped dead.

Wearily, Ishtar returned to Carnac. She wandered through the stones stretching into the moist sky. The ocean still hissed. As the moon slid behind a mountain of cumulus clouds, Ishtar rested her forehead against the rough flank of a phallus. "Aaah, what will be-

come of my children? Ritual must precede wisdom. Where is my Star?" She lifted her long woolen skirts and slid her vulva down the seaslimy ridge of a leaning stone. She reached her ivory arms to the sky, shivering, longing for her Star to return. Then she descended into the long barrow under the earth leading to her chambers.

Someday she would find the right woman to take over the wisdom. And the world. She curled up on a stone and slept before her Star.

3

Ishtar sat on a bench in Miami's Bayfront Park. She smiled at the purple silvered pigeons cooing at her sandaled feet. A young man wandered along the palm lined walk, into a grove of blood red hibiscus, and she watched him stretch his mouth to accommodate a small gleaming gun. The pigeon perched on Ishtar's ivory shoulder jumped slightly at the explosion. Someone called the Law. The Law arrived in a truck with cages, careening down the narrow palm path into the grove where the young man sat upright, tomato red, against a palm tree trunk. Two policemen jumped from the truck.

"Holy Mother uh God."

Ishtar, unseen, nodded graciously.

"He wants a blanket, Jess," the older policeman spoke laconically.

"He gone for sure?"

The older policeman prodded the boy's hip with the toe of a black polished leather boot. "Jess, you git his wallet for me, hear? See if he's anybody." He walked away to lean against the truck.

The younger policeman kneeled, pushed back his goggles, extracted a wallet gingerly between his thumb and forefinger. "Thirteen bucks, liberry card out Dania way, Monkey Jungle ticket, punched."

"Git the blanket."

The boy coughed suddenly, erupting a stream of blood over the policeman, who leaped backwards, wiped his boot off with a handkerchief, balled the handkerchief and tossed it behind the palm.

"Got some on your pants too, Jess. They gonna want a cleaning."

"God damn."

"Kid, ain't he?"

"Likely 22, 23. You got K2R on the truck?"

"Blood always wants dry cleaning. Well now, Jess, we call the coroner or the ambulance?"

"Ambulance means we gotta ride down to Jackson with it. It's on to four now. I go off at half past."

"Since when we ride with red blankets?"

"Since the sergeants got sensitivity trained."

"Shit, git the goddamn blanket on to him and call the coroner and tell him he don't have to hurry long as he gets on about half past."

"Jess, how bout you drive on out to call, hear? So you can pick up a couple a cokes? And if you see a Pat Boone poster up, take it down for my kids, hear?"

As the cage truck pulled away, the older policeman took off his helmet, wiped his forehead with a sleeve and put one foot up against a palm tree behind him. He balanced his helmet on his raised knee and fingertapped it aimlessly.

Ishtar, the Great and Terrible Mother, whom they had not seen, heard the young man moan from under the blanket. Her pigeons cooed peacefully in answer. Ishtar picked up her Burdine's shopping bag with its hot pink and orange suns and walked to the Bandshell because she did not want the Law to ask her questions or find the Pat Boone and his Choir of White Christian Businessmen poster in her bag. The aimless tapping irritated her. She tore a feather from the purple breast of a pigeon and cleaned her teeth of pumpernickel seeds with the stalk.

"Cacogenics," she announced to the sky. "That is the problem here."

At the Bandshell, the Youth for Christ Club of the Allapattah Baptist Church was cleaning the stage and the dressing rooms. The last night Jim Morrison and the Doors had desecrated the Park with their performance and this night Pat Boone and his choir were coming to Miami to save the children.

Ishtar watched a young boy scrape Jim Morrison's semen from a footlight. She sat in a front seat and smiled at him and he blushed at her great beauty. She let her feathered thighs fall open and exposed herself to him. He stopped cleaning the footlight. She stretched out her thin hand for his Easy-Off. The boy smiled and passed the can to her. She sprayed it into his eyes.

Ishtar placed a talent of silver in each burned eye since she had no smaller change and covered his tortured face with the poster. From her Burdine's shopping bag she drew a bundle wrapped in the Miami *Herald* Comic Section. She unwrapped her furca, laid it in her lap and traced tenderly the copper of the cursive *e* she knew so well, then folded the Comic Section into a colorful pyramid hat, Mary Worth at the peak, and tucked her long hair neatly under it. She often forgot and ruined her curls in storms. Twisting her carnelian mouth at the sky, she cupped her breasts, the furca flashed blue arcs and she commanded El, "Flood. Small."

Around her a torrential rain sluiced suddenly through the park. The older policeman, cursing, pulled the blanket from the boy and reversing it, bloody side up, tented it over his head. The Youth for Christ boys and girls, except for the one at the footlights, scrambled to a bright mustard school bus. Its rubber doors snapped closed over the sounds of the shrill voices singing. Ishtar liked the weaving of the words and allowed herself a moment to listen. "The prettiest girl I ever saw. The prettiest girl I ever saw was sipping cider . . ." Blood and semen washed into the sidewalk cracks. Beyond the Bandshell, the royal palms bowed to the ground under the wind. Ishtar walked to them. A chorus of whistling palm fronds swept the ground before her feet in terror. And she spoke out of the whirlwind.

"Praise Ishtar, the most awesome of Goddesses, I am come back."

The palm fronds whistled.

"I am the Gleaming One, the Torch of Heaven, the Light of All Peoples."

Soft amber tears ran across her cheekbones and dropping to the grass, hardened into stones. "The heavens weep. I am unknown, unloved and my children are lost. The singer pours his wasted semen into empty skies. The suicide pours his blood into barren soil.

Her face contorted, terrible in anger, she wrenched the backrest from a bench and drummed it mightily again and again into the seat.

"Praise Ishtar. I am the Mother. Damn you with your nightsticks, your crumbling tablets, your wooden crosses. My children are sick on your stale wafers and your false wines and your Thou Shalt Nots! They are all bad hash, children. It is Mother you should eat. You hear me? Mother!"

She cupped her breasts with trembling hands. The furca flashed blue in the shopping bag. On Biscayne Boulevard the drawbridge at First Street shot up precisely as the school bus with its singing children reached it and the bus smashed into the steely tendril section over the river, hovered in its web, then plunged forward in the Miami River.

"They are all bad hash!" she screamed to the children bubbling in the sewage. "It is Mother you should eat."

Ishtar collapsed on the splintered bench. The furca sizzled as it cooled in the rain. She ended the rains. The palms stood straight; the fronds calmed themselves. The sun was hot copper innocent in the blue sky. Ishtar rent her comic pyramid hat, lamenting the children drowned and the claw footed bench broken and shredded the papers of her hat into long kitetails. She threw the kitetails over the silent face of Biscayne Bay. They drifted north.

Ishtar noted her needs on her shopping list. The afternoon news attributed the bus disaster to a freak electrical storm. Although Ishtar acknowledged the accuracy of the word disaster, the wrong turning of the Star, the word freak deeply offended her. She flew north that night, the shopping list clutched, like the branch of peace, in the beak of her mouth. She would find an earthly woman who tended toward the divine and was more in keeping with the culture. And she would teach her divinity. And then she would rest. Shape-changing always drained her.

Ishtar's Shopping List

I need a beautiful woman.
I need a band for music.
I need a son and/or lover.
I do not need a son or a lover.
I need three by five cards.
I need rubber bands.
I need new long-life batteries for my furca.
I do not need to, but I would like to get laid.
I need some new underwear.
I need to follow the Thruway to Exit 39.

The girl, Colleen, worked behind a counter in a drugstore in Miami. She wore a horsetail and a pink mini-skirt. Her boyfriend was in the courtroom.

"I saw Jim Morrison of the Doors," she said. "And he pulled down his pants."

"How far?"

"To a point midway between—between his waist and his knees."

"Would you care to describe what you saw?"

"Oh, no!" The horsetail shook, the shoulders shook and tears ran over her clear white cheeks. Never trust a girl who claims she is pure. "He put-put his hand on it."

The jury caught its composite breath.

"And, and he said an unusual word beginning with an f."

"Indecent exposure," the judge said, calling a hasty recess. Colleen's boyfriend escorted her from the chambers, comforting her.

It is not difficult to understand why a rock star, having reached the limits of adoration among the people, will then offer himself to the world as an all-purpose God.

And Ra spoke. "I even I had union with my clenched hand; I joined myself in an embrace with my shadow. I poured my seed into my mouth, my own. I sent forth issue. I wept over them and there came into being men and women from the tears."

One might even speculate as to whether men did not create the larger forms of society after they despaired of being able, by magic manipulation and many pulls of their genitals, to bear children. Childbirth is the last stronghold.

"Do you experience the same reactions at your concerts that you did at least until a year ago—girls going crazy, et cetera? Or is it all a myth?"

Morrison: "You know, that's the funniest thing. Sometimes it happens and when it does, it's all very mythical and strange. It just seems to happen out of some ancient ritual that somehow people have buried in their minds. At other times it just seems like a big put-on by the audience, which is very sad, a send-up when they pretend to be all jazzed over what you're doing and they're actually just doing it to be funny and that's very . . . but sometimes a very strange thing happens. The music or

29

the night is just right and you hit a peak that's so heavy that people just can't help kind of becoming a herd, a strange, ancient crowd celebration. But lately I think . . . I don't know, ah, shit, I haven't performed in a long time."

Morrison exposed himself in Miami and died in a bathtub in England.

"In Australia, for example, each time we'd arrive at an airport, it was as if De Gaulle had landed, or, better yet, the Messiah. The Beatles had come. The routes were lined solidly with people; cripples threw away their sticks; sick people rushed up to the car as if a touch from one of the Beatles would make them well again; old women stood watching with their grandchildren, and as we'd pass by, I could see the look on their faces. It was as if some Savior had arrived and people were happy and relieved that things were going to be better now."

"What is your belief in God?" the reporters asked Dylan.

Dylan replied: "Well, first of all, God is a woman. We all know that. Well, you take it from there."

When the trial resumed, Miami Police Officer R. E. Miller, who was patrolling at the concert, testified that Morrison pulled down his dark leather pants to his thighs and exposed his testes for fifteen seconds. Miller said he did not observe any underwear and could not tell whether or not the pants were down only in front.

"Morrison took his genitals in his hands and shook them. He took his shirt and threw it into the audience. I did not observe any underwear at any time."

"What did Mr. Morrison do then?"

"I observed Mr. Morrison pulling up his pants and then I observed him on his knees in front of another male member of the group. I further observed a white female on the stage with Morrison, after his exposure, and he had his arms around her and was hugging her."

And she handed him an apple and got him in the bathtub in England, later. She chose him.

4

When the Morning Star rose over the bittersweet drumlins and apple groves of Syracuse, where she had been going, Ishtar stood on the median of a superhighway, her nostrils dilating at the pungency of gasoline, rotting apples and manure. She waved an arm gracefully and flagged down a bakery truck, climbed aboard displaying her feathers, and exchanged her favors for four dozen packages of Hostess Cupcakes and Hostess Twinkies. Ishtar and the laughing African who smelled wonderfully of lemon and was much more satisfying than the stone phalli at Carnac, chuckled at sunup. The African shoved Twinkies into Hostesses and licked the spilt creme of the centers from Ishtar's fingers. Ishtar loved his brown fingers and perfect pink-mooned nails. He pleased her greatly. He drove her to a steel and glass supermarket where she would fill her shopping list and waved good-by energetically from the cab of his happy truck.

There was a parodic sense of Eleusis about the shopping plaza, rising as it did from a vast concrete apron beneath a spread of drumlins. A fountain sprayed in the center of the apron; beribboned poles of light encircled it; bushels of tomatoes, corn, piles of watermelons and potted plants were stacked, like first fruits, on wooden plank ziggurats. The neon pine tree swinging in the light breeze pleased Ishtar. She loaded a shopping basket with Cupcakes and Twinkies and pushed it into the supermarket. The manager watched threateningly from his glassed cubicle. She touched her breasts slyly and muttered: "Your member shall torment you until sunset." Then she built a perfect pyramid of Cupcakes in the shopping cart and a corbelled dome of Twinkies on the end of a checkout counter. Finished, she tied an apple green paper hostess apron around her slim waist. Her woman with the band and the boy would be in soon.

"Hey, Lady," the squirming manager finally rasped at her from his divider. "You got authority?"

Ishtar unfolded a green puffed paper hat on which she had inscribed in gold ink HOSTESS and placed it carefully on her curls. She smiled up at him.

"They teach you how to build them pyramids up to Hostess? Wish my bag boy coulda seen." He lifted his sergeant shaped paper hat and scratched stringy hair under it. Ishtar waited patiently for the woman. A bag boy came in stiff in his linen apron. Ishtar was excited. The bag boy blew her a silent kiss and took his station at the checkout counter. She nodded at him and mouthed, "I'll meet you in the Produce Room."

At last, at midmorning, the magic eye doors swung open and the woman entered. The bag boy followed the woman's behind hungrily, blowing it a kiss as it disappeared into a wall of Wonder Bread and Miracle Mix loaves. Ishtar forgave him his disloyalty. The doors swung open again and a husky manchild, his legs like columns, wearing camp shorts with many pockets, zippers, whistles and knife chains, burst in. He stopped at the Cupcake buildings, admiring them. Ishtar smiled nervously as he examined her. Then he shouted in a gravel voice: "Mother?"

"Right." His mother's voice came back, vibrating powerfully along the aisles.

Ishtar's neck pulsed with excitement. The manchild walked toward the loaves of bread and his mother's voice. Ishtar, the Terrible Mother, among other things, smiled politely and considered the new woman. Her hair was too straight. Her clothes were a workman's. But the slight hook of her nose, the pinkness of her cheek meat, the Tartar slants of the bones, the statuesque frame and the bare feet were satisfactory. Ishtar ran her trembling hands over the pyramid and dome. It had to be correct this time, enough of Snow Whites and False Queens. She would forego the lettuce leaves and the bag boy. There was no time for play.

When the mother and the manchild stood in the checkout line, Ishtar smiled at the manchild and waved a Twinkie at him invitingly. He pulled the mother's sleeve. She shook him off and bent to unload her food cart. The bag boy watched, looking down into her shirt and the full white flesh between the lapels. She lifted a heavy case of cat food, grunting at the effort, caught his probing eyes and straightened up with hands on her hips. "My turn. Unzip your pants and I'll watch *you* load." She grinned and stared at a growing bulge in his jeans while his face reddened and swelled under the white leprous splotches of acne cream, like a mushroom. He unloaded the cart. Ishtar clapped delightedly and waved a Twinkie at the manchild again. The manchild approached her. She knelt and caressed the warm tan skin of his shoulders. He reached for the Twinkie and slipped it carefully into a back pocket, zipping it closed.

"Where are your two front teeth, little love?" Ishtar asked of him, running her hands along his arms. She wished to bite the fat of his forearm. He looked over his shoulder at his mother and whispered to Ishtar:

"I pulled them out. Both of them."

"Aaaah." Ishtar filled the remaining pockets herself, smoothing the gabardine over his small body, zipping as she went. "Nice. Correct."

The mother pushed her basket by them. "Let's go, Beast."

Ishtar and the bag boy watched the dungareed hips roll vulgarly.

Many features of initiation rites suggest that they are in part sacrificial offerings to a female goddess. It is all written in your books. Spence and Gillens, Barton have reported numerous instances in which the initiates present their foreskins, blood or teeth to women. Among certain natives of Victoria, Australia, on arriving at manhood, a youth is conducted by three leaders of the tribe into the recesses of the woods; being furnished with a suitable piece of wood, he knocks out two of the front teeth of his upper jaw, and on returning to the camp, gives them to his mother. Loeb (and others) is convinced that circumcision was a sacrifice to a female goddess. He follows Barton, who holds that originally all Semitic circumcision was a sacrifice to a goddess of fertility. This placed the child under her protection and consecrated its reproductive powers to her service. Bring home something nice for mother.

After Ishtar purchased a restaurant size can of halved pears, she followed the mother and the manchild out to a rosewood Plymouth station wagon, calling to them. "Here, take the rest. Take them, I'm finished here."

The mother's periwinkle eyes were bored and haughty. "Thank you, no. He exists on Hostess Cupcakes and Hi-C. We don't need anymore." She turned her back regally.

Pleased with the combination of the vulgar and the regal, Ishtar also turned her back, ignoring the refusal. She opened the car door and dismantled the pyramid of Cupcakes onto the seat. Three orange tiger cats stretched and yawned with snakelike jaws on the black leather seat. The mother, watching her, took a Twinkie from Ishtar's shopping bag, leaned against the car, squeezed the creme forward and licked provocatively off the top. Her boy moved behind her, whispering loudly in the gravel voice. "She's gonna give them all to us. Is she kookoo?"

The cats eyed Ishtar; their heads simultaneously followed her hands. When the Cupcakes were all in the car, Ishtar held up her palms and the cats licked them with warm sandpaper tongues. Then she dumped her shopping bag of Twinkies on the floor of the back seat and slammed the door. She turned and faced the mother. She fixed her with her best basilisk stare, lifted her skirts and ruffled apron and displayed, with a pelvic jerk, her feathered crotch. The mother shoved the manchild behind her. She laughed loudly, though, crumbs spewing onto her fair chest, flashed a hand forward and plucked a feather. Ishtar yelped. Her eyes burned with rage and amusement. She dropped her skirts.

"I am Ishtar," she spoke in a threatening monotone within the mother's dwindling laughter. "I am Ishtar. You will eat one Cupcake a day for seven days at the rising of the Evening Star. Nothing more. They are marked for you. On the fourth day you will cleanse thyself. On the seventh day you will have wisdom. On the eighth day you shall grow feathers. On the eighth day you shall be Ishtar also. You have been chosen."

The mother wiped tears of laughter from her eyes. Ishtar muttering, caressed the manchild's behind swiftly and secretly, sent her cart sailing across the parking lot and sauntered away, tossing her apron and bonnet into a pile of charcoal briquets, which instantly burst into bright blue flames. At her back she heard the Mother's car leave, tires skidding from the concrete plaza. "Drive carefully." She waved a pythic finger after her.

"You gonna get feathers, Mom?"

"Don't be silly. If anything, I'd prefer a silky tail."

The manchild leaned over the seat and counted Cupcakes. The mother patted his pockets. A cat climbed into her lap as she drove, scratched a nest between her legs and slept, purring heavily. The mother grinned and slipped the feather inside her bra for safekeeping. That night she wrote a line from Anaïs Nin under the slant-eyed Chinaman's heads in the phone directory. "She was spreading herself like the night over the universe and found no god to lie with."

It didn't seem to be her thought, but she welcomed it as it articulated something long hidden within her. She put the child to sleep and masturbated gently with Ishtar's feather, wishing her husband the same accuracy, and dreamt of pine trees and puffball mushrooms with tiny streams of ancient mushroom powders bursting under her fingers from the dusky centers. She didn't know, on awaking, where she had learned about puffballs.

The elder Ishtar, after leaving the supermarket, rented a small room in the sleet gray YWCA near a library. The ladies' room at the library was amazingly decorated with Sumerian terms. She passed the seven days, remaining in her room and visiting the library, translating the Gideon back to Sumerian, working through pages and pages of garbled instructions, recipes and mushroom prayers. Someday she dreamed to correct the man-made Bible that had been so monstrously rewritten after she had been slain. Ishtar was tired of destruction, tired of being called a virgin, and tired most of all of the ever recurring claims by upstart males that they created the universe, the world and man. Remembering viciously, she pulverized pears at dusk every night, added the roots of a large female mandrake and mixed the potion in Genesee beer, a local product. She ate the mixture each night as she had instructed the mother to eat, and waited, greatly impatient for the woman to realize her chosenness. And each night, crosslegged, Ishtar held her breasts and directed her energies into the suburban mother. And each night Ishtar entered wisdom into the dreams of the mother. Then she herself would lay her hands under her head, her tiny feet tucked beneath her on the stiff mattress of the iron bed, and listen. At last, on the seventh night, she rose, opened the window and blew puffs of frosted air into the black as the new Ishtar received her final wisdom in the shade of the night.

"Cunt," she began, "is from the Sumerian *cunnus* and means burden. Fuck," she continued, "is from the Sumerian *furca* and means cross, indicating a point of meeting. All cookies," she went on patiently into the night, "are cognate, as are bread, bagels, and language." The lessons continued until sunrise. They included the terribly important recipes for balancing sexuality, for preparing mandragora juice for ecstasy and general comments on the state of the world, which was, of course, degenerate.

On the eighth day, the mother discovered not feathers but fleas. On the eighth day, the boy unclenched both fists as the mother spooned honey and penicillin into his mouth. Two tiny boxes, engraved in gold by the dentist FOR THE TOOTH FAIRY, black and clear plastic tephillin, lay in the palms of his fat hands. Inside them, through the clear covers of the coffins, the mother saw the two front teeth, long, grotesque, ivory. The boy swilled his mouth with water from a paper cup and spat noisly into the sink. "You keep them, okay, Mom?"

She nodded at him and took them in her hands without looking. The teeth, even at a distance, shot a needle of pain into her stomach. "Didn't it hurt you, baby? Didn't it really hurt?"

He touched her arm gently. "Do I get money for the ones I pull out?"

The mother pulled him within her arms. "Baby, don't do it anymore. Please. Listen, a secret. I'm the Tooth Fairy and there's no cash for do-it-yourselfers."

He nuzzled against her breasts with his head. His hair smelled of his father's styling lotion, almondy. "Can I name them?"

She clicked the rattling boxes at his delicate ears like castanets.

"Can't I name them like babies?" He nuzzled in deeper, hurting her nipple.

She pushed him away. "Listen, kid, I have the babies around here. You want to pull out your teeth, that's your business. But I have the babies, get it? Go. Ride your bike or something. Like a boy. Go!"

His face loosened, ugly, and his voice shrilled, much like Robert when his power was approached. "When did *you* get to be the Tooth Fairy?"

"You gave me the teeth, didn't you? That makes me the Tooth Fairy."

"But . . . oh, okay. Okay." He swiped and knocked over a half-filled coffee cup. It broke in the kitchen sink.

The mother raised her right arm and pointed her finger at the ceiling. It was a signal her son understood.

"Okay. Okay. I said okay!"

And it shall be as a sign that the Lord's law shall be in thy mouth. That the tephillin must be square was revealed to Moses upon Sinai and also that they must be wrapped around with the hair of a beast and sewn with its sinews. He who purifies himself and washes his hands and puts on the tephillin and reads the Sch'ma and prays, he is accounted by the Scripture as one who has erected an altar and offered up a sacrifice thereon, for it is said, I will wash my hands in innocence, so will I compass your altar.

"Come back here and wash your hands!"

The boy obeyed. The mother attached the plastic tephillin to a chain and wore it on her graceful neck. As the boy stomped angrily past her, the mother spoke: "Hey, Beast. Come back here. I've got something for you too."

She held out a yellowed circle pin to him. On it was an apple shaped shield of blue with white stars. Inside the stars was an old slick-haired mustached man.

"Who's that?"

"That's Teddy Roosevelt. He was something of a great hunter, something also of a pig, but he had some good words. Here." She knelt and pinned the button on his shirt. "Walk softly. Carry a big stick."

"Gee, thanks, Mommy. Thanks a lot. That's cool."

"Fair enough," Ishtar the Terrible Mother said to Ishtar the New Mother. "Fair enough." The New Mother smiled over her son's head in acknowledgment. "It won't be easy," the Terrible Mother said to her. "Initially, you must take care of those fleas."

"When do I get the feathers?"

"Make room for the feathers."

"Who are you talking to, Mom?"

"Get out and ride your bike, please." She stood tall and regal and pointed her warning finger to the sky. The son raced out of the kitchen.

"What fleas?" the new Ishtar asked again. But the old woman was gone.

The old Ishtar descended in the wrought-iron cage elevator to the lobby of the YWCA and made plane reservations for Mount Ararat, from whence a vessel would depart. The desk clerk, overhearing, couldn't remember having heard the name of the airline before, but then she hadn't traveled much. Ishtar was joyful. The new Ishtar, however, had fleas and was horribly discomfited.

5

It is teeth, as you have surmised, with which I have problems. Not my teeth, particularly, except for incidental fillings and cleanings, but with teeth. My father, I may have told you, died from . . . no, I am always careful to say died after he had had a tooth pulled. I am due this very moment at the dentist's. I will not, however, honor my appointment. Then Robert will receive a bill for a disappointment, which is exceedingly clever but this is the level of humor one learns to expect from my dentist, who, as the chairman of the Temple B'nai Israel Cemetery Committee, collects funds to repair desecrated graves. I am charged for not coming just as I am charged more for sugarless gum because it has no sugar. I will tell Robert as he sits at the desk reading the insertions on the cumulative bill with the five dollar charges for disappointments that if I must pay the dentist for not coming, then he must pay me when I come, or at least when he comes.

Robert is not at all amused. I can repeat verbatim what he has answered and will answer: "Look, Ishtar, you have three alternatives." The fingers go up. "One, you keep your appointments with him, which you obviously can not do. Two, you find another dentist you prefer or, three . . ." I can not emulate the deep gloom ridden voice here, "Three, you don't care for your teeth and you'll have all kinds of problems and that will cost me a fortune." The fingers are down into a knotted fist now. My father's teeth are, I am sure, still strong and solid and gleaming goldcapped in the terrible purple velvet lined open-mouthed coffin I had to look into before half the town and all the family when I was a child. Finding another dentist has absolutely no bearing on the matter.

This week, however, I have an acceptable excuse. I have fleas. And it is excruciating, I will tell Robert, to sit still in the dentist's chair while I am being attacked by my fleas. I do not know which of my four animals has given me fleas. Perhaps all of them are responsible since crossbreeding brings strength and durability. I have employed every manner of salve, ointment, balm, hunting procedure, soaking, Pristeen and Scope to no avail. Even Ammens Powder. I have had all the cats and the dog washed thoroughly at the veterinary hospital. I have treated my bedclothes with Pine Sol and Lysol. Fleas, I find from discreet questionings, lie in soft warm places as mohair upholstery, wool carpets and pubic centers and they leap, straight up and down, to bite skin on the move. They are vicious and rarely miss and their bites swell and rage with itching and I scratch and dig until I bleed from cavities in my legs and thighs. It is as if there is some devilish hand sowing them. I lie in bed stiff and still until I feel the stinging bite, fling back the covers with a scream for power but find nothing. The flea is gone. Perhaps, I have imagined hopefully, the fleas are white like the mircrocosmic pills on my Wamsutta Permaprest, but no, even on the dark floral patterns, no matter how quick I am, I find nothing. Perhaps the fleas change color like chameleons. They are not to be trusted. I do not understand what that woman has done to me. It is a desperate situation and Robert, from whom I have not been at all able to hide this information, is continually and unsympathetically awakened when I shout and disturb the entire kingdom of our peaceable bed. He will not touch me in love or desire.

Although Robert knows nothing about teeth or fleas, he does, however, know music.

He knows music very well. And when my hairdresser, who wears no underwear under knit pants and blows hot whiffs of himself into my ear and down my neck and slips hairclips into my lap so he can snatch them out and is not to be trusted, said that his rock and roll band needed an investor and a manager, I decided a band would be good for Robert. He whistles a great deal, tonelessly when he is sullen, plays strong major chords on the piano and I have seen him, with his enormously long daddy legs, jump into the air and kick one ankle. "He can make a lot a bread off us," Nino blew into my ear at the beauty parlor. And I thought, as a leavening agent in the desert of Robert's work ethic, a band would be fun. It isn't that Robert wants the money. He doesn't care about money as long as he has enough and his demands, really, are minimal. So Robert became an investor this week and the manager this week and now will make decisions about recording, playing weekends, salaries and insurance on equipment. And I will take care of the day to day heartaches, rather like a mother, which include girls, wives, penicillin shots, clothes, egos, mothers, lunch, poster designs, radio tapes and whatever it takes to keep seven bad ass men contented. They are not boys in age. They are men. And it will give me something to do. My son, after all, is in school a full day.

Under the stage in a dimly lit room with a dripping sink and a cracked mirror, the Demons prepared themselves.
"The man's out there with his old lady. Lay it on," their leader told them as he sprayed his hair with Adorn.
"Dig."
"You see the pockets on his suit? Filled with bread."
"Class chick," another remarked.
"She foreign or something?"
"Around here," the leader answered, "class is foreign."
"I wanna eat her knees."
"You're real class yourself, Nino." The leader spilled cologne on his wrists.

"Big leader don't lower himself to eat," someone else added, grabbing the cologne for himself.

In Hagar Qim on Malta in the forbidden third temple a hidden chamber is behind the altar. A tube bored at knee level in the rock slab wall emerges at ground level in the penetralia. The priests speak through the tube, howling, moaning. They terrify the earthly visitants with sounds from the beyond and echoes from the dead. The Great Mother who is the source of all things, who maketh the wadis run with manna and honey, enters her temple.

With thee, thy seven lads, Plump Damsel, Daughter of the Mist, with thee, Dewy, Daughter of the Showers. Thy face thou shalt surely set toward the Mountain of Concealment. Take the mountain on thy hands, the hill on the top of thy palms and descend to the House of Corruption in the underworld and thou shalt be numbered with those that go down into the earth. Go down. Yea, thou shalt know annihilation as the dead.

She comes. The Goddess from the great above she set her mind toward the great below. My lady abandoned heaven, abandoned earth, to the nether world she descended, leaving the phone number with her babysitter, reincarnated, reblooded, in skins of mink and boots of cowhide and kohl on her eyes, seeking her immortal lover in the great below. Tammuz, long have I wept. Behind Ishtar walks Moses with a vest and cash in his pocket and a set of laws scraped with bleeding fingernails into the rock of ages. Ishtar is happy to have toes again.

"Why the hell should I invest in these guys?"

Ishtar taps her fingers on the scarred tabletop to the jukebox music while Robert finds his own answer. Once she herself had a band. Once she herself had dark demons who whistled down the highways in terror, scourging heaven and earth of unbelievers. They had not been ordinary. These boys in the band, as Robert explained, were ordinary.

"I don't need the money."

Ishtar smiled benignly at Robert.

"Ishtar, I can make something of these boys, create something."

Robert will never be happy until he is able to have a baby. Until then, for a sense of power, he will sell anything. One of my sons, giddy Jack, sold me, his own mother, for a handful of beans. The beans, as the legend goes, contained spirits and Jack thought he could bring them to life. He could do nothing with them and, in defeat, planted them. He had hoped to make babies without me. Nice boy. He sold me, in my image as cow, down the road. Robert is rankled by my power of birth, also. Although he thanks God every day that he was not created a woman, he has been a Mason, a boy scout and a fraternity man. He has been initiated in all their secret ways with the doors closed and the lights out. The rituals are all the same. They are trying to imitate birth. They can not. Have you ever seen a bar mitzvah? It is the quintessence of male stupidity. The rabbi and the father and the cantor dress as women and pray to a male god to bring the boy to manhood. A boy can come to manhood only through a woman. Out of sheer frustration, they sell things.

"Do you realize what kind of money one hit record could make? With personal appearances as a follow-up?"

Ishtar nodded. The appearance at Fatima unintentionally had brought the pope a fortune.

"That's the leader over there. Jesus, I never noticed it before. He looks queer. How can I sell a guy like that as a sex image?"

Ishtar looked in the direction of Robert's nod. Ishtar fixed the boy in her sight and waited as his eyes slid over her languidly, dextrously, then blinked as he recognized something and disappeared under heavy fruited lashes. Pain had shown for only a sweet perfect moment. The pain had given her a sudden orgasmic rush, a joy in her belly. Ishtar wanted to see more of his pain. He was not ordinary.

"He won't be so pretty when I finish with him. If I can sell polyesters, I can sell a band. It's all in the packaging.

Follow the laws of good merchandising, you can sell anything. Even your mother."

Robert laughed. His laugh is false. If it is beautiful and you are Moses, you either fuck it or sell it. Robert fears his desire for the beautiful in other men. He fears that which is womanly in himself and fights with himself. He will make the boy over in his image. To sell. Since there is nothing else he will allow himself to do with the boy's beauty.

We both watch the boy. We are both insatiable in differing ways. He talks to a young girl who moves in flutters about him, touching him, touching the cloth of his cape. His cheekbones are slicing and hungry. His skin, outlined by long soft black hair, is taut and sallow. His eyes, large and soft, intelligent. From a strong pedestal of shoulder rises a thick and graceful neck. His teeth are even. His smile, gentle. The cape, black outside, blood red inside, exaggerates the hunger of his lips and jawbone. He is not ordinary.

"Why change him, Robert?"

"I think he's queer. We'll worry about that later. You're going to have work to do if I take this band. Get you out of the kitchen. You're always complaining about the kitchen."

Ishtar yawned to cover her interest in the boy. Can I this time love a man without ruining him? Year after year I have killed my lovers. It was with Tammuz' death I was most wounded, for he was the first. There has always since been a vacuum in my soul. I have searched for years in the wilderness, on golf courses, among wadis, in forests of stone for a gentle juicy poet. But I have been reduced, betrayed, annihilated by my men and never truly loved. Faithfully I have slaved in their butteries, a thousand butteries, unending kitchens of adobe or stainless steel, and still I search. Now I am here in this underworld of rock and swamp creatures, half-formed, semi-conscious if at all, and I am afraid that this boy too is Baal, is Marduk, is . . . is any one of those who would love me, then fear me and then, in fear, annihilate me.

In glorious agonizing pools of existence, everything repeats. I throw the stone, but often, too often, I am betrayed and swallowed. I am fed up with that number. I wiggle my toes. I am pleased with their feeling. I was tired of the claws and can now wear pantyhose.

He tells secrets to the girl. I feel hot jealousy now.

"It's from a circus. In England." He puts a corner of his cape into the girl's young hand. She rubs it sensuously with promise against her cheek. "Gets me in hot water. I drive this red Caddy, see? You chew Sen-Sen? Nice. So I get stopped on the highway with the cape and the stage makeup. Three in the morning. My hair teased. The cop he does a double take and starts ripping up the car. Upholstery, shakes out my talcum powder, all the time calling me fag."

He waits for the girl to laugh. It is important that she laugh. She laughs.

He continues. "Rips up the dog I got in the back. With lights in its eyes? Everything. Finds nothing. Had it in my hair." His hands run through his hair. They are infinitely old against the silkenness of his flowing hair. Lettuce picker's hands roped with veins and new scratches.

I would lick them. Ah, Tammuz, is it you again? The lover of my youth? Wash him with pure water, anoint him with sweet oil, clothe him with a red garment. Let him play on a flute of lapis lazuli. Let courtesans turn his mood. How long have I bowed low, sat and wept for you.

And Marduk, who sucks the breasts of the Goddess, who slew the Goddess Tiamat and was worshiped in a pavilion made of her skin, sits on the pavilion. Somewhere. I can not see him. The room is hung with Schlitz signs rather than harvest fruits and palm fronds, but no difference. It is the same cult hut of the wilderness, the land of the immortal, where the heroes die only by violence, never age, by speeding tickets and bad hash. It is the cult hut where I bring them to one with the God Head, where they find their immortality within their mortality. "You want head, you want head?" the obscene little girls scream from the dance floor to the musicians on the altar. They are only phallus worshipers and have denigrated themselves to nothingness. But there is a chance. Where there is a Will there is a Way and I am here to show you the Way. The red, green and blue cloud pillars of spotlights and cigarette smoke descend over the ancient tabernacle. It is the holder of that which is sacred. That which Moses stole from Egypt: my Ark. It is the same as the Holy of Holies in your synagogues. It is all the same. We keep coming back in other clothes. The light operator sits on a support beam and works the neons and the musicians sit in the pine plank womb of the Great Mother, the place of initiation. It doesn't matter where it happens. As long as it happens. It is night and it is the time of the Great Mother. And the musicians sit in the sukka awaiting the Messiah, but She comes instead. It is in my womb that thou shalt become a man. In no other way. Here, I say to Enki, sit thou in my vulva and I shall heal thee. Tonight be a man in your pavilion, the paved loin of the Mother Goddess and the temple virgins with their demisermihemmies vulvulating, offering themselves to the sons of the Muse in my name. Ah, I have dreamt in a den of snakes. I have been a divine woman sleeping beneath the sea. I grant my gift to those who love me. And now, here on Butternut Street at the Crossroads of America, etc., I re-emerge. But not yet. Not quite yet.

"Does it interest you?"

I give Robert my attention. "What?"

"The band. Getting out of the kitchen for a change."

"I don't necessarily wish to be out of the kitchen."

"You women don't know what the hell you want. I'm going back to talk to the boys before they go on."

Silently I answer him, sliding my eyes over the boy's body again and feeling rushes through my skin. I have descended to save the world. I will not fight you for this one, Robert, this boy whose fruits I covet. I give you, Robert, I address his back and he walks away, these seven creatures from the swamp of your civilization, to mold into your product. If they were mine, I would bring them to immortality and manhood. You would package them to sell. Perhaps the monies and the sense of power will help you. It will only be a sense, never enough. But go. Play. Be happy. I have work to do. So get off my back and shape their destinies. Just don't mess with mine. Housekeeper and whore is what we want. And all the stops in between.

"Get in line. I seen her first."
"She wants to see Nino, yeah. Somebody loan Nino a sock for his jock. A rubber hose?"
"Loan me your hair spray."
"Maybe we'll make it big and you can buy your own fucking hair spray for a change."
"Yeah, and maybe you can take lessons and get talented."
"And maybe you can knock off walking in front of me when I'm singing."
"It don't matter how much you got. It matters how you use it. And I use it better than you. Ask your old lady." And they laugh at each other and mask the hunger in their faces and climb the stage.
"Which one is she?"
"Black dress, fur collar, long hair. Her name's Ishtar. Old man Moses says it means womb."
"Shit. No one calls their kid Cunt. It means star."
"*Isteddu accurtu a sa luna; tristu chi é deponne.*"
"Meaning . . . ?"
"My mother always says it at night. Star near the moon. Sad is he who it strikes."
"You're pretty heavy, Mack. Knock the poetry shit, huh?"
"I repeat. I wanna eat her knees."
"Shut up."

"Okay, leader."
"Let's go. One, two . . ."

Long ago and far away, Ishtar was hungry. "I am hungry," she howled from the walls of her city. "Hungry!" She spied Gilgamesh, a hero of Babylonia, returning from the great Cedar Forest where he had slain the dragon Huwawa, whose mouth was fire, whose roaring was the storm flood. Gilgamesh had washed his grimy hair, polished his bloody weapons, wrapped a fringed cloak around and fastened a sash on his waistline. Ishtar saw him approaching her city, Uruk. He wore a dazzling tiara. Ishtar raised an eye at his beauty.

"Come," she cried from the battlements, her hair flowing in the sun, her garments whipping around the luxury of her body. "Come, Gilgamesh, be thou my lover. Do but grant me of thy fruit. Thou shalt be my husband!"

Gilgamesh placed his hands on his hips, his legs, like firm cedars, on the ground. He examined her beauty. "Hah! Ishtar. What am I, a poor man, to give you, that I may take thee in marriage? Can I feed you food fit for divinity? Can I give you drink fit for royalty? And how long will you love me? Which of thy men, thy shepherds, pleased you for all time? Listen, Ishtar. I will name your lovers for you and tell of their fates. And you will know my answer."

Gilgamesh, with his fringed cloak and flowing sash, climbed the ramparts and stood with Ishtar. She gloried in the closeness of him. She did not glory in his words. "Tammuz. The lover of thy youth? You ordered wailing year after year for him after sending him to the Netherworld. The dappled shepherd bird, you were not satisfied with men alone, you loved and broke his wing and he cries forever, "My wing, my wing." And the lion, perfect in strength, you dug pits for him, seven and seven pits. Then for the stallion you ordained the whip, the spur and the lash and condemned him to run forever and drink muddy water. Then the keeper of the herd, who heaped up sacred ash-cakes in your honor, who slaughtered goats for you daily, you turned him into a wolf so his own herd boys drive him off and his own dogs bite his thighs. Ah, that is not all. Ishullanu, your father's gardener, who brought you baskets of dates and brightened your table, you raised your eyes at him. You went to him when it was dark and the gardens were empty and said, "O my Ishullanu, let us taste of thy vigor. Put forth thy hand and touch our modesty. And Ishullanu said to you . . ."

"How do you know, this, Gilgamesh?"

"All men know your ways."

"They dream of me."

"They fear you too. You are fatal food."

"It is their manner that is fatal to them, not myself."

"Ishullanu," Gilgamesh continued, stopping up his ears with his forefingers, "Ishullanu answered you in the garden, 'What do you want from me? Hasn't my mother baked in your name? Haven't I eaten your holy breads? Why, now, should I taste the food of offense and curses?' He was man enough to spurn your destroying love. And as you heard his talk, you smote him and turned him into a spider. You placed him in the midst of a web and he cannot go up and he cannot go down. If you would love me, you would treat me like them. I will love Enkidu, my friend."

"That is unnatural. Enkidu is almost a beast, a wild man. I am a woman. It is necessary that I am loved for the love of the heavens."

"I will dwell with Enkidu. I do not want you."

Then Ishtar mounted the higher rampart of the city, sprang on the highest battlement and offered a curse. "Woe unto Gilgamesh for he has insulted me." Ishtar assembled the votaries, the pleasure lasses and her temple harlots and set up a wailing for she had sent the Bull of Heaven to kill hundreds, but Enkidu, the friend of Gilgamesh, slaughtered the Bull of Heaven and tore out its heart.

Enkidu, from below, from the marketplace, yelled at Ishtar above. "Could I but get thee, like unto him I would do unto thee. Your entrails I would hang at thy side."

"Beast," Ishtar hissed. "Beast. No one shall go up. No one shall go down."

Gilgamesh built of lapis his own Bull, offered oil to his own god and washed his bloodied hands in the Euphrates. Enkidu and Gilgamesh embraced each other as they went on, riding through the market street of Uruk. The people of Uruk gazed upon them. Gilgamesh said to the lyre maidens, "Who is the most splendid among the heroes? Who is the most glorious among men?"

And the lyre maidens sang, "Gilgamesh is most splendid among the heroes. Gilgamesh is most glorious among men."

Ishtar, enraged, mounted to heaven. The rivers dried. The clay shattered. The wheat burned. Ishtar left and the women did not bear, and the animals had no young and the trees remained barren. The mother opened not her door to her daughter. The child they prepared for food. One house devoured the other. Like ghosts of the dead their faces were veiled. The Womb was bound and issued not offspring. The Mother had left in fury. The temples were empty and strangers entered not the great circles and paths of regeneration. The priests ate from her coffers. Ishtar abandoned her people.

They deserved it. Ishtar ate peanuts and threw the shells on the floor.

"Rise, oh my folk, from the dust of the earth, from the checkout counter at the A&P, from the greasepit at Midas Muffler, rise and garb thee in raiment, in see-throughs and tight bells and midriffs baring your first fruits, stuff your holy 32A padded apples into highrise bras and glue your lanuga eyelashes on and drape yourselves on the steps of the sukka bandstand and suffer, succubi, and raise your childlike voices that turn shrill in your demiurge and the hemisemidemiquaver of your voices shall reach the great ones on their pavilion. "Hey, you. You with the mustache. Eat me. Eat me. You want head? You want to go down on me?" Beat your hosanna in the meat market marked with magic markers proclaiming these seven lads. And yes, there they are on their pavilion now near the bar, on the altar, neath the ladies and the gents, and the folk from the dust of the earth shall worship them because someday, someday they may be great. Why not?"

"Phallus worshipers," Ishtar spat into the broken peanut

shells on the floor, cursing the girls who begged near the stage. Slender hands reached to touch Nino's member and he backed away, whispering huskily, "Later." And Ishtar spoke her incantation to the peanut shells, remembering her own band of demons, lost in the dust of ages. "They were seven. They were seven and again they were twice seven. Spirit of the sky, remember them. Spirit of the earth, remember them. They who have revolted cause the gods to tremble. They spread terror over the highways and advanced with whistling roar. They were capable of bringing down the sky. Suspending the earth. Making springs to dry up. Sweeping away the mountains. Conjuring the spirits of the dead. They weakened the gods, put out the stars and lit up hell itself. But they were extraordinary. I fashioned them myself. This band of Robert's is ordinary. And he will fashion them into paste-up images of manhood. I would make them immortal. Ah, if they were ever to be remembered, her demons, she would remember them with a member as large as Nino's, which, according to the stretch of his knit pants, was considerable. I castrate. I devour. I remember. I heal. Come to me.

Ishtar amused herself as she watched the band by restoring the shells to the peanuts immediately under her feet. She did not understand the music. It was without focus. Of course. The strength of the beat increased.

She worked faster restoring the peanuts to their shells. When she was a child, music had always been taught and mechanical. Indeed she had taught herself, picking out "Song to an Evening Star" with one plump finger, translating circles of ink to matching keys on her grandfather's organ with its carved pushes and pulls and stops until one Saturday, standing on a curb, a Legion parade passed and she heard the drums and wanted to march. She had not known music like that. She wanted to march simply and mindlessly in forbidden directions when the drum beat inside her chest and she had cried wildly until her father lifted her and held her to his chest. But the drums were beating in there too. Six men played their instruments and Sonny sang. Somewhere behind him drumsticks rose and fell. An open-backed organ far from the front line microphones displayed intricate, knotted multicolored bowels. Ishtar strained to see the back row but could not. She could hear no melody. It was sound, rupturing and total. Her ears vibrated with the mad noise. Nino stopped to wipe his forehead with a towel. The trumpeter shook spit on the floor of the stage, the guitars listened to themselves, tuning to a private perfection and then Nino sang again, but this time his voice was different, oddly broken, keening, melodic. The drums thundered and fought him. His voice rose above them. The horns bleated, rising finally until the melody snapped and Nino stopped singing, picked up maracas and began to move in pelvic jerks. Ishtar was entranced. Robert was beating with his palms wildly on the tabletop, grinning.

The music spread from Nino's mouth to his body, ululating and grinding, caressing. A strobe light covered him and his body fragmented into stills, snaking on a thousand joints, orgasmic. His member was erect and he danced, somehow, around it. The room beat with the strobe, like the inside of a stomach wall, pulsing in every cell. Nino was screaming now, punctuating an open spot in the music and in her stomach. Nino's scream was inhuman. Somewhere between a female dog in rut and a zither. It tore at her nerves. It hurts, the music said to her. It hurts, Mother, right here. Nino stopped. A high note, a lamentation, growing softer and softer from the organ, trembled into the distance from somewhere behind the organ player's ribs where the pain must have been greatest. She stretched to see beyond Nino. It was the boy in the cape. And she grew frightened.

"Let's grab the ball and run, baby. We've got ourselves a band." Robert took her hand.

In the chamber of fates, the abode of destinies, a god was engendered, most potent and wisest of gods. In the heart of Apsu was Marduk created. He who begot him was Ea, his father. She who conceived him was Damkina, his mother. The breasts of the Goddess he did suck. The nurse that nursed him filled him with awesomeness. Alluring was his figure, sparkling the lift of his eyes. Lordly was his gait, commanding from of old. When Ea saw him, the father who begot him, he exulted and glowed. His heart filled with gladness. He rendered him perfect and endowed him with a double godhead. Greatly exalted was he above them, exceeding throughout.

Perfect were his members beyond comprehension, unsuited for understanding, difficult to perceive. Four were his eyes, four were his ears. When he moved his lips, fire blazed forth. Large were all four hearing organs, and the eyes, in like number, scanned all things. He was the loftiest of all gods, surpassing was his stature.

"That Mack, he's the best looking one of the bunch. And intelligent."

"He's the tallest, too, is he not?"

His members were enormous, he was exceeding tall.

"But Nino is hung. Jesus Christ is that kid hung. We keep him center stage. He's going to be our image."

Robert was excited, grinning, drinking quickly in large swallows. Ishtar left to go to the ladies' room.

"What male is it who has pressed his fight against thee? It is but Tiamat, a woman, that opposes thee with weapons. O my father-creator, be glad and rejoice. The neck of Tiamat thou shalt soon tread upon."

Mack could be Robert's weapon against her. It was a weapon that would strike close to her heart. As it had been before, the overthrow of the Mother.

Tiamat, she who bore us, detests us. She has set up the Assembly and is furious with rage. Mother Hubur, she who fashions all things, has added matchless weapons, has born monster-serpents, sharp of tooth, unsparing of fang.

With venom for blood, she has filled their bodies. Roaring dragons she has clothed with terror, has crowned them with halos, making them like gods.

"Stand thou up, that I and thou meet in single combat." When Tiamat heard this she was like one possessed. She took leave of her senses. In Fury, Tiamat cried out loud. To the roots her legs shook both together. She recited a charm, casting her spell, while the gods of battle sharpened their weapons. Then joined issue Tiamat and Marduk, wisest of gods.

They swayed in single combat, locked in battle. The lord spread out his net to enfold her. The Evil Wind, which followed behind, he let loose in her face. When Tiamat opened her mouth to consume him, he drove in the Evil Wind that she close not her lips. As the fierce winds charged her belly, her body was distended and her mouth was wide open. He released the arrow. It tore her belly. It cut through her insides, splitting the heart. Having thus subdued her, he extinguished her life.

He cast down her carcass to stand upon it. The lord trod on the legs of Tiamat, with his unsparing mace he crushed her skull. When the arteries of her blood he had severed, the North Wind bore it to places undisclosed. He split her like a shellfish into two parts. Marduk created heaven and earth.

Of course. And Ra insists to this day that he masturbated and took his seed into his mouth and spat out the first children. They are both fools. But they fight well and I am no match in fisticuffs. Furthermore, I would really rather make love in single combat.

Ah, baby, which one of you is it this time? Perhaps you will be sweeter? Perhaps we can make it this time.

There is no mirror in the ladies' room. My eyes are bleeding and I need a mirror desperately. Flies circle, helpless, above the toilet around the light pull. It is how I feel. Slowly and carefully, the blood running cold at my trembling fingertips, I prepare myself for the toilet. The toilet is green emboweled, the room hung with flypaper and the stench of the netherworld encompasses me. Disease crawls over the flaking toilet seat. A fly lands on my kneecap and I kill it between my fingers.

"*They are olive and sallow and the one, the leader, in the dark, sitting up at his organ, in shadow profile, looks like a lizard.*"

I do not need him. But I have seen his hurt and I remember Marduk of the enormous members, who sucked the breasts of the Goddess. I have seen it all before. And the red silk and the black silk of his circus cape and the bad eyes and the Circe female mouth ready to once more annihilate the Queen of Heaven. But there is a sweetness in him, a sweetness in the even smile of his teeth and the pain of his eyes. I am not sure I want to hurt this one. I am intrigued with his mustache.

Ishtar smoothed her pantyhose over her legs with one hand and walked out, past the leader, who was bent over his keyboard intent on the music. She wiped the remains of the fly on his pants leg as a sign. He thought it was a caress. She was not certain what it meant except she had wanted to touch him.

6

I have been at last to the gynecologist. I have been there in utter humiliation, as a fornicator in the Inquisition. I have slept with the devil and confessed that his skin is cold and his penis hot as the glowing coals of his eyes and his smell is foul and I have been myself befouled. I have been shaved and cleansed, powdered and sprayed. Shaved for my sin. Now, not only am I not a member of the Jewish Community Center, but I have fleas. There is a vast difference between being fleabitten and having fleas. I am a carrier. I will not achieve full regrowth until three months have passed, he has told me. I inquired about a hair piece to the gynecologist's great goatlike amusement and my complete degradation. When I arrived home from the gynecologist's an older woman stood crying at my doorstep. She had run over my cat, Green, and held it, mutilated and tire-marked in a First Trust Bank shopping bag. I was not certain the cat was dead so the woman and I drove with the sadly bloody cat to the Japanese veterinarian, who pronounced Green dead and I, raising the bank's bag over my head in the reception room, sobbing, blessed my cat and passed her on. People waiting for appointments shielded their children from my display. I felt responsible for Green's death. I knew then that Green had given me the fleas and there was an as yet undefined relationship between the death of the cat and the removal of the fleas. It was as if to become a member of Green's kingdom, I had to accept and really know Green's suffering with her own fleas. Green gave me her fleas so she could believe in me. This is of course utter madness.

I kissed her bleeding head in the reception room and handed the attendant my sad offering for burning. The woman, still crying, suggested I move from my neighborhood, where there are now many cars, too many for animals to deal with. She cried and handed me her card. She sells real estate. You don't think there is an as yet undefined relationship there too, do you? That in this way she lists new houses first? When you live in the land of Ra and Dio, anything is possible. I feel somehow that I have sacrificed Green for what purpose I do not yet know. I am certain her death relates to my having been shaved.

There is a Samsonian defeat in all of this and I can not blame it on Robert, as I wish to, who lay in his bed when I emerged from my Phisohex bath and laughed like a schoolboy at my girlish plump, neatly plucked naked triangle . . . my cooky, as my mother referred to my parts. I threatened to re-circumcise him with my regrowth as soon as I had regrowth. However, immediately that night something odd began to occur. I dare not ask the doctor. He will only shred me again with his barnyard laughter and his old razor blade. And I am not sure that it is something to dislike, this new condition. It is not to be belittled. I believe it is rather special and I tell you only so you can understand all of this. Rather than a stiff and whiskery regrowth, I am soft and downy on my cooky.

I can't go on about it.

Which is why I shall return again and again to it.

I have seen in dreams a raven jumped by a weasel. The raven was black and old and I think perhaps wise, the kind of raven one sees scudding across the full face of the moon. It pecked in a field of limestone boulders like frozen whale bones, pierced here and there with bits of sphagnum moss and spongy grasses. The weasel, thirsted, leaped from a white rock onto the raven's back and the raven fought, whirling, screaming, but the weasel held. And then the raven with supernatural power took to his skies over the sea. There he wheeled and dived and wheeled again and again trying to shake off the weasel. The weasel held to the raven. Terrified or tired or satisfied, his grip loosened and the weasel plummeted to sea, feathers still sticking from his mouth.

I might mention here that it is amazing what a simple change like this can do for one's personality. Better than a nose job, of course. I feel so much more complete and complex, albeit rather giddy. I have refused this week, while I am healing, to go to the factory and Robert is upset but understanding. He is very gentle and fascinated with my new growth. He is too astonished to laugh or to tease me any longer. He seems to take a sort of wondrous pride in the down. He fluffs it with his Luckies breath while the cat, Blue, sits sphinxlike spread between us, watching, often taking little nips at Robert's breath. I look also. We can only see the movement of the down under Robert's breath but Blue, I believe, sees the breath as reality. Blue walked over the first evening of my down, sniffed and then rolled with his back across my belly and underbelly. He approved and accepted this change in me, which is nice. Although I shave very often under my arms now, almost savagely, nothing happens there. When I say to Robert in bad moments, "Once a queen, always a queen," he responds, "With feathers." It has become a litany between us. Robert is not the kind of man to tell other men about his personal life. No one will really ever know of course unless I so choose. But I will most likely never return to the gynecologist. I do not like gynecologists. I am sure they are all perverted and not even polymorphously so. They know only one place. I can not imagine sleeping with one. I have tried to and I can not.

Which reminds me. I must take my son's fangs, which I believe his gerbils have now spirited into their fetid cage in the kitchen, to the dentist for his examination. My son extracts long bloody fangs from his seven year old mouth. They are not his canine teeth, I have discovered. They are from different parts of his mouth. Rodent teeth, thumbnail long, which initiate a deep and grinding horror within me. He is losing his permanent teeth, speaking of odd choices of words, this genetic monster of mine whom I love so madly. I diligently gave him quarters for his lost teeth and he had always been convinced that I was the Tooth Fairy. I will not pay him for the permanent teeth. He has also thought for years that I had a tail and laid eggs.

I believe knowing about my feathers will also upset him and draw out more of the precious teeth. His father will buy him new ones. The feathers can be destructive, I imagine. But they can also give me power.

It is not my wish nor has it ever been to use my sex to bargain with Robert, nor my feathers. But it is a position, this bargaining, into which I am forced. The feathers give me a new wedge. Robert, after all, at one time in his life, rose every morning, bowed and thanked God for not making him a woman. Now, let him be grateful then to me, for without me, I am beginning to realize, he is not a man. This is a new and interesting idea and I have to consider it. Robert thinks that money is stored up energy against the time when he is weak. I wonder if he really has stored up energy against his weakness for me. It is not energy he stores; it is hate. I wonder if I could send him plummeting into the sea with feathers in his mouth as I go scudding across the moon. I'm being totally irresponsible. I need to ask him to put money into my once and again overdrawn account. I must do something today about my teeth and my son's teeth and as I plan my day, two orange cats sharpen their claws against the sides of my suede sofa, which is granting the cats a new energy by its very richness. In some respects Robert is right. He is correct about taking care of things and holding back rot and decay. But I must in the future sort out very carefully those things about which he is incorrect. Now that I have feathers, I seem, untangled, to see things more clearly.

"See and hear the Demons at the Inferno. The Inferno, where it all hangs out. The Demons. The Inferno. Where it all hangs out."

The owner of the Inferno was crippled. He wore red, blue and white horse racing plaids over his shortened leg and his normal leg. His shoes were brown and white gum soled saddles, mismated for the ungrown foot. Ishtar drank tonic water in his office high above the floor of his vast warehouse dance hall. A perfect Russian wolfhound licked her ankles.

Robert was in New York, conversing with a minor, but heavily invested, recording company interested in the first album. The owner of the Inferno had called Ishtar with a quaver of hysteria in his voice. "Your band," the owner had complained, "your band's fighting me every step. They cut short on the sets; they stretch the breaks to forty minutes sometimes instead of the twenty. Don't play requests. The kids are talking about them. Bad ass guys. Listen, don't get me wrong. I got twenty off-duty cops in the lot parking cars and bikes. I'm almost up to two thousand kids on weekdays, which is terrific. Like your husband says, they draw. But they still gotta have some stepping on. They gotta work with club owners no matter how big they are. And they're bad ass. The kids turn off and then you don't get record sales up here."

The boys had played four nights and had a week and a half to go on contract. Ishtar had flown unhappily to Buffalo that evening. Annoyed at the soot on the snowy face of the city, she wore a black silk dress cut low under the arms so the white sides of her breasts were displayed, depending on how she sat. She sat carefully in his paneled room. "So talk with them, huh? I don't want any more screwups. Right now, they're on break and they're ten, nope eleven minutes into the set time.

Probably getting laid, uh, excuse me, in the dressing room. The kids know and they're sore."

Ishtar sat coolly listening. Then the owner led her, bobbing on his gumsoles, to the projection room. Jimmy, her projectionist, sat with his knees to his chin on a high stool, his face gargoyle lit from below. Jimmy dipped his head from the light controls. He was choosing cuts of meat with his spotlight, concentrating, touching wantonly like a mad butcher the torsos of three jerking girls dancing to the canned music. The owner pointed to them. Their faces were swollen also in the sharp lights of his spots, their hair Pythian puffed, their eyes hawklike, unfocused, turned in on the bird bones behind their makeup masks. Ishtar sorrowed for their emptiness.

"You see," she whispered to the wolfhound who understood her and the owner who did not, "they hope. They wait for the music to make something happen, they wait for something to fill the spaces between their eyes. They come hungrily each night, thinking it will happen from the music."

"Hey, Ishtar, they're waiting for the Demons because they dropped three clams at the door."

Ishtar chose to ignore the owner. People had always thronged to stages and altars and threshing floors because they were assured of something happening when Ishtar was in charge. "And these sad children," she spoke silently now to the wolfhound, "the girls in their cheap bellbottoms, their frayed acetate ruffles, their new shoes turned at the heels already, soles warped from the salted snow . . . see? And see the boys with their legs like matchsticks and Trues wrapped in the half-sleeves of their T-shirts, see them? Ungenerous bony-assed boys in lightweight pants. Ah, out of the swamps they come, impure, fireflies, to hear the Demons because the Demons are out of the same swamp, you understand, with the same rotting chickens and Fords in their backyards and the same good mothers who iron their shirts and cook their sauces at sunrise." The wolfhound responded to Ishtar's wisdom by licking her ankles, his tongue rasping on the stockings. Ishtar's blood danced to the movement of the tongue.

Below in the sea of children, the heat held light pillars of cloudy blues and greens. The pillars rose between the ceiling and the floor. Acrid stenches of pizza, garlic, beer, urine, cigarettes hung longer and closer in the heat. Behind her counter, a pizza waitress wiped the back of her neck with a towel and repinned an elaborate french curl. A redheaded girl, standing far from the stage, alone and ignored, waved a large balloon magic-marked HEY TWENTYMILES! Fronds of Genesee beer signs and plastic clovers festooned the I beams. The faces of Marilyn Monroe and W. C. Fields, like unholy parents, moved, blown-up across the walls while Popeye grinned from the ceiling. A multi-faceted fixture rotated, casting traces of light in widening pools on the shoulders and heads of the children. It would have been, Ishtar sighed, a magnificent place for a mass initiation rite.

"I got eighteen, nineteen hundred at three a head." Someone popped the redheaded girl's balloon and she cried into her hands. The crowd hid her.

Ishtar frowned. The owner hit Jimmy on the shoulder and sent him to the dressing room to find the band. "Ever see this light show work?" he asked Ishtar as he poured Three-in-One oil into a basin below the projector and sprinkled in powdered paints of bright colors. "Really simple."

"Good effect," she replied, watching carefully. There was so much to learn, having worked only with the fire of heaven, the auroras and lightnings.

"That's a classy bunch a groupies your guys have. Those ones only come for the big groups. I can always tell a group's going somewhere when they show. Can't see them from here." He leaned against the wall to relieve his good leg. "That's why I took the bother to call. Otherwise I'd fire the bunch a them for breach a contract. Nino, that Twentymiles . . ."

"Twentymiles?"

"Ventimiglia. The girls call him that because, well, he's well-endowed."

"Oh."

"And if I were you, I'd keep Mack from him. I think Mack's got the hots for him. That Mack. You know what he does when I tell him something? Walks away from me. Just walks away." The owner shifted his legs and waited for Ishtar's agreement.

"Is your leg a birth defect or an accident?" she asked, not completely kindly. The owner bent to pat the wolfhound's head as his face grew brilliant over the horse plaids. "Birth."

"I'm terribly sorry," she answered, now sincerely.

There were long dog hairs on her black dress. There were long dog hairs on his plaid pants. She wanted to be rid of him.

"Yeah, well." He brushed and picked at himself. "I gotta go turn up the heat. They drink more in the heat." He commanded the dog to remain in the projection room. "Sure appreciate you coming up. Management's real important in this racket."

"I don't dispute you, baby."

They shook hands solemnly.

7

I myself have a great curiosity, recently acquired, to be eaten. By a man with a mustache. You understand why I have not taken advantage of the flesh in the rock and roll band. I am terrified of social disease. Frankly, I am grateful that my terrible pubic itches were fleas rather than anything social. I will soon need advice. Being bright does not help me. For when I ask questions that are purely and honestly naïve, I am not taken seriously. I still do not know whether social diseases can be transmitted from kissing. Perhaps from groupie to boy to pen to contract. Could it be, I would ask if I knew someone who would answer, that if Mack has relations with the groupies in the usual attitudes he tells me the seven assume with five or more in a small bed in Painted Post and then Mack kisses me in Horseheads . . . ? Isn't it odd that the lower classes who are most likely to carry diseases continue to assume all these breeding variations while the upper classes who are most clean rarely vary their position. Things are changing though. I am told. Perhaps I will be involved in the change.

My gynecologist is the past president of the Jewish Community Center and condemns me because I joined the European Health Spa instead of the Center Pool. If he condemns me for that disloyalty, I can not ask him about other disloyalties. The groupies complain to me that the seven Demons wish only to assume odd positions and there is something I do not feel free to describe that is an act which is very distasteful to the groupies and they complain constantly to me about it in my position as mother. Promise as the boys do, they continue to perform in this abominable manner. It could be, therefore, that this cross polident pollination from pistil to stamen to stem as it were . . . ? No, nor from toilet seats, my mother always said.

I can not ask Robert either. He, I suppose, knows the answers.

Recently we traveled on a vividly hot day to an afternoon concert at a small agricultural college in Morrisville. Robert was driving. He had told me to sit in the back and write down the names of songs as Mack recited them to me. Name, artist, studio, time. The list would be submitted to a Scranton disc jockey preparatory to our playing Scranton. We stopped for a Dairy Queen. He sucked the breasts of the Goddess, it was said of Marduk, and I watched nostalgically as Mack licked the curl on the top of his pistachio Dairy Queen. Robert ordered a butterscotch sundae. I, nothing. Mack offered me his cone. Robert turned and said, "I wouldn't eat that if you knew where his tongue had been." Mack laughed. Obviously Robert knew something. He did not know that Mack and I were holding hands under my notebook. I can't ask Robert. Mack has a mustache.

I often think that another five minutes in Mack's red Corvette in the rain in the Savarin Thruway parking lot with the lights of midnight trucks bleeding across the silvery pavement, or in my bedroom listening to tapes of disc jockeys talking about the Demon's music, or lying on the red plastic couch in the rehearsal hall which was once a chicken coop behind Mack's house on moist summer nights writing words for the songs he plays shirtless, on the upright piano, I often think only five minutes more and we would stop looking so hungrily at each other and finally make love.

But nothing. When I ask him why not, he will answer, "I'm content." His Adam's apple chokes him and his eyes are ravaged and his lips turn white and he is content. So. I do not want to push him too far for then I would totally terrify him. He may be waiting for me, or he may be simply holding me at bay to use my power over Robert to his advantage. I am not undesirable and he has whispered to me in all of those perfect above-mentioned places and more at other times, on trips into New York and Chicago where we are alone for uncounted hours, that he wants me. I say nothing.

After all, I am there.

He told me once over a pair of runny English muffins at the Poughkeepsie Savarin that he was afraid of me, physically. I laughed. Robert trusts Mack more than he trusts the others and so I am to drive with Mack only. That is why we are alone so much on week nights. Weekends, Robert travels with them. I am growing more certain of this power I have every day now. Mack recognized it early. That is why he can not ball me, as he says. I am beginning to recognize it also. It is a dreadful thing, this power, something like a magnetic box inside me that draws men, women, children, teenage boys, animals and teeth towards me. Robert calls it charm. I know better. I often know when it is charm only, for there are deposits of lipstick on my teeth from the particular smile. Other times, I do not know what it is that trips the magnetism. If I did know, and could control the power and use it to my advantage, I would be very happy. Recently returning from New York City, where I had taken tapes to Atlantic records and was offered by the person next to me on the airplane a newspaper, I used, unwittingly, my power. I had only noticed his pink shirt sleeve as he read and I watched the black shapes of night moving across the moon. I was very tired. "No, thank you," I answered kindly. "I am so tired that reading would make me cross-eyed." He folded his paper, gathered his effects, and as I looked up to see why he was thus leaving in mid-flight, I saw that he was already cross-eyed. He changed his seat. I had hurt him. I do not know why I even mentioned cross-eyes. It may be unintentionally in some way, that is my power which draws my son to pull out his permanent teeth and leads me to harm people.

One does not deal with power lightly. I have burned compelling incense which my Jamaican maid gave to me and brought Robert home at midnight from distant places. He drove and when he arrived, to my terror, three times in succession during the span of a fortnight, insisted he had simply decided to come home. I have not told him exactly why he had returned. I have made a pencil lift itself in the air and turn around. This also frightens me and I will not try it again. I do not want to be susceptible. Once I admit to my power, I admit to all sorts of spiritual dark browed enemies who may wish me ill. Mack's mother, who is an accomplished Cook of the Week and has black strega eyes, may have guessed how hungry I am for her son. I avoid her.

I have always had a pre-pubic fantasy about power. My fantasy began at the time I was wearing someone's Boy Scout pin and being tied up in basements in cowboy and Indian games. Still, far into puberty, when I am tied by my own fears to the dentist's chair or the gynecologist's table, I escape by dwelling on this wakened, still satisfying dream.

The dream is: I am a queen, tying handsome, rude, crude and nude men of pagan origins to posts, ordering them beaten while I suffer, visibly in conflict but nevertheless watching because it is my duty to inflict this suffering upon them and upon myself. Hatred smolders in their smoldering pitless eyes and then, forgiving, I heal one in my room, a palatial syconium, and give myself to him in sorrow, contrition and Brueghel abandonment. Come and I will heal thee. I suppose it is one of the reasons I so want Mack, because he does suffer and, related to Robert as I am, he suffers indirectly at my hands. Robert is rather inhumane to them all. I truly hope Robert's judgment falls upon their heads. I know the seven Demons are out to get Robert but it will never happen. He is much too strong. Anyway, my dream is quite a dream for a little girl. And it is lasting. Even when the dentist flashes his X ray into my genetics, and I receive his death while he wears a rubber apron and leaves the room, even then I use the dream to escape. It is possible, now that I think of it, that the dentist's X rays are the cause of my son's fangs and the reason why he can not cut a straight line with his first grade scissors. However, I must attend the dentist because I can not be both cunning and lingual, which is my hope, with four month old fermenting rye bread seeds in a decaying mouth and so eventually, armed with my dream and my growing power, I will sit in his chair. Not this week.

Ishtar stroked the wolfhound's back. She went into the office and called her maid. The smallest dog was due for a shot and needed to be taken the next morning to the veterinarian's. She had forgotten to leave that message. The band took its place on the stage. Jimmy returned to the projection room and Ishtar sat on a spring backed couch, stroking the wolfhound and considering the sad children below. Her son was well, although the maid thought he had begun working on another tooth. Ishtar was not happy. She wished to sit quietly with Mack. When she had glimpsed him, he was surrounded with groupies touching him, rubbing near him. She had seen the ugly groupie again, near him, but not next to him. She had begun to notice the girl who always lingered just outside the inner circle of the painted lovely girls around Mack. And Mack? What was his interest in Nino? Was that what held Mack from her own arms? No. She refused to consider it. The door shut beyond her. The set was over and Jimmy had left again for the back room where the groupies visited the band between sets. It was why the boys were in so great a hurry to finish playing. And the poor hungry children waited in the heat below. Ishtar felt grief rise in her chest. She stood and called to them from the tiny window of the projection room. They did not hear.

HANSEL AND GRETEL

It was winter in the Black Forest. There was no sunlight. The people in the towns, hungry and cold, strayed deeper and deeper into the dark forest for wood and food. Ishtar heard often their boots, heavy, Teutonic, stomping across her paths. Although hunting was necessary once the peoples broke the original taboo and ate meat, Ishtar had never learned to like hunters. She had watched one from behind an elder tree near her ginsengbread house, trapping her cat. Screaming at him would have betrayed her house. She bit her lips. The house was for the children whose lives she hoped to illumine and whose stomachs she hoped to fill. She had baked long in preparation for this time and the house, rich and fresh, was standing ready for them. The children would come soon. She sorrowed for her cat.

It had happened before. The people were reduced to eating cats; they would next eat their children. And yet these children, with the same dark blood as their fathers, would be better eaten and gone, would they not? Ishtar, shaking her head in her mirror, remonstrated with herself. "Not the children. I am here to save them."

At last, one night, she heard the crying of children in the forest. She smoothed her hair and sent a snow white dove to lead the children to her house. They came and with great excitement, Ishtar listened as they broke off bits of her house. There had been so little ginseng left and with one cat gone and most of her stores run out, she had only the precious gemstones left for magic. But the gemstones, so hidden in the terrible forest, so far from the sun, could produce little power from the heavens. Ishtar prayed that what the children received from her house would be enough. With their thick-necked redfaced fathers, these children needed ever so much lightness to balance their over-dark blood. Ishtar made her voice soft and leaned out the door.

"Nibble nibble gnaw. Who is nibbling at my house?"

"It is only the wind," a child answered.

Deceitful, they were, and easily turned to thievery. They would need much help. And yet they were the first and if she were kind to them, the other children of this dreadful country would come and eat from the sweetness and partake of the light.

Ishtar called pleasantly into the night. "You may tell the truth, children. I know you are hungry."

They looked at her without trust. She smiled. They dropped their eyes. Their mouths were sullen. Their eyes were slitted.

"Dear children, who has brought you here? Do come in and stay with me. No harm shall happen to you." Ishtar took them both by the hands and led them into her house. Then she set good food before them, milk and pancakes, with sugar and apples and nuts. Afterward two pretty little beds were covered with clean white linen and Hansel and Gretel lay down in them and thought they were in heaven. They were of course closer than most people.

Ishtar worked hard, cooking them every sort of meal and adding her recipes to balance the children's systems. "Why are you afraid of me, children? I will not harm you."

They would bow their heads and continue to eat. Gradually they became more trusting and looked directly at her. They were not, however, grateful and their eyes were smaller than most children's. One day, Gretel placed her warm little hand within Ishtar's own. The child's lips trembled. "In the town, the mothers and fathers are cooking their children. First they cooked the dogs, then the cats. Then if a child is bad . . ." She and Hansel looked sideways at each other. Ishtar felt great compassion for them.

"Come," she said with spirit, "I will show you my jewels to cheer you. These are jewels with which I draw power from the sun and the planets."

"You aren't going to eat us?"

"Heavens! I have a house of food. I do not eat children."

"Even on Passover?"

"That's an anachronism." Laughing, Ishtar poured aprons full of her jewels on the kitchen table, her precious emerald tablets, her magic egg amulets, her scrolls of lapis lazuli and a collection of dead men's teeth. The children cast sidelong glances at each other. Ishtar said nothing to Hansel although he had pocketed an emerald and his eyes were small as pig slits. Ishtar gathered up the jewels quickly. She hoped, soon, fed and happy, Hansel would return the emerald. Knowing the son, it was believable that the parents were capable of eating their offspring. It was the times and the blackness of the forest and it had been too long since the races of man had mated with her daughters. The divine strain was becoming weaker and weaker. Which was why Ishtar had returned.

Ishtar asked the children every morning: "Do you feel sweeter now or still angry?"

Every morning, they answered: "Angry and hungry."

But still, they seemed sweeter and Gretel often offered Ishtar her hand and Hansel, without being asked, fetched wood for the fire and fed the cats. Soon she would have to send them back to tell other children about the house in the forest where they too could find food and happiness and safety. Perhaps the girl would stay and help with the baking. There would be much to do if the rest of the children came and much to do if she were to bring light to the people of the Black Forest. Ishtar was happy with her work. Each night she tucked the children in gently, wrapped hot sweet buns under their pillows and a dish of chocolate mousse by their nightstands. She sang them to sleep.

Hansel asked again and again to play with the gemstones. Gretel begged to learn the magic of the oven and the many colored vessels in the kitchen above the athanor. Finally one rainy afternoon, Ishtar, with Gretel's hand in hers, said, "Gretel, tomorrow I will teach you my baking secrets so you will never again be hungry or lack wisdom."

Hansel asked also to learn the baking. Ishtar felt it was wrong but he pleaded so and his eyes seemed so much softer than those first narrow eyes, she promised the next day to light the athanor and teach them a few of her secrets. "Tomorrow morning, first thing," she promised them as she tucked them into their little beds.

When Ishtar awoke to her mourning dove's call, she saw the two children stuffing gemstones into their pockets. All the colored glasses in the laboratory were shattered.

"Stop!" she called from her bed. It was useless. Her feet and hands were tied with the thongs of her own sandals. She distended an eye and pulled the other into a slit. She cursed. She howled. Hansel dragged her to the oven and Gretel, sweet Gretel, gave her a push that drove her far into the athanor and shut the iron door and fastened the bolt. Ishtar howled horribly at them from behind the grates. "You have betrayed me. I fed you. I gave you my secrets. Ingrates!"

It was Gretel who threw in the match. Ishtar no longer cared. They were not worth her while. The children ran home through the forest, their pockets bulbous with jewels.

Forever after, their children and their children's children and their children after them told the story of how Hansel and Gretel threw the wicked woman into the oven and took all of her wealth. Everyone in the Black Forest wished in their black hearts they could do the same. They finally did.

Ishtar never returned there.

I have often done better with children than those Teutonic thalidomides. And it is within the children where the energy lies. These children now, of the Inferno, below me, are sad and waiting. I feel that I am, in some way, expected. And it is this expectation which stirs the power in me. I call to them again. A few hear me.

"Rise, oh my folk," I call to them from the projection room over the noise of the jukebox. "Rise, oh my folk, from the dust of the earth." Some look up. "Rise, oh my folk, from the checkout counter at the A&P, from the greasepit at Midas Muffler." I have more of them attentive now. "Rise and garb thee in raiments, in see-throughs and tight bells and midriffs baring your first fruits, stuff your holy 32A padded apples into highrise bras and glue your lanuga eyelashes on and drape yourselves . . ." The jukebox is turned off. ". . . and drape yourselves on the steps of the sukka bandstand and suffer, succubi, and raise your childlike voices that turn shrill in your demiurge and the hemisemidemiquaver of your voices shall reach the great ones in their pavilion." They are giggling, but attentive for I too have a nice rhythm.

"Hey, you. You with the mustache. Eat me. Eat me. You want head? You want to go down on me?" I am speaking their language now and they are quite attentive. "Beat your hosanna in the meat market marked with Magic Markers proclaiming the Demons. And yes, there they are on their pavilion near the bar, neath the ladies and gents, and the folk from the dust of the earth worship them because someday, someday, they may be great."

"Why not?" they call up to the wall of the projection booth. They cannot see me.

"Why not?" I answer. And flashing the words on the walls with a bounding ball I lead them in singing to Moses. "Go down," the ball bounces. "Go down, Moses." They sing, aware of the entendre, and I sadly slice the wolfhound into bloody quarters with the misericorde from my shopping bag, aneling him with Three-in-One oil as the children sing.

"Bright oil, pure oil, shining oil, the purifying oil of the gods, oil which softens the sinews of man," I murmur. "With the oil of the incantation, I have made thee drip. With the oil of the softening which is given for soothing, I have anointed thee. The oil of new life I have put on thee. Depart now."

I lay each of his parts at the legs of a stack table covered with tortoise shell Contact paper and build a small fire of papers before the table. I address the soul of the departing dog: "For your strength, I shall heal your master's lameness," and then I leap over the fire and the stack table clumsily, but effectively. It has been a long time since I have made that particular leap. I am sorry I do not have a captive or a simple puppy to sacrifice at this time. And no river to toss them into. I need the strength derived in this way. But, these are new times. I sprinkle water and oil from the light projector basin onto my forehead and then I prepare an entertainment for the children. I turn in the same place, my arms stretched above my head and I call down for them the Skirts of Heaven onto their walls. I play curtains of auroras for them across the dance hall. As the curtains open, enlarge and burst like coronas into myriads of vertical colors flooding the room, the children gasp appreciatively and wave up to the projection booth. They know, although there is only a small hole in the wall, that a specialist is above.

"The aurora borealis," I begin rather pedantically, "is the orgasm of the Queen of Heaven, as a thunderstorm is the orgasm of her lover. Her orgasm is multi-faceted and beautiful. His is singular and terrifying. Even noisy." I allow my voice to sough over their backs. "These are the Skirts of the Queen of Heaven on your walls. I am the Queen of Heaven, the Great Goddess, et cetera. There is no sin beneath my skirts. Sin, my babies, is a fantasy." I turn the aurora up into its high frequency electric blues. "The original sin was my murder. That is when sin began, when the first wife, the first mother was banished. But I am back.

The children stir restlessly. "Listen not to their tales of original sin. The church hangs you up and shakes you down as they did me from the Tree of Life, for I am the apple and it is I that must be eaten for knowledge and joy. But they rip you off too. Sign nothing. Promise nothing. Don't sell your soul for their redemption. You have no sin. Remember the Hostess. Jesus is bad hash. Partake of me." I shift the blues to purples and finally to the iron ore red of the mother lodes and down to the umbers and blacks of nighttide. The children become silent as the colors change; their faces lift expectantly.

As I rotate the light of dawn on the Eastern Wall, their faces wait as cornucopias to be filled with the sweet fruits of my knowledge. I love them.

"I am the apple, my loves. Paradise, the Garden, the Star of David, the Star of Bethlehem, the Star of Solomon, Lady Luck, even Lucifer. But I didn't fall. They ripped me off. Now they offer you stale wafers and false wines, but no sweet fruit, no ale, no cakes, no solace. I am the alewife; I am the Hostess who bakes; I am the mother. Tell them that you know me. Tell them I am back and have told you the truth."

They laugh, clapping. "Good show."

I squirt the entire container of Three-in-One oil, in the basin and add pigments wildly. "Here. Here is what happened." On the side walls I show them foolish Adam, thick-lipped and doughfaced, chasing a sow through a lonely forest of ferns. The children roar as Adam mounts the sow and dives away from the bite of her tusks as she fights him from her back. "Don't jest," I tell them. "How do you think we domesticated animals for you. Adam, after I subdued him with my love, it was given to him to love the animals." Adam is heaving, working hard on the sow, who snorts and bucks obstinately.

The children shout encouragement. "Go to it, Adam. Go to it."

"And now, here he is coming back to my Garden. See how tired the poor man is, legs wobbly, shoulders hunched, scarred. Surely humping wild beasts is a job fraught with danger and I did feel sorrow for him. There he comes now, followed by the rutting females. The work is not over with the cows, the pigs, the dogs. It was then my job and the job of my women to soften the beasts with food and affection. And see, first the female animals, then the males follow them into the Garden. Our first flocks. I nearly lost Adam over a she bear but he escaped and we chose to leave bears wild. Men were more in demand than bears. I myself loved the lion and the steed. But my love doesn't truly domesticate. Adam subdued all these beasts with his only weapon and within time, flea-ridden, spent and odiferous, he would return to me. I had my sacrifices too. This last Creation, yours, was the most difficult. Yes? A question?"

"Cats?" they call up to me.

"Yes, cats. Cats came curiously but were never subdued.

There, there!" My voice breaks with excitement as I remember. "See my sons? They are half-divine. Cain and Abel. Your idea of blue blood is not without basis. And see how they hold their mother? Was I not lovely then and divine? They being much cleaner and more sentient than their foul father, who was not in any part divine, I took pleasure from my sons. And their father . . . see how he ruts the ground with his foot in his jealousy. "Ha!" I shout at the wall. How I despised Adam. "Ingrate. Narrow-minded hotbuttocked tree dweller!" I change the picture to an open plain. Things will be sad now and I steel myself. "Now see, see how he turns son against son and I weep there by the yucca, beautiful even though ravaged with the grief of my son's murder. No one, not even his father, shall take my son again. No one. Adam, you see, had hoped to have me for himself by killing off his sons. Nice man. But I am for all mankind. So I departed. See me leaving? Do you like that gown? The heavens collapsed of course. My Star fell and I wandered desolately. Aah, how long . . ." My voice fades out. It is terribly dramatic and the children are with me.

"What, child? I can't hear your question."

"Eve?" I spit into the projection bowl and curtains of green light shiver unnaturally around the scene on the walls. "She was the second wife. Adam produced an image of woman he could deal with and subdue. I am first. Not that maidenly simpleton, see her? Adam created her from the lower parts of his hairy beastie body. He had little knowledge left and could not create beauty. See that nunsuch face. Mincemeat. Botcher. See how she hides her parts in false humility. Miserable wretched usurper. That sweet cowering dumdum, children, is the major source of your problems today. She is sin. Eat all the apples you want, Eve. They won't work on you. Do you understand, children?"

The children clap. Now I diffuse a creamy lactescent light through the room. The children wonder at it and reach to touch. They cannot. They applaud. "I am the apple," I shout happily over their heads for want of anything better to shout. "Eat me. I am the body of wisdom. Know me. I am back."

"More," they shout. I adore an audience. I am a Star again.

I cannot lead them ahead unless I begin where they are. To show them Ur, to show them Babylon, to show them my glories would be of no avail. They don't know the words. Decisively, I turn the walls into the golden living walls of the First Temple in Jerusalem. I make the walls flow with Cherubim and palm trees and sinuous snakes intertwined in divine copulation as the children shout in awe and astonishment. I show them the bronze doors of the Eastern Walls and drape the seven precious veils from the ceiling of the dance hall to the stage. I carve the Eastern Gates with light and place the great golden chalices and silver hangings on the ark of sittum woods on the stage. The children turn from wonder to wonder until I bring in very gently, my hands trembling, the two Cherubim, their golden wings intertwined in love, their faces turned to each other glowing with joy. The Cherubim gaze calmly at the walls of the dance hall. One winks at me. They look upon the children and smile upon them. Then they turn and fold their golden wings decorously over each other.

"They're real," many say to each other. One child reaches out to touch them through the thin veils. I am forced to throw a terrible electric charge with my furca into his curious hands. I magnify my voice. "Touch not the Holy Ones. They are the angels. I bring them to you and I bring to you the beauty of love. Clap your hands for the Holy Ones. Help them."

The children clap obediently. A few seem to be crying. The Cherubim change the rhythm of their embraces to the rhythm of the children's hands. The children's rhythm quickens. The holy act reaches toward consummation. I rupture the embrace.

"Don't stop!" they protest. "Let them finish." There are angry fists reaching toward the wall of the projection room.

"Pray then, children," I advise softly. "Pray for their happy consummation. Pray that they be together in love and the heavens will be right."

I can see the magenta veils moving as the children's lips move in broken half-remembered prayers. They have no words. But they are sincere. A few are on their knees so the others behind can see. I rest my chin on my elbows over the projection room and abandon the light show. My tears I feel streaming across my cheeks. My tears land in the oil basin and mix with the paints and dyes and the Three-in-One oil. I sigh mightily. I am lonely. There is no god to lie with. As I watch, the Cherubim, vague and amorphous now behind the sunset of the shimmering veils, consummate the act to the children's prayers.

The children cry and shiver. I do not wish to terrify them with the destruction and the carrying of the Cherubim in cages of ridicule in the streets of Jerusalem. But it is all over. I splash blood from the wolfhound's stomach into the oil basin. It is not until the walls begin to bleed of themselves, the temple scene fading from them, that I flash on the images of tortured monks and decapitated saints and then at last Mary, looking very much like Eve, holding her bloody son in her lap.

"It's real. It's really real," a girl screamed in the proper hysteria. All the children were on their knees. "I felt her."

My voice thunders cataclysmically. "This is not real. Now you will see what *is* real!" And I turn the projection machine on my own face and play myself in triumph on the walls as whore, mother and hag of death. "That, kids, is real. I'm Mother." I turn my voice into a calm commercial tone. "Hope you enjoyed the show." There are a few giggles, evidently of relief. I had frightened them too much.

I can still hear the echo of the girl protesting. "It's real. I touched her."

Older children begin to laugh at her. The laughter is doubtful but necessary.

I turn Mary and Jesus to Marilyn and W.C. I put Popeye up again and I stamp out my small fire. I throw rags on the hound's body and flee. There is not time to clean up and I am sorry. As the manager comes running down the steps, I trip him and he clatters in agony downward. He will heal properly. I escape. The band begins to play. I hope Robert doesn't hear about this. I'll blame it on the feathers.

8

Ishtar, her gown greasy with Three-in-One oil and stuck with clumps of dog fur, rounded the warehouse, howled back at a passing freight train and strode mightily, smugly, along the uneven sidewalk toward her motel. She picked at the fur on her gown.

"Hey! Wait up!"

Ishtar stopped. She did not wish her contemplation interrupted. The voice came along the dark sidewalk, then embodied itself as the ugly groupie under a streetlight. Ishtar was curious. The groupie ran, gangly, grasping a cello by its neck, like a dead brother, banging its tailpiece over the sidewalk cracks. Ishtar leaned against a store window and waited. The girl was impressive. A velvet cape of black with mutton sleeves flapped around her as she ran, its hems spread and gathering sidewalk slush. The girl's face was hawklike, unsoftened by cosmetics, sharpened by corrugated hair, sticking out, two black washboards, from the sides of her head. Over the neck of the cello, her hands were white and big, ugly and powerful. She was not pretty as the others were. Ishtar, who had her own images, wrinkled her nose in distaste as the girl bent on her knees before her, covering the sidewalk with her cape in a large dirty circle and breathing heavily. Ishtar waited, not unkindly. She felt sorrow for this half-woman who fit so poorly into the scheme of present things. The girl unscrewed the tailpiece of her cello.

"I guess I broke my tailpiece." She removed it from its

socket, stuck a clot of gum from her mouth into the socket, tucked the gum around the hole and patted the cello. "There." Masking tape and flag-striped bandaids held the bottom of the instrument together.

"I am hurrying."

"I'll keep up with you."

"And where are you going, child?"

The girl laughed and stood up, smoothing the cover of her cello over the wood. Her laughter carried into the night. "I'm twenty. No child. I catch a bus near here. But I'll go where you're going." Her eyes were brazen, unabashed.

I do not wish to be with this person. But there is something powerful in her hands and her laughter, riding as it does into the night, something that was not in her aura when she sat with the groupies. "We will talk here. We will wait for your bus together."

She leaned her cello against the window of the drugstore. Inside a clerk watched them. The cello was soft and rounded. The girl's body was angular. Ishtar waited. The girl squeezed moisture from the filthy hems of her cape. "You manage that band, huh?"

"Yes."

The girl busied herself with the cape. Ishtar grew annoyed. She examined a pyramid display of vibrators in the drugstore window. They were black and white and rainbow striped. They seemed hopeful. The clerk grimaced obscenely at her. Ishtar surpassed him with a few subtle maneuvers of her fingers.

"I want to be in the band. I'm good."

"It is my band."

"I just want to be *in* it. I don't have to take it from you, do I?"

"Which young man do you want?"

"That's not it."

"I have seen you with the groupies. You and they know only the worship of the phallus. They and you disgust me and turn my bowels into clay. I have waited for you here. You will tell me the truth."

"Okay." She covered her cheeks with her hands. Ishtar hoped she was discomfited. "Mack." There was something alluring about the movement.

"You may not be in the band. You may not have Mack."

The girl examined Ishtar closely. Ishtar stood still. "I want both things. I don't look like you. I don't look like the other girls. But it doesn't mean I'm not interested." She grabbed Ishtar's arm. She was very strong. Ishtar grew curious, as though standing on the edge of a distant precipice. "I've done it. I mean, they think that's what I want because I hang around and once in a while I get picked up. But it's no good." Her grip tightened. "I mean, is it good?"

The Queen of Heaven shrugged. "Depends."

I do not wish to share anything with this dirty-hemmed girl. I am one. It is my band. I shall have Mack. I am jealous. That has always been a fault of mine, but how can I, who is one, whose name is one, be less than a jealous goddess? But there is something new glinting inside that face. It is something I recognize in my own face. But not Mack; Mack is mine. Yet she is strong, too strong, for the other half-men. Women have not been sisters for millenniums. I am wrong to trust her. I do not like her. She has not been loved by someone who knows love. No one has been initiated yet. I myself have chosen Mack. I do not like this person.

"One of your breasts seems uneven."

The girl was silent.

"You would do well to shorten your cape. It is stiff with filth."

"I can pick up Mack's amplifiers with my hands." She splayed her hands over the drugstore glass. "You have a husband. Mack and I talk a lot. We have to stand in corners or in the kitchen by the beer cases so no one can see us. Because I am ugly. He doesn't say that. I know. He talks to the others but he's just doing it for effect. He told me himself he has nothing to say to them. I told him I'd sleep with him or do anything for him, even blow him, if he wants, but he just kind of looks at me. Just looks. Why? I can pick up his amplifiers. I can drag him away. I have very strong hands. I play the cello so much that my right breast is all muscle. There is hair around the nipple."

"Who are your parents?"

"My father he makes glass. He installs it, I mean. And my mother, she's at home a lot and she's disappointed in me because she was beautiful. At least she says she was. You can't tell anymore. All the men in my father's family way back made glass. His name is Glazier. I just call myself Claire. I don't use a last name. I thought the musicians would be better in bed because they have feelings. No way. I watch you a lot. I want to be like you."

"Come, I will buy you one striped like the rainbow."

The girl pocketed the vibrator within the folds of her coat. The bus rumbled out of the night. The girl pulled her cello by its neck, racing down the sidewalk, her coat trailing in the dirty snow. "Shorten your coat," Ishtar yelled after her.

Ishtar fixed her hair in the drugstore window.

I do not like her. I do like her. She has strength. Her nose is strong. Aah, but I am so much prettier than she is. So much. And then, smiling, chiding herself, she walked on thoughtfully to the motel. She would have been, in another age, a great beauty, this girl. I suppose she will have to have Mack. But I am first. First. That at least. And my breasts, of course, are even and smooth. Foolish child, there must be ritual.

"Dig super cool," Nino announced at breakfast in Buffalo.

"Make like you know me." A newly bearded young man in purple pants and orange shirt slid into a seat at the long table. "You guys the Demons?

"Don't look at me," Sonny, the trumpet player, answered. "I was doing U-turns under the sheets all night long."

"Heard you had some light show. Who does it for you?"

"I'm the leader. We were on break. You a cop?"

"How'd you guess, Mack, how'd you guess?" Nino hissed, and waved a weak wrist in contempt.

"Look, you guys are in trouble. Not with us. They tore down the Inferno last night. Burned it to the ground."

Ishtar laughed loudly and then stopped as everyone stared at her.

"Hundreds of cats, old, young. Piece by piece carting it away and they're in the churches now calling for the Mother of God. They're telling the bishops they seen Her. We're gonna get you out of town before they tear you to pieces."

"Anybody want my undies for a relic?"

"Do they claim also that the walls bled?" Ishtar asked politely.

"Yeah. Some kids say they tasted it and it was blood."

"See," Ishtar addressed the group. "They always claim blood. Lourdes, Fatima, Glendalough. It can't be Jesus unless it bleeds. So they convince themselves by making it bleed. No god is stupid enough to come down and get ripped up just to prove himself. What for? This is . . ." She touched the orange sleeve. "Mass hallucination, War of the Worlds, that kind of thing."

"That's what downtown's saying. I'm Polish Catholic myself and I never seen anything like it. Some in wheelchairs. They even took beer cans for relics. And then the folks who believed started to fight with the . . . well, it was pretty bad and we want you guys out of town before anything picks up again."

"Would you tell us how the people described the show?"

"Look, some kids swore they touched two angels which were, uh, observed to be fornicating."

"Fornicating, I do declare."

"Shut up, guys, he's helping us." Mack glanced at Ishtar,

who held a beatific smile on her face and closed her eyes.

"These strobe images. You get pictures flashing on at a sixty-fourth of a second, all you do is hold the basin, swish the stuff around. It's just a dish. Nothing weird about it. The bar, the heat, the music . . . chicks get hysterical when Nino takes off his shirt for Christ's sake."

"Listen, the owner's dog got cut up. That's for real. And they say the dame told them to go to their priests and tell them there's no original sin because the sin was knocking off the mother and now she's back. That's what's cooking at the churches. You guys better go. They won't give you time to explain it if they find out who you are."

"Yes," Ishtar agreed, opening her eyes. "It is time to pull out. Withdraw. Who ran the show? Did you mention that?"

"I told you. The kids said it was the Mother of God."

"Aren't they *stupid*? After all that. God *is* a mother." She stood up and smoothed her skirts. "Thank you for helping us."

The boys followed her out. Ishtar was proud of her band. She was more and more concerned about breaking the contract. Robert would not view the event lightly.

9

It is Sunday. Robert waits, a thunderhead, at my kitchen, dark and threatening. He must know about Buffalo. Sunday is not my day. This Sunday will be most unpleasant. I am squeezing navel oranges and not pulling enough juice. Robert enjoys fresh orange juice on Sunday mornings and it is the least I can do for him particularly since he seems so silently angry. How much he knows I can not now deduce. Because the juice burns the inner skin of my fingers, I walk naked except for my fur slippers, my underwear and the long red-brown hairpiece from a Kyoto geisha shop. The hairpiece I have attached to the inside of the elastic band of my lollipops and my tail swings invitingly at my calves while I prepare my family's breakfast. I am threatened by Robert's silence. The Italian hour plays softly. My son takes his cereal bowl. He does not want me to cook for him. Robert's silences are more threatening today than his words.

Sunday is a day of rest for Robert only. He has not asked me yet to drive to the factory. Angry as he is, he will likely not ask that I go with him but will be angrier that I don't. Later, if the black and white stepped pattern of the *Times* crossword puzzle pleases me in its design, I will fill in the words. Words are edible, power sources. I work my mouth around them and derive their energies. Sentences do not interest me particularly. For instance, while I am squeezing these oranges, Robert has been saying in stark groaning chains of words such things as "I will not break the law. You will not break the law. We will not break the law."

These pronouncements may refer to the taking of drugs and the destruction at Buffalo, or they may be an answer to my suggestion of worldwide Cupcake factories using specific Sumerian ingredients that I spoke to him of earlier in the morning when he had awakened in a gentle mood. There is a lull between his sleep and his waking. He does not fight. He is loving and he nestles his head in my soft parts and I speak to him. Then suddenly he is awake, lunging around the bedroom dangerously, looking for things which I pray from under the blankets are where they ought to be. These are not godlike pronouncements he is making, although he sits above the breakfast table tapping cigarettes, reading the comics and waiting for me to serve him. He in fact sounds rather petulant. He has never enjoyed my feeding him. It is perhaps why I am such a good cook, having at least attained countywide note with my quiche lorraine and cabbage soup. It is a torture for him to be physically dependent upon my skills, good graces and putting away his clothes in the correct places. It is why he is quick to find fault, for he hates the dependency.

The yellows will not run when he jabs the eggs I will soon give him. They will be too hard. I do not like the jabbing for I know what eggs are. They should not be eaten lightly. I and my son do not eat eggs, considering the eating of running foetus quite unbearable.

"Is that clear, Ishtar?" He had spoken. I did not hear. I will agree.

Into the lilting matrix of the Italian hour, the announcer injects crystalline Anglo-Saxon. "Sears and Roebuck," and I, cracking an egg, smile at the unwitting wisdom. I do not understand the Italian. I enjoy its flow. Sergio Franchi sings about his mother. Robert waits.

"We will not be involved in drugs in any way, commercially or privately."

I rub Corn Huskers Lotion between my fingers and nodding my head in agreement I sit myself on a golden yellow breakfast stool and drape my tail carefully to one side.

"And if your precious Mack . . . if I find anything on him, I'll have him arrested. I'll throw the book at him. I'll have his ass kicked in."

Robert continues. His tempo is increasing. My nipples are antennas, grossly exaggerated in the curved reflection of the Sunbeam toaster. They will understand when the toast should pop and will warn me before it burns. Robert, watching the stainless steel nipples, forgets that his juice is freshly squeezed and swallows the pulpy clots, coughing them into his napkin. I smile secretly. He has not yet put down his paper. He is now reading the financial section. Before while I spoke to him of Cupcakes and factories and an entire civilization living on the chocolate and mandrake roots of my Hostess Cupcakes, and like happiness, being sold on every street corner of America, of the world and the mothers of the boys operating the factories while Robert sits far above them all, overseeing and designing new ovens and machines and checking quality control, he laughed suddenly between my words. He was reading Dagwood Bumstead. I continued to spin my dreams of edible records, of spruce beer and pears and happiness and wealth enough for the boys' contentment and his own peace, of peace between man and woman, of wholeness for everyone and of a connection again to the powers of heaven. He laughed. But what can I expect of him. He went to the bookstore to buy a copy of *Intelligent Life in the Universe* and when he arrived, forgot the title. He is not the kind to consider other worlds, particularly the inner world of his own dread supernatural. Why does he laugh at Dagwood Bumstead? Dagwood Bumstead has never been funny. The hatred between the two is abysmal and I wish to remove it. I can.

Somehow, my mother would say, you must begin at home. I do not think though it will be possible to change Robert without sacrificing too much of myself. And yet I know I must, in the words of the youngsters, get it together, so I can be a goddess in my kitchen and a cook in the universe. Only then will I be happy. I wish to be recognized for all that I am. I believe it is too late for Robert. I must begin someplace.

We worked with diligence that winter, the three ugly sisters and myself, separating lentils, within which, you understand, were spirits, from the ashes of the world. Often my doves came to help me. The good into a dish to throw. The bad into the crops can go. Later mystics will call this simple process reincarnation. I had to hop all that winter for I had lost my slipper during the night of chaos whence I had dispatched all of these souls. I hopped in order that my holy heel, uncovered, would not touch the ground. Although I had lost my golden slipper, I did not regret the destruction and I was willing, with the help of my fine ugly friends, to clean up and save from the ashes that which ought to be saved. A dismal oil lamp burned eternally in the chimney corner, for it was a poor house, but I was not disheartened with the lentils and the cinders. I was in hiding, you know. And there is no better place than a kitchen for a mother goddess to go unrecognized, particularly a poor kitchen in a poor country house away from the palaces.

Naturally there were dozens of young slavering hard-on princes scouring the land for me. The kingship was empty; the land barren; the wells dried up. And I, the sovereignty of the land, besmirched and dressed in rags, refused to be bothered with these sweating aspiring princes who came seeking the kingship. I alone had the power to confer this kingship upon them. I needed a rest. I did not have the energies yet to uphold another weak character seeking his manhood, another lover protecting his fragile potency from his fears and I was tired, so tired, of tiptoeing around the cages of the barbaric emotions of these men who needed to rule the world. I was tired of bringing them up to flower. So I changed shape often, from pear tree to dove to swan to gate post until at last I found this good, albeit poor, home. Few men sought the ugly daughters and they could use their energies to save souls from the cinders. Ugly girls, of course, try harder and often have better spirits. I hid. No man would find me, not even the Foot Fetishist.

Of all the princes, the Foot Fetishist is most aggressive in his search for me, and he, this great perspiring, unconfident, sweat-palmed beast, has always been after my foot. I'm certain it was he who stole my slipper during the night of chaos. The slipper has no power without my foot, but men have been known to busy themselves in odd ways with shoes. It is more than drinking from my shoe that he busies his princely gross self with. I know, in his slovenly closets and besmirched bedclothes, he has deposited many a handful of offering in my name, in consideration of my foot. Often, he calls great palace festivals, rounding up all the women of the countryside and slips my now unclean sacred slipper onto their innocent but mortal feet. Oh, he is ill, this one, and he would do well to be plowed under with the rest of the no-good beans. Often it is his men coming through the green copse beyond our poor home in richly trapped horses carrying jewels and gowns for girls of the neighborhood. He wants only to be my royal footholder and control the power of the land. He has my shoe and I am somewhat weakened. He follows me.

At last, as was inevitable, for the people needed me, he appeared. He announced yet another dance and counted us. I had to appear. I could not avoid him the entire dreadful evening. I stood tiptoe all night to keep my heel from the ground. He insisted on dancing with me. I hopped away as soon as the music ended and he called into the night behind me: "No other shall become my wife but she whose foot this golden slipper fits." There were many things I wished to do to this pig of a prince, but he had my shoe and my powers. I raced, hopping through the forests, keeping my naked heel off the earth. I changed shapes all the way home, rabbits, white rats, pumpkins, a horse. He did not find me. But the next morning, his retinue were at the door of our poor cottage. I cowered in the fireplace.

The good ugly sisters did their utmost to fit that slipper on their feet and save my life from the Foot Fetishist. I will never forget them for their devotion and their sacrifice. One cut off her toe; one cut off her heel. It was without avail. I was found and he, with his yellow pointed teeth, his twitching loins, and sweating palms, took my foot in his hand and slipped the befouled slipper upon it. That was it. Do not think I lived happily ever after at all. The only advantage received from that stage in my career is that I was able to stop hopping. You may hear other versions of this tale.

It is still Sunday. I am still in the kitchen. I am still preparing Robert's eggs.
Let us begin, then, with eggs.
There are no fertilized eggs in Syracuse.
I have sought them. As you have.

Near daybreak there shall be a great calm and you shall see the Day-Star arise and the dawning will appear, and you shall perceive a great treasure. The chief thing in it, and the most perfect, is a certain exalted tincture with which the world (if it served God and were worthy of such gifts) might be tinged and turned into most pure gold. Pow.
Once you gleam the totality of truth, the details will fit. At your point in space, degenerate in knowledge, you do not know what to do with the report of a human footprint in the stone bed of the Pacific Ocean floor or a picture of an adobe house on the moon taken by Apollo 12 or why you buy Easter eggs. You would have to know larger concepts. That Mu, the Motherland, for instance, lying once between South America and India, blew to bits 12,000 years ago and her colonies, Atlantis, Ireland, Britanny, the Basque Highlands, Crete, Dilmun, Catal Huyuk—there were many more —lasted somewhat longer until all the original knowledge and language were dispersed, leaving only that solitary footprint on the sea floor and Easter egg hunts on the White

House Lawn. You've read too quickly. Go back. See the sentence about language and knowledge? I want you to understand that everything came from one source, that language and knowledge were all one and from one. Myself. Civilization is given.

It is entirely appropriate that you continue to seek the egg at Easter. For Easter is Ishtar's holiday. I find it offensive that you are reduced to buying sterile eggs at this holiday of regeneration and that I myself must order mine from New Jersey. However, since I have always been the source of knowledge, it amuses me to begin once again with the egg.

The egg.

I have twice in this life attempted to produce eggs. Once in mechanically acceptable circumstances with a junior egg hatchery purchased at Chanukah for my son in order that it bring forth on the New Year. And once through private body functionings. The second act was perhaps to justify the failure of the first. I can not however blame the failure on the machine. The failure is to be laid upon the malaise of the milieu. I have never failed at words. Often I have been euphemistically referred to as The Word. I am neither The Word nor The World Egg. I am The Lady who is The Source of All Things.

"Sorry, lady," the egg farmer, who was either one of my obscene phone callers or had just dashed in from his henhouse, breathlessly apologized. "I got only this one rooster and he's running into fourteen, fifteen hunnerd hens a day. No telling when he catches one how many he's caught before, strain's so weak. Try the Experimental Farm ferinst Pompey?" Pompey is to the East. Ferinst is Middle English, quite antique, meaning over against.

I ignored his suggestion, not wishing mutations on my kitchen counter, and ordered two eggs from New Jersey, filling out the coupon attached to the plastic domed hatchery. Check one, chicken, turkey, pheasant, other. Next to other I printed plainly in large letters, goose, golden. Times change. Hope remains.

It was dead winter. The package from New Jersey sat in my RFD nest for hours. I lay the cold speckled eggs which were neither golden nor goose into the hatchery basins within the dome, filling the third basin with warm water to keep the shells moist. I ought to have placed them between my legs, but I had much walking to do. I prayed over my menorah, which, contrary to Yahwist teachings, represents the seven planets with the top candle none other than the Queen of Heaven. I called down the power of each planet to the eggs. I plugged the cord of the plastic womb into my Universal appliance center and I spoke to, cared for, protected, the clear dome's contents as if Snow White lay within waiting her time. In order that he raise not his voice nor slam doors near the eggs, I strained Robert's juice and cooked his eggs to perfection. And no soul, for the entire gestation period, crossed hands, feet or fingers in my kitchen. I myself wore nine needles on a tricolored thread around my neck to magnetize the astral rays toward my kitchen and bring my son's eggs safely to life. My orange cats, like the Three Old Ones, sat around the womb, heads tilted, watching and listening for hours each day. I felt they could sense something I could only hope for. Luck, who not only is a Lady, but is from the same source word as logos, lucifer and means wisdom, light, power, might bring me a phoenix flapping against my Spanish ceiling beams. Phoenix, by the way, originates from the same source as Venus, Penis, Phoenicia, and Phoenicia is the place where circumcision was first, according to your histories, practiced in my honor.

"What are they going to look like? When will they get here?" My son inquired daily.

"At daybreak," I would answer him. "There will be a great calm. If you have served me well and are worthy of such gifts, they will appear on the first day in the first light of the New Year." That is a method I employ when I am unwilling to do something prayed for. I patently blame it on your unworthiness. It gets me off the hook. Being much like you, please understand that I at times enjoy wallowing in the same stubborn, lazy, halfhearted trough you often occupy. If you are Olympian, you are necessarily careless.

At last it was daybreak of the New Year. According to *Anderson's Tales of Paradise, Harvard Classics*, Volume XVII, page 311, "there resounded a clap of thunder, so dreadful that no one heard the like and everything fell down. And he opened his eyes and the Star in the distance, the Star that gleamed like the Paradise that had sunk down, was the morning star in the sky." Do you remember what happened with Moses and myself when you first met us? Venus became a planet. Pieces of her, small stars.

Whatever manner of pterodactyl horror was within fascinating the cats, I shall never know, for the thin-shelled embryos burst dutifully at dawn perhaps to our digital dial alarms, and scrambled themselves ferinst the plastic dome with a green and red shmear not at all traceable to the archetype of Snow White or the Philosopher's caskets. Obviously, I had not been served well and my son was not deserving of gifts. The cats leaped to hide in the attic insulation. My needles swung sideways around my neck.

I stared into the membranes lining the dome. I stared into the pia mater, the mutated pia mater of the plastic dome of the plastic brain and within I saw *Herodotus' Map of the World According to the Brain of Man*. I saw *The Ventricles as the Abode of the Soul according to Albertus Magnus* and *The Seven Spirits which Abide in the Brain According to the Museum Hermeticum*. Aah, I saw Calvary, the bare skull. I saw Golgotha, the burial place, and I saw the skull of the hoarfrost giant, Ymir, forming the walls of heaven. The world is a large sick body of which you are the cells. And I was sick at the horror in my Universal appliance center and I, like Tiamat, the Great Mother, pulled the plug and tossed the whole mess into the snow below my kitchen windows and raced to my bathtub, where I am able to renew a limb or a psyche. I have learned with bad recipes to throw the whole thing out and start over again. Adding an arm, or kindness, or technical abilities or even oregano, doesn't help when the original eggs are rotten. Some things are not worth saving. It is all the same, you know. Eggs, cauldrons, craniums, universes, chalices, pools, grails, bathtubs. All attached.

That you must understand.

And that you, buying your world eggs at Fannie Farmer, seeking regeneration and power, seeking them under Nixon's lonely footprint on the White House Lawn at Easter, I lament for you. That you do not know Me, that you are degenerate in the knowledge and lost your connection to the heavens. I come to teach. I come to connect. Reddy Kilowatt. I come to restore the power.

Can you use ferinst in a sentence yet? You must begin to look backward. The globe, green, steamed in the snow. Soon the early morning's snows covered it entirely.

Now I place the eggs on the table. Robert folds his newspaper. He has realized that I am not listening to him. My son, pinked milk running from his chin, looks up at his father and begins to pick at a tooth in the recesses of his mouth.

"If you're going to do that, Buddy," Robert reminds him rather kindly, "leave the table. The boy should eat eggs," Robert reminds me unkindly.

The boy takes his cereal bowl. He does not look up at me. He goes to the family room, where he is alone to watch television. I would like to go with him. I would like to help him escape from this pain. Since it is my power, though, which brings him to pulling out his own teeth, a divine demonstration of his power over both his body and my emotions, my helping him to escape would be further destructive.

I have found that power must be used with discretion. I do not know why he must prove his power. Robert tells me that it is my fault the boy pulls out his teeth because I am too willful, headstrong, demanding and the boy is rebelling. It is now the plan for Robert to be his friend so that when I am too strong, he can turn to his father. For a while I believed all this until the boy gave me his teeth. Although I am not at all certain of this, I now blame his problems on Robert. Whether I am right or wrong, it is easier this way to bear the gaping holes and the bloody fingers. I believe the boy wishes to defend me and has given me, in this grotesque, thoroughly archaic manner, his pledge.

Robert asks me a question. "Do you have any explanation for the disturbance in Buffalo, Ishtar?" His nose becomes thin. He is controlling his anger to derive information from me. It is his way. I give him little.

"There is unrest among the boys."

"You think it's Mack, Ishtar? I have to *bring* groupies to him. Don't you ever notice anything queer about him?"

"He is kind. He and Nino are fine friends. Nino is so masculine, you know, with that ridiculous penis of his, he would never befriend Mack, if Mack were not a whole man." I think this is well said.

Robert is concerned. "Ishtar, who always gets the coffee and doughnuts for the boys? Who do I always have to get the girls for? I tell you, he's not interested."

"There is nothing wrong with him, darling. He is a sweet and gentle person. Perhaps none of the cheap girls are what he wishes. I prefer him to Nino. I find his constant erections offensive."

"It's funny. The kids . . . well, it's a hell of a gimmick." Robert uncovers his eggs and sticks them with his tines. "Don't start protecting him too. One son is enough." The eggs do not run. Robert's upper lip tightens and puckers and his jaw juts forward, Neolithic. Wow. He stands, looks beyond me, and shovels the eggs into the Moloch of the Waste

King, where they are eaten along with an unsuspected Design Research spoon. His anger is Captain Marvelous with comic book zigzags of lightning escaping from his body. Waste not. Want not. I waste. I want.

"I'll bet he started something in Buffalo. Nobody wants a queer around."

I will not blame Mack. I will protect him. For whatever danger it may bring upon me. His gentleness is of value. "It was an Act of God."

"That's another spoon! Don't you care about the spoon? God damn." He stands before me. "Do you know what that means? That means I don't collect on the contract and we've lost five thousand dollars because that . . . that mess in Buffalo has been determined an Act of God."

"I care about the spoon." I am desperate to agree. I have no heart to fight with Robert today. I am deathly tired after my appearance Friday night. I would rather make love and restore my energies while the child is in the family room. I do not wish to fight with Robert over Mack, which I will have to do, or with the Waste King now wrestling like the Angel Michael over the strangling spoon. I am prepared to believe Robert will blame me or Mack in some way for the event in Buffalo and he can not really know my responsibility. He has no significant reason yet to know doubt. He does not yet know my powers. As all men do, he suspects them. The boy comes up again.

He asks for more milk. I pass my hand through the steam of the teakettle, preparing water to add to the cocoa mix. Robert drinks no stimulants. He is dynamic and can not sleep easily. "How *do* you account for the destruction? You were there."

I shrug. Droplets of steam course from under my breasts to the lollipop elastic. "Act of God." I speak meekly.

"Bull shit. We both know better."

The boy's fingernails on the milk glass are bloody. I am not supposed to react about his teeth. I am supposed to react about the spoon. Robert continues to rave about an Act of God and his inability to collect on one. The boy is trying to show me his fingers. He draws little bloody lines on the white of my lollipops, fingerpainting his pain.

"Sit down, Buddy," Robert tells him, "while your mother and I are talking." The boy stands near me. "I said to sit down," Robert repeats, and I can see the inside silver of Robert's teeth. One fell out once, the day I met him, in a college cafeteria. It came out planted in a crust of Italian bread, a land claim in the name of the Queen. I was overjoyed. But he mumbled and pocketed the tooth, which was false anyway, and I did not see him again until it had been properly replaced. We never mention it. Instead, he gave me a fraternity pin and later a diamond ring. You know what it was I really wanted. Right now I want to leave. I am tied to the fake beams of the Spanish kitchen with anvils on my ankles. "An Act of God could be worked up into a good gimmick, but you and I know it was drugs and somehow your friend was messed up in it because he's a mess." He smiles at me, baring his teeth once more. "Your mother will make you some eggs." I flip my tail at the stove. I obey for now.

But I am not going to sacrifice either Mack or my son to the power of this man.

"I want a poptart, Mommy."

We compromise. "While you eat these golden scrambled eggs, I will demonstrate how mother chickens lay eggs. I will draw a picture with my mons veneris, for where and what is the word de—mon—strate if not lines taken from the mons? So." Robert raises an eyebrow over his financial page.

I squirm. I cackle. I sigh. I dip. I rise. I cackle once again. I moan. He chews. He swallows. Robert reads, unbelieving. The plate before my son is clean and I, in a penultimate cackle, slip a Grade A from my bathrobe pocket and twist it victoriously between my thumb and forefinger. Astonished, my son runs with it to the refrigerator. "If you make more,

Mommy, we can sell them." I do not like that remark. He leaves, returns, dressed to play outside, and tell his friends of the newest marketable wonder at home. He pauses.

"How come you couldn't make the others into chickens if you can lay eggs?"

It is a consistent Godhead these people need. They do not understand absurdity as a function. "Perhaps the cold."

He removes the egg from the refrigerator egg tray. His eyes change, shifting. He wears down-lined, star-decorated warm-up pants and a Mighty Mac jacket, a young Orion, holding the world egg, twisting it as I had. He says nothing.

"Perhaps it was the machine," I offer. "The shells became too hot and broke."

He resembles his father, who smiles benignly at his son's great cleverness. I hate. I am glad I have my son's teeth in the plastic box around my neck.

"Perhaps it is a time of sterility. The eggs were not fertile. The mule does not spring upon the jenny. The wadis run dry."

"Ishtar," Robert remonstrates. "You are going to confuse the boy."

He is not confused, *this* son of mine. He pronounces slowly with the familiar Mosaic menace: "Animals with tails do not lay eggs. It is a Law." And he throws the egg against the ceiling.

His father laughs loudly. The egg ricochets from the Spanish beams. The albumen, stalactitic, hangs, and I laugh venomously. I laugh as only a Medusa laughs. I rattle the teeth at my son. It is the only way to deal with his logic.

"Snakes!" I scream, shattering their laughter. "They were serpent eggs from New Jersey. They were serpent eggs, green and spotted speckled serpents eggs. Thousand of snakes died in your hatchery like sperm, dying, squirming, under the globe. Snakes!" He draws away. His father shows horror.

Let him, my son, have a supernatural and let me feed it well.

The albumen reproduced itself asexually, sadly, from stalactite to stalagmite, rising on the carpet of the kitchen floor. The yolk remained above.

My son jumps fitfully in the snow. The poptart patriarch of the Jews becomes the Patrick of the Irish stamping out the snakes. "Don't go under the apple tree with anyone else but me!" I, Mother of All Things and Source of Lamentation, scream from my window. There is a picture scratched and painted in a South-West African cave wall of European women with delicate Saxon profiles. They are Amazons with raised bows from the stone age. They have tails. If it were necessary, I am certain they could have laid eggs. If it mattered.

A lament he made, a song.
About his going away and sang
Our Mother
The Goddess with the mantle of snakes
Is taking me with her as her child.

"If you serve me well and are worthy of such gifts," I scream at my son, and pull the window shut. I will take them both, my son and Mack. Mack with his fruitful beauty will give me much pleasure. Mack, who knows his female soul and his male soul, is what I hope my son to be. Neither of them will I allow Robert Moses to forge in his brazen image. It will be more difficult than bringing life to rotten eggs. Already Robert provides Mack with young girls. Already Robert has taught Mack the red and black ways of the account books. Already Robert advises Mack on his loves and his cars and offers him money.

"If you can't fuck it, sell it. If you can't sell it, fuck it."

Sorrowing, I have watched Mack, sleepy-eyed, a shadow of beard on his face, glancing slyly at me in the kitchen from the dining room. He sits for hours with Robert at the slate dining table and tallies small sums of monies and clips Thruway and motel receipts for the records. He is learning the Law too. Robert will get neither one of them. I will fight him.

As I fight to bring men to their manhood, I will fight to bring Mack and my son to the fullness of theirs. In fullness they will know power. In fullness they will know me. For I have been the Chaos, Tiamat, who preceded and fashioned all. I know the patterns. I have been the skin Marduk sat in after he slew me. I have been the skin of the Tabernacle and the loins of the Torah and I have been the jungle hut where the boys became men, and I have been the sukka hung with the gourds of my breasts and the grapes of my nipples and the figs of my vulva and the Tree of Life. I have been and I will be and Here I am Again in the omphalos of Eleusis, in the underground of the Pythian, in the penetralia of the living Leviathans who would seek me for their circumcision, who would seek me to be men. My Star fell and left only the Evening Star and the Morning Star to which I sing a song and no one can put Humpty Dumpty together again. Except me.

So flay yourself, baby, for the Great Mother has returned. Come, Mack, I will say to him, what hurts you? Come, sit in my vulva and I will heal thee and you shall know ecstasy. I descend. I wash the floor of its egg.

Robert turns pages in his paper rapidly. "Do you want anything else to eat?" I ask from the floor because I am amused.

He is too intelligent. "From you?" He walks out, calling for the boy to shovel snow with him because the band is coming over at noon.

I watch them in the snow working together. I will have to remove the child. An Act of God, it will be. One cannot jail or sue or condemn an Act of God. It is. An Act of God is beyond the Law. I am beyond the Law. And I am beyond Moses. Eventually, which is cruel and unfortunate, I will be called upon to prove that I am the God his Law refers to.

There was snow on Robert's long and kinky hair when he came inside. Ishtar moved against him and twisted the hair into two tiny horns. She had been forgiven for he touched her waist with his icy hands. "Come, Horny Hardhat, it's your hour. Let's pretend." The boy had crossed the street to play with a friend. Robert led her into their bedroom. Ishtar, lying back across the bed, considered appearing at the sergeant's desk in a metropolitan police station in a class B movie, Mack's bail folded tightly into an evening purse. She sees him behind bars. She knows she loves him. He is sallow and pained. He is released from the jail into which Robert placed him on his turn in a pusher campaign. She takes him with her. "Why are thy cheeks so wasted? Is sunken thy face. Is sad thy heart."

"And I better not catch you taking anything either."

The wind whips through their coats as she and Mack walk away from the police station to find a class B hotel. They chew roots in the mussed bed on stiff torn sheets.

"No drugs, Ishtar."

Ishtar fought the temptation to laugh at Robert, standing above the bed, his pants off, his arms crossed to pull his T-shirt over his head and his lips lemon shrunk again pronouncing his commandments. Under her bed even now was a Bendel's box filled with mandrake roots.

"Come, pluck me, Robert." She closed her eyes and imagined Mack touching her as Robert was. Mack has not lost altogether that which is soft and valuable and is given by woman. I could teach him to heal. I will teach him to sing when he loves me. I am tired of grunters. Robert grunts.

The Italian Hour gives way to the Manon Forum. Robert collects the hopeless wads of Kleenex from the bedroom floor and leaves to read the financial section in the den. Ishtar washes herself. She hears the Moloch disposing of shells and rinds, belching noisily and rattling crystal in the cupboard above. Robert rewarded her, she realized, by finishing the dishes.

Outside, in his red-plaid Pendleton with his wife in black mink and rabbit après-ski boots, the Republican Chairman of

Ishtar's County walks past her house in the frozen morning as he does every Sunday, along the still street where apple trees and unbending willows line the perfect lawns. Stands of pines form barriers between the two acre plots. The Chairman frowns at the pair of silver Thunderbirds and the red Cadillac sedan in Ishtar's upper driveway. The Chairman and his wife stare at the shivering coterie of young men on Ishtar's porch and the young men look back curiously. The black mink wife twists her mouth in distaste and continues to walk to the fields at the end of the road.

Ishtar's willow tree, around which the upper driveway circles, had fringed and knotted quipu riddles in the snow at its base during the night—delicate mysterious lines and unknown histories. Now its fingers lie absolutely still against a periwinkle noon sky. Her star and tulip magnolias and rosebuds are boxed in redwood winter coffins. The two orange cats in agreement leap from the upper reaches of a pine tree, spring across the snow, paws meeting in midair, and bound onto the flagstone porch. They rub their luxurious coats against the thinly clad legs of the boys on the porch, who ring the doorbell a second time. Robert strides through the mushroom, moongray living room and Ishtar listens to the muffled voices of the boys and the plaintive miaows of the cats beyond the double doors.

I do not stay with the men while they discuss the contract they will not sign. Often I carry in coffee and cakes. There are sandwiches laid out in the kitchen. I wait for Nino to come to me with his pants to alter. I do not know quite why his own mother does not do this for him unless it is either a recognition of my motherhood or an invitation to touch him and I am glad to touch him. At last he knocks on the bedroom door with his old pants over his small arm and his new loose pants on him. I have my pincushion waiting. It is an apple.

I beckon to him to stand on a velvet padded stool before my mirror. He balances himself with one hand on my shoulder as I crawl around the stool.

I smooth my hands over the corduroy which lies smooth and flat under my touch.

"We don't want that contract," I tell him as I touch him. "It is not a good one." I place my thumb in imprimatur on his buttock. He will not support the contract any longer. His buttock is not as tight as I had expected. I enjoy men. I mold my hands in the air, recording his shape in lines. He is a bantam man but he has come to me and I am pleased.

"That's too long. They should break over my shoes."

He bends to touch me once. I push at his knees for his straightening. I pin around both cuffs, smooth the fabric from waist to ankle and I know him. I remove the pins from my mouth. I have not swallowed any. His nails are digging into my shoulders. It is no longer for balance. I understand what it is he wants and since everyone else is quite taken with the contractual efforts, I shall make one of my own. I proceed, although his nails still dig uncomfortably into my skin and I wish he could stand still and in balance without hurting me. I do not understand this need to hurt while I am thus giving pleasure to his body. There is something desperately incorrect.

"Oh!"

I draw away. I am deeply shocked. He persists in pressing me down again but his power is not like mine and I very gently replace his member and examine his eyes. They are hidden. "I am sorry, Nino. I did not understand this before."

The sides of his jawbone twitch.

"You do not have to tell me." I sit on the edge of the bed. He stands before me and I offer him my arms. He covers himself. "Sit, relax."

"No." He shifts one leg forward, posing. "It doesn't make any difference. It's better this way. You can enjoy it forever."

I speak, in wonderment. "It is unlike anything I have seen, yet quite perfect, beautiful in its perfection. But it does not function. Aah, that is why it is always erectile. It is bone."

He wears bangs across his forehead and his hands are delicately veined.

"Well." His chin is high and rugged now. "It never stops, Baby."

"Don't consider me as Baby. I think that you suffer greatly and you do not enjoy then your personal life." I begin to cry for him. I am also crying for me.

"Well, now you've seen it. I gotta go."

"Nino," I grab his thin arm. "Where does it come from? How is it done?"

He can not pry my viselike grip from his arm. He grows very angry. "Rib. Okay? I'll show my scars when they turned my cunt inside out. You can cry over that too and get your kicks."

"It is nothing to be ashamed of. It is very fine. From the rib of the Goddess was made man. It is that way. You are significant of a new beginning."

"And if you want some copy"—he had not listened—"you can just tell them that Twentymiles, the best hung rock star in the Northeast, has a clit. Okay? You tell em. What a gimmick. Twentymiles, he never comes. Just goes on forever. Okay? You think they'll enjoy that?" He is watching himself over my head in the mirror. He is fascinated with his image. "You can make me a clown and you can make a fortune off me. I'll even give you the name of my doctor. Maybe you can get some before pictures for the album cover. I could write a book too when I retire from show biz, huh? About me and Mack."

He slams the door and white chips of paint fall to the olive green carpet.

"Oh."

I stick pins into my apple. There are deadly secrets in apples, in trees, in snakes. I know the secrets. I will not cure this person, who, whatever he is, man or woman, is not whole. And he shall stay far from Mack with his poisoned half-ness. I tear the pants I am to hem into shreds and flush them away. I hear Robert call out sharply about the septic tank bubbling but I do not respond.

10

It is in Monday that Ishtar finds delight.

On Mondays, her cleaning lady leaves the house vapored with Pine Sol, the semen of pine. On Mondays, she anoints herself in Jean Naté oil, rubs her body with Mentholatum and waits for the phone call. Monday is obscene phone call day. Ishtar's picture is often in the Sunday papers as Cook of the Week (a shortcut with veal cutlets), collector of artifacts and Welder of Metals (she is shown with her torch). Because she understands loneliness, she welcomes the stranger on the telephone dutifully, speaking gently to him through the slice of crystal quartz lying between his heavy aspirations and he receives the power of her words.

"Remember me, baby?" the stranger asks huskily. He is lying down.

"Aah, I shall remember you, stranger. I shall renew your member until it is strong and lives once again. Remember. Yes, this is she. Have no doubt. I used to call Santa Claus when I was a child. I understand. Yes, I wear bras. You are hooked on bras? That is quite amusing. I am also. Yes, I cut out the nipples. Oh, you saw my picture and you have it pasted on the ceiling of the bunkroom aside the stable? Up to Pompey? The sacred stall for the sacred goat? Bring me your goat and I'll divine your future by his heart and his liver and you will always be remembered. No, I don't shave my legs. All the way up until you reach the feathers. I pluck.

"That's right and I make little bunches and fasten the

stalks with tight green rubber bands, snapping rubber bands. Come under my shell. Lift the tab, gently, and I'll change you into an egg and bury you in the sand with my sandy claws and you will be born again. I lay eggs and I brush my teeth with Pristeen, almond flavored, and place a pomegranate between my breasts. Do you happen to know a good dentist? Oh, white, everything white. And I just cut away the bra and wear only the straps for snapping like rubber bands because I am the Great Mother Snapping Turtle. Come, come. I will heal thee.

"Is that enough? More? Of course. Allow me a word of advice while you're getting your towel ready. Wear lipstick when you drink coffee. It tastes better because a greasy mustache improves the taste of food. I have always wanted a man with a mustache to go down on me. You aren't listening but I can hear your breathing. Og, Ishullanu, I placest thou in the midst of Mother Bell's crystal web and thou can not go up and thou can not go down. Ready yet? Go, go down, go down and while you're going down, oh, Moses, I'll just take hold of the Tablets of Fate and the horns of your goat and your Snake Banner and when you call me again, call me Ishtar. Return to the Breast of the Great Mother. That's where it all hangs out. Snap. I cut away the straps and just wear the nipples."

"Uh, pardon me, missus. I can't hold on the phone no more. Me hands be in me pockets."

"Glued. Ride, mother, ride. I dun it wi' the missus. A yardman, that's what I'm wanting. Oh, my Ishullanu, let me taste of thy vigor. Bring me your fruit. I've never had a descent gardener. A yardman with a mustache. 'Hi, there, sweet potater, dig ya now, plant ya later.' Listen, I adore the Farmers' Market with the sweating Italians selling lettuce and ruby red plums and cantaloupes. Yardmen give you throat cancer. We get uterine cancer because we have lost the teeth from our vaginas and can't defend ourselves. Do you happen to know a good dentist? You're more than welcome. Until next week? If my line is busy find a tree with a knot hole. Glue your thirteen wisps of goat hair around the knot hole. It is your mother. Christ returned to the holy wood of his mother's arms and the log of the cross became a magical bridge over which the Queen of Sheba would not walk because of its holiness. When you are finished with your libation, place stamps or coins in an envelope and mail to the Psychedelicatessen Venus Church. Sathergate Station, Berkeley, Cal. It's the only church we have left. S-a-t-h-e-r-g-a-t-e. Right Thank *you*. Of course I love you. Don't forget a return envelope. You'll receive a feather and a chant which can be chanted in groups, not necessarily in unison. Bye. Oh, no. I have to be at the dentist's glory hole quite soon. Call back. Oh, sorry. P O Box 5673. Zip 92801.

"Hello? Oh, perfectly all right. Are you tapping my line or his? Of course. S-a-t-h-e-r-g-a-t-e. Whatever it was worth to you. No, don't send anything to me at all. On Mondays before noon. Yes, you can abbreviate his middle name. Next week then."

I sat on a hillock of trefoil in the school yard. My son was up at bat. He and the team members wore maroon caps and shirts. The other team wore green. My son's team, sponsored by a dentist whose own son played a poor outfield, had their shirts emblazoned in white. Clean Tooth Team. There was a score. I did not know what it was. Other mothers knew but I sat apart from them and their inattentiveness, which I considered inexcusable. I was attentive. Robert Moses stood behind the pitcher's plate as temporary referee. My son was up at bat.

Previously the catcher's older brother had explained the rules to the emblazoned children. My son had difficulty in understanding a rule and the older brother, massaging my son's nicely combed hair in a rather insincere gesture, explained once again. "If the pitcher hits you, you take a base." This of course makes no sense and I could read my son's confused face under his now unkempt hair. If the pitcher hits you, you hit him back. If the pitcher hits you, you hurt. I understand my son. First base is not a just reward for being mutilated by a hurled ball. But it is in this way in which goals are established in this country as they were in Sparta, and here, from my trefoil hillock, I understand and he understands that first base is a reward for either hitting or being hit by the ball. So be it.

It was not surprising therefore with the goal of the muddied pillow established, that my son, after witnessing in distress his own father calling two strikes and three balls against him as I tore trefoil from the hillock as if it were my own hair, declared that the final fast ball hit him.

"It hit me."

The mothers of the green team hissed. The coaches and my son's father looked to the pitcher, who was smaller than my son and had a ferret-pinched face.

"I did not hit you!" the pitcher yelled. The green team cheered for him.

"The ball did, stupid. It *grazed* me."

"Yeah, I heard it *graze* him," said the green catcher, impressed with the new word.

"He's not even on your team," I heard the catcher's coach admonish the catcher. "So don't defend him."

My son's father and the two coaches walked to the base of a triangle toward each other, my husband down the bisect of the triangle in the setting sun. They met at home plate over my child.

"It grazed me. Slightly."

The two coaches looked to the boy's father for a decision.

"It wasn't even near him," yelled the pitcher.

The catcher shuffled his feet uncomfortably.

"Well," said my son's father, a Solomon he isn't, "I'll have to go along with the rules. If he says it grazed him, he must know. Take a base," he muttered to my son, and returned to his place behind the pitcher. "Let's play ball!" he called out heartily. The triangle dispersed. The game continued.

When the game was over, the sun set, the packs of Teaberry gum distributed to my son's winning team, my husband, silent and stern, drove us home in the moist evening, and as I cleaned the soil from my fingernails in the living room, he beat my son in the bedroom.

I do not know if he beat my son for lying, for being hit by a hurled ball or for humiliating his own father. It matters not. After beating my son, his father considered himself vindicated and correct. My son, his dirt-smeared face plowed deep with tears, advised me, unconvinced by the power in his father's hands, that he had really felt the ball.

I shrugged. I did not know what else to do except to make them both chocolate pudding, which they ate warm. My son ate with his eyes closed. My husband said to my son, kindly now, "Why don't you open your eyes so you can see what you're eating, Buddy?"

"It's chocolate pudding," my son answered. "I can taste it."

"Well, Buddy, why are your eyes closed?"

My son rimmed the empty dish with his forefinger. "I can't open my eyes because my father is blind."

My husband left the table.

My son licked his fingers clean.

I myself wished to partake of my own heart.

Peter Lupus, from Mission Impossible, uses gingseng root, he reports, "as a rejuvenator, an invigorator, a reactivator and an aphrodisiac." He interests me. Once, I and my Druids gained wisdom and power by magnetism, drawing the celestial fires, the astral fires, through the sensitivities of such items as mistletoe, mandrake, gingseng, three-colored cats (my cats were three and colored but not three-colored) nine needles. Beyond all, my Druids used eggs. I was the magnet superior, of course.

The author then expresses himself of the opinion that the Druidical eggs were almost certainly artificial and of various color, some blue, some white, some green and other variegated with stripes of these colors. Serpent eggs were believed to be impregnated directly from the solar ray and the preparation of these mysterious eggs represented the process by which the body of the Druid was caused to generate within itself the serpent of wisdom. The Druids themselves were called snakes as they were masters of the serpent power. The serpent power was not evil, but wisdom. You remember what Patrick did for my religion.

It is this manner of gaining wisdom, this immaculate conception, in which woman draws into her body the powers of the planets by means of the cats, metals, drugs, plants and produces . . . well, your *New Testament* disguises the alchemical work as the Son of Light. We didn't have children. We produced power. We had children only when it was necessary to populate the fields or recreate ourselves. The process of stimulating and fascinating the powers was the same process we used to stimulate and fascinate men. That process was reduced to the laboratory as an alchemical marriage and all the knowledge was lost.

Almost.

The womb was a glass casket, a vessel in which the Brothers of the Rosy Cross were buried alive. It leaves little to the imagination to redefine the Rosy Cross. The womb was properly called the Philosophic Egg and suggests Snow White as a vestigial tale. Aah, to have a tail to flip and swing in anger or in passion to curl around a sleeping lover. The cave was in Brandberg, South-West Africa. At regular intervals the philosopher, breaking the shell of his egg or womb, took up the concerns of life, later to retire once more into his shell of glass.

This son prefers poptarts to eggs. The poptart box reads slip thumb under tab and lift gently. It is the way to treat all syconiums, which are collective fleshy fruits in which the ovaries are borne within an enlarged, more or less succulent, concave or hollow receptacle. Gently.

There was a night when Robert was in Canada. I needed

terribly to run in the fields. I neglected to pick up the babysitter, driving past her home. I ran and returned much later, burning with new energy, to find I had abandoned my son. My son, though, was eating simultaneously, happily, from four boxes of poptarts. Chocolate-vanilla Frosted, Concord Grape Frosted, Strawberry Plain and Brown-sugar Cinnamon Plain. The more anxious he became, I assume, the more he ate. It helps, you understand, eating. My mother lies dead/bleeding/both in a ditch and has abandoned me. What shall I eat *now?* He was rather pleased that I had forgotten him and had, as so often these sons do, gotten into the secrets and blamed his stomach ache and pain on me. Literature will later have it that I opened the boxes of poptarts and forever after the world suffered, gripped with colitis. It is the way men twist our truth because of their own guilt. I was Pandora, as you may have surmised by now, the Woman of One Thousand Names and One Personality, the All-Giving.

It was my box.

I was willing then to share, as I am now, the mysteries, when man is ready. You might explore the obscene connotations. There is more truth in fairy tales and obscenities than all of your written histories. It was Epimetheus who opened the box. From the damage, you know he wasn't ready. His name translates to Afterthought, which he was. I was first. I had warned him steadfastly to stay away from my mysteries. Hands out of the cooky jar, Afterthought, I warned him. I stopped baking then and there. He became a Jew or a Christian, something modern and disconnected, I do not recall which, and lay all the guilt on my shoulders, changed the story and blamed me for both hunger and pain. By the by, while Afterthought was into my cooky jar, Prometheus, or Forethought, was playing with matches and stole the sacred fire. Kids are not to be trusted. My sons have been a source of great disappointment to me and the world. But I keep trying.

11

Of course I know they are with each other.
    Claire sits in Mack's lean red Corvette, twisting yellow and blue wires together. The wires hang loose under the dashboard. Claire is self-conscious as I warned her not to let Mack touch her. Mack is cool because Robert warned him to stay away from Claire. Claire feels very large in the small car and wishes to be smaller. Often she squeezes her knees with those hands or draws that cape over herself. In her lap lies my notebook. I have given her some incidental information along with directions for the slaying and dedication of a pig in preparation for a particular event I am planning in relation to Cupcakes. They are now driving toward the Agway Experimental Farm. They there have a plethora of cleanly and clinically bred pigs. There are other things I have told Claire. She wears that cape still. Rain threatens the afternoon.
    The car speeds along a narrow state road. They have talked sporadically, distantly, about record charts and new bookings. Mack has questioned Claire about her music. Claire has offered to jam with him. He has answered without enthusiasm. He fears Robert. Claire hums. She doesn't know what else to do. I understand. There is so much deep within Mack that can be sensed, one begins to feel that mundane conversation is not valid.
    Claire pushes the glove compartment closed. "There. Light's fixed."
    "Much farther?" Mack doesn't thank her.

"She says take a left on Route 20, drive a mile and a half to an Exxon station, and look for an Agway Farm sign. Do you want to hear her lament for killing of a suckling pig? Or would you prefer the proper sanctification for the act of plucking the puffball mushroom?" This is wrong of Claire to do. I do not like her contempt.

"That's really there?" She has aroused Mack's interest at my expense. It is one of the least attractive aspects of modern woman—to sacrifice one's sisterhood in order to snare a man.

"Where do you think she finds this stuff?"

"You believe in it?" Mack asks.

"I saw the light show. And, you know, what can I lose by believing?"

"Yeah." Mack considers that. He has much to lose. "Yeah. You know, I never told this to anybody but my mother is kind of like Ishtar. Evil eye and that kind of stuff. Counts acorns for good luck. When my father died, she went and told the bees." He rubs his forehead. "I mean, she comes home from the hospital and says in this strangly voice, 'Kid, pop died,' and runs out to the hives and tells the bees. Then . . . then she comes back and it's okay to cry. She cures headaches with water glasses. All that kind of stuff." Interesting. Etruscan, I imagine.

"Where does she get it from?"

"Her mother. She said her mother owned a bakery in the old country and they grew up baking and praying. My mother, she prays in front of the oven when she puts something in. Hey, you know what? She's Cook of the Week next week. Watch the Sunday paper."

Claire is not impressed. She is struggling to turn the conversation toward herself. I am, however, very impressed.

"I guess they both got something." Mack says.

"It's crazy, though, you know. Ishtar takes a can of pork and beans, and she shakes her head . . ."

"Were you over there?"

"She's . . . she's teaching me some stuff." Claire smiles mysteriously. "She shakes her head. 'Pork,' she says, 'sacred to the Goddess, eaten only on Her days. Beans contain spirits. Flesh of redemption. Spirits of redemption.' 'This is a sacred dish,' she says, 'and now, packed in tomato sauce.' And then she throws out a half dozen of them that she just bought. I think she's nuts. I mean, why did she buy them?"

"Jews don't eat pork." Mack shrugged. "Who knows? I dig her." He is tempted to defend me. Then he remembers Robert. "Listen, I should tell you something. Uh, don't break your back doing favors for the guys in the band. They're a bunch of assholes. Like today, you shouldn't do them any favors like this. They, uh, don't want you around. You're supposed to turn off the groupies."

"*You* want me around?" Claire is strong.

"Well, it's not actually up to me. See, it's business. The more chicks we have around the better we look. Shit, I like you, Claire. I've never been able to to talk to anybody until you. I like your head. I walk up to those chicks and I say, "Hey, you wanna fuck?" And they do or they don't. It's a business. I don't mean to offend, but it's a business. Part of advertising. The more we bag, the more records we sell, the bigger crowds we draw. The guys follow the chicks who follow us."

"So?" Claire puts her nose against the window.

"I don't love it. I mean, after I play, I'm beat and then I gotta go out and perform all over again. You know about the charts?"

"Sure I know about the charts." She doesn't. "So?"

"The point system. You know they keep charts on all the upstate bands. How we play. What we drive. How we ball. What we wear. Christ, you know I just went out and bought all this new underwear. This new bunch—the stewardesses . . ."

"They aren't stewardesses. I sit with them."

"Well." Mack is defensive. "One I know is. They get out

there and scream for us. And cry. You ever have anybody cry because you're so good? I'm so good, me, they cry for me in front of the whole audience. That makes us, Claire."

"You mean you just walk up to them, say, 'You wanna fuck?' and they do?"

"Yeah, that's the way we do it."

"Okay." She continues to look out the window. "I wanna fuck."

The corners of Mack's mouth turn white in anger. "Oh, for Christ's sake, shut up. You're not one of them."

"I wanna fuck."

"Shut up, Claire!" His anger is justified. She is being ugly.

"And I have to go to the bathroom so let's stop at the Exxon."

"You can go in the woods. I want to get this over with."

"I'll go where I want to."

"You sure can turn guys off. You sure can. Look, all I'm telling you is don't sit with them anymore and stay away from the guys in the band." Mack drives past the Exxon sign without stopping.

Claire is sorry. She wishes for long eyelashes and to be small and giggle in his car. She attempts the mysterious smile, but she is empty inside. They find the farm. Beyond a sloping gray barn, there is a complex of new green and white aluminum barns. Claire points to the correct barn down a dirt road. Mack drives to it. Claire leaves the car, relieved to be uncramped and away from the white corners of his mouth. "There's a guy watching us. Get turned around," she directs Mack. "I'll be fast."

All the pigs in all the pens stand as Claire enters. The barn smells of Lysol and feed. I have told her that dreams come true if you sleep with the pigs. I have told her pigs have great power. She smiled when I told her this. Over the pens hang forms and charts. Thermostats are clipped to the screenings. There are hundreds of pigs in the long barn. One sow stands, clumsily, threatening Claire with dull red eyes, grunts, collapses on the sucklings about her. Claire laughs at the sow. I like her laugh. It fills the empty barn. She extricates a slippery pink suckling, tucks it under her cape and races through the labyrinth of pens to the entrance.

She laughs as she runs. She has forgotten Mack's insults. The man in overhauls starts calling to her, many times, each time more insistently and closer. Claire doesn't hesitate. She tosses the squealing pig in the rear of the car and claps her hands over her head to make the man disappear. He doesn't. Mack spins his tires in the mud, splashing his white hood and windows as he roars out of the farm area. The pig is soon lulled by the motor and sits quietly behind them. Fat drops of rain fall on the windshield. They turn into a hollow road between gentle green hills of firs. I hope Claire doesn't forget to pick the puffballs for me. As a reward for dedicating the pig I shall teach her how to use them as an aphrodisiac. It is not an important secret, but it can be amusing. There is a problem. The window is fogging. Behind Mack's head a pale steam rises and then is followed by the hearty smell of fresh vomit.

"Mmmm. Who cleans the car? Your goddamn pig is carsick."

Claire reaches behind Mack and rubs the bristles between the pig's ears. "Forgive Mack, piggy. Poor experimental pigs. You have charts too, don't you? What did you do, baby? Eat the lining of my cape and get sick? Poor baby. And there, sitting in your own . . . oh, look what a good piggy! She ate it all up!" Mack opens his window and rain pours in on him. Claire feels vindicated. She has forgotten to be gentle.

The forest I chose is primeval. A silver mist surrounds it now. The rain is light and as they stare into the rows of trees, the forest grows blacker. Claire takes the pig and climbs from the car. Both Mack and I appreciate the way she looks against the forest. She sees his face soften. "Come on. Forests are groovy in the rain."

121

"Nah, I'll wait . . . shit, I'll come. Give the car a chance to air out."

"Hey, Mack." Claire stops him as he rounds the car. "You ever get Ishtar in the sack?"

His face flushes. "What the hell does that have to do . . . ?"

I am astonished also.

"I just thought I'd give you something valid to get sore about. It wasn't my fault the pig tossed up her cookies, for God sakes." She smiles at him. "Still sore?"

"You win. Okay. You sore at me?"

Nice children. In another age I would have them lost in the forest and eating nuts and berries for the rest of their crazed lives. However, I need these two.

"Nope." Claire tucks the pig again under her arm and stalks off into the spruces. The floor is spongy. Horsetails spring like minarets at the roots of the trees. "I'm disgusted with you."

Mack takes her arm. "I wouldn't go to bed with her. Christ, she'd turn me into a frog if I didn't satisfy her. You want me to carry the pig for a while?" What can I say to all this? I shall not comment any longer.

"I'll carry the pig." Claire walks faster. They can hear the rush of water ahead of them. "You're not in any danger of becoming a frog. You have to be a prince first." I laugh in spite of myself. Mack laughs also.

"Thanks a lot. Hey, Claire, you still want to fuck?"

"Are you *kidding*? I'm holding out for a prince." Neither of them is sincere. Excuse me, I said I wouldn't comment.

From subterranean clefts under the beds of slate water pours into the ravine. Claire picks her way over the slate teeth tartared with lichen and club moss as far as she dares, then a little farther because Mack is watching, steadies her legs against the rocks, lifts the piglet high over her head with one hand and with the other hand takes the notebook from her pocket. Mack is shivering on the brink of the ravine above her.

"C'mon, Claire. Throw it."

"The rain smeared the words," she calls up to him. "I forgot what she told me to say."

"Say anything. I'm freezing."

"Do you think it matters?" she yells.

He spreads his hands. "Don't know."

"Well. Uh . . . well, good luck, pig." The small body bounces against the slate teeth and then falls, screaming, into the wild waters, unblessed. Blood fans out behind it and it is gone. Claire and Mack stand still, shuddering slightly and then remember each other. Mack holds out his hand to help her up the side. They walk quietly together. He keeps her hand as if he had forgotten he held it. The rain has changed to mist. I do and I do not wish to watch the next part.

"Don't watch," Claire tells Mack. They have found the puffball clearing, the water faucet stuck into concrete, the circle of old trees. Claire is going to urinate behind a tree. I do not know if her embarrassment is genuine or not. "I did it once in the woods and wet my sneakers."

"Go on. Stand downhill."

"Let's just find a gas station."

"Unh, unh, we promised to get the mushrooms for her." That loyalty is not his motive, I can assure you now.

Claire runs, her face bright with excitement and shame in the dark tree paths. She trips on a thick root and catches herself. When she returns, still bright-faced, Mack's arms are above him against a tree, crossed and he grins at her.

"I miss a joke or something, Mack?"

"You never told me you had such a nice ass." She doesn't. It is too bony.

Claire swings and punches him in the stomach. "Bastard." But as she wishes, he grabs her and slides his hands down to the flaring of her thighs. "Bastard," she repeats venomously, moving against him. I join her in her imprecations.

"Really nice ass." Mine is far superior.
"What's Robert going to say? You're not supposed to be seen with me."
"Shh."
"I'm not even pretty."
"Shh, Claire."
"We have to get the puffballs for the old lady."
You were right. I shouldn't be watching.
Mack closes his eyes and kisses her forehead. "Let's just talk a little. Let's just talk a little."
"I'm bad for your image." She is challenging him.
"No one's watching, Claire. They all left. You're okay, Claire. You're okay, no kidding." Mack kisses her on the cheeks, on the chin, on the nose but not on the lips. He has a method. Never kiss on the lips until they start stretching out for you. He kisses her face again, teasing, letting her move toward him. Damn, I wish it were me. She moves toward him on the grass, on the moss. I know what is in his head.

When their tongues come out, you can get a hand on the tit. When you get the nipple going, you should stop and whisper, "Let's talk. Let's talk a little and then let's get together." He whispers it now. It doesn't sound right to him. Claire is watching him warily. He closes his eyes and pulls at her clothing. He tries the words again. "Let's talk, Claire, and then let's get together." Her body is oven warm against his.

"Wait, Mack." And she pulls away. "The mushrooms."
The what?

And then she is back, sliding off her underwear with abandon and sitting cross-legged. Mack assures himself. Kinky, kinky turns you on. "If they're good enough for her, they're good enough for me," he hears her say.

Chutzpah. Hubris. What shall I say?
"Jesus, Claire." He will not look.
"You mind?" She smiles my smile. Bitch.
"No, it's . . . it's great." She breaks the puffballs with a thumbnail, spraying the dusky centers into the palms of her

hands and powdering herself in preparation. It is meant to be a secret act.

Mack watches her tongue move across her lips. He thinks she might be exciting herself for him as she works. He isn't certain. Championships, he remembers from the signs in the Liverpool High School *Gymnasium*, are conquests, not bequests. The best way to win is to get out in front and stay there. The only way to swim faster is to swim faster. Some psychiatrists see in their impotent patients fears of incest, men who associate all women with a mother image, with teeth in their maw, smoking dragons, spider ladies. He watches her tongue. Every punker has a good excuse.

"Where'd you learn that?"

"Ishtar." A lie.

"Jesus, Claire." The normally aggressive male withstands this challenge but the more passive male eventually becomes impotent because of his fear and hostility toward woman. He drops his eyes to watch as Claire touches herself, easily parting the dark hair between her legs. He'd never seen a chick touching herself. Although he's seen a lot of things. He's only got two arms and two legs same as you. You can't climb the ladder of success with cold feet. The only way to swim faster is to get in there and swim faster. Every punker has a good excuse.

"You'll like me, Mack," Claire tells him.

"Oh, yeah, I'm sure. Hurry, huh?"

"I'm good."

Dr. David Jonas says about 75 per cent of patients coming to his Institute of Sexual Maladjustment are under age thirty. If you can't win, make the guy who beats you break the record. I never feel good, like a man, until I'm in a chick. And then, when I'm in, I feel sure of myself. But I don't want to hear a chick say I love you or anything like that so I put my hand over their mouths. You see, he is afraid to know women as people.

Claire is finished. "I have a good body," Mack hears her

say. "I really come quick." She lies on the ground next to him. Her nipples are magenta in the cold, full and succulent. One is smaller than the other. Her body is too hard and angular. Dr. Otto, Chairman of the National Center for the Exploration of Human Potential, says men are beginning to perceive women as sexually demanding and possibly insatiable. No man is a failure until he gives up. Never let a punker beat you. "I never wanted anyone else like I want you, Mack," he hears her whisper.

"Good. Great." Her tongue explores his mouth. He touches her breasts. On time.

He takes little bites around her breasts. One has long fine hairs circling the nipple. She trembles. I don't know if chicks actually ejaculate. When they blow me in the back of the truck, they get on their knees and there's always a wet spot on the floor where they were kneeling. So maybe they do. *Something* happens. If the goals have not been achieved, and sometimes when they have, the man may become impotent because the amount of psychological energy and physical energy consumed has been so great there is none left over for romance. "Shh, don't talk."

Claire is good. Everything works. She responds to all the tricks on time. She seems almost ready. Therefore it is time for Mack to remove his pants. He has always been good at timing chicks. He wants to see her face when she comes. He is glad he wore the new blue underwear. His blood jerks in great dark pulses. It is time to whisper, "Touch me, feel me." "Touch me," he whispers. "Feel me." Her big hands envelop him and he shivers. When you're out in front, stay out in front. The best way is to get out in front and stay there. The lucky swimmer is the guy who makes his own luck. They can't beat you, if you can't be beaten. In some cases the effects on the male ego can be severe enough to leave deep emotional. . . .

"Mack?"

"Shhh."

He wonders how long she will come for and what her face will look like. He wonders if she will really come. He massages her and kisses parts of her body, working down to the catreek smell and the musky puffball powder. He allows himself to imagine it is I. If you stay in one place on them too long, they stop responding. He stops thinking of me. You got to move around, bite a little, blow a little, lick, squeeze, vary but keep going down. When you're tired, the other guy is just as tired. Claire is squirming against him. The guys better not find out about this one. He listens for her breathing and moves one leg over hers, pushing her legs apart with his knee. It is a smooth movement. He can't remember who told him about it. A diamond is a lump of coal that stuck with it. Sometimes girls ask me to do something another way and it messes everything up. I like to do it my way. Thus a young man today often finds himself or thinks he finds himself being judged on his performance. The time to start is now, not tomorrow. The difference between good and great is just a little extra effort. Never let a punker beat you. A diamond is a lump of coal that stuck with it.

"Mack?"

"Shhh."

"Mack! God, Mack!" Claire howls under him as her body contorts. Wow. He stops, surprised to watch the great force passing over her and see her face. She tears at his shoulders while he watches. "Mack, please!" But he has nothing for her. He tries to enter her uselessly.

"Nothing?" The question came from deep in her throat.

"Nothing."

He stared into her face. She was weeping. "Too fast, Claire. Too fast, I guess. I'm sorry. I was too excited. I guess." He rolled away from her warmth and he began to shiver.

When she took her hands away from her face it was no longer naked. They tried to smile at each other. "Jesus, I'm sorry, Claire."

Dr. Herbert Otto of La Jolla, California, agrees that the

attempt by men to laugh away or ignore the liberation movement is indicative of the threat to the ego structure posed by this force. Claire wiped her eyes with the backs of her hands. "You look," she said bravely, "like a priest who just farted." She tried to be funny. It wasn't funny.

"I'm sorry, Claire. I don't . . ."

Her face broke again. "Oh, Mack, Jesus, Mack. I'm sorry." Then she wrestled his head with her great strength back to her breast and held him while he struggled and beat his fist into her shoulder, dumb with anger.

"Let go. Let me go, Claire!"

She cried. He could feel her chest heaving. "I gotto go, Claire!"

Claire covered herself with her cape and watched him dress and walk away. She hitchhiked home because she didn't know what else to do.

Hah hah.

One does not reach ecstasy with contempt for the origin of the ecstasy. You fly too high, Icarus. You go too deep, Gilgamesh. You lose. Remember me, baby, or I shall not remember your member when you need it most. I will not tolerate this vanity, or this contempt. The words do matter. Not the least of mine loved without first saying, "May Ishtar be satisfied." Not only that, I whisper to Claire, whose eyes do not meet mine as we plan our baking event, I will have the first fruits of my labor with Mack, not you. I, first, will be satisfied.

I have worked here with something less than an Arthur and a Guinevere and something more, I hope, than an Adam and an Eve. I use the best materials I have at hand these days. Mack has properties of beauty and sensitivity and knows his origin from woman. Claire has strength and can laugh at large things. They will be put into balance. Neither of course is ready and that is my labor. You will have to understand that holy grails, Excaliburs and singing stones are hard to come by these days, as are princes, kings and rightful heirs. All I had was that steel spigot stuck into the concrete and the mushrooms and the polluted ravine into which Allied Chemical pours its process. It's no Paradise. But I'm trying.

12

I still don't understand why we're going," Claire asks from the seat next to me. "Why can't we just bake the Cupcakes ourselves?"

"It is because, my child, your world understands commercial packaging. And I, after all these mother-fucking years . . . another Sumerian term . . . am going commercial."

There is rooted knotted anger in my voice and Claire understands at least not to question me further. We drive silently now. The mothers have finished working their rosaries and as we pass the Montezuma Wild Life Sanctuary, they open wicker baskets and remove their crocheting tools. The winding of threads and clicking of the crocheting tools is a friendly sound and I am lonely.

Grace, Mack's mother, sits behind us. She is Etruscan, I am certain now. She has honey in her fields and mandrake roots near the rhubarb. She is wary of me and has come with us this night in order to inspect me. She sits with her friend in their pastel coats and soft little mink collars. They are large and comfortable women. Both have been Cook of the Week. When they stepped into my Country Squire this night, they lifted their fur-collared boots carefully over the muddied slush, much like tawny African queens whose feet may not touch the earth and are carried proudly on golden stools. I am pleased to be associated with them. They crochet as we drive, pink lacy mandalas.

We stop at a Savarin on the Thruway. They warm their hands over steaming coffee and pour heavy spoonfuls of sugar, stirring with wooden sticks. They turn the pie display, which contains foamed coconut cakes and pale clotted cherry pies, and they laugh deep and sonorous over the paucity. "Garbage," one pronounces. There is no discord. The waitress blushes. Claire hides a smile. "Can I get you something else?"

The mothers ignore her. They untie silk bandanas from beneath their chins, displaying masses of anchovied Dynel. Under the Dynel, their faces are stony, furrowed like old fields. Their eyes are ancient. Yellow diamonds, mother's rings, bride's rings, are on their knotted fingers. An occasional stiff gray hair sprouts from spreading velvety moles on their chins and cheeks.

Claire asks for aspirins. I do not trust her. She is begging for the sympathy of Mack's mother. It is well perhaps. I do not want Grace to know my hunger for her son. The power in her pitchblende eyes is degenerate, but still useful.

"Poor child," I say. "You have a headache."

Ignoring me, Grace waves the blushing waitress over. "Hey, chickie, a cup of tea. Leave out the teabag, okay?" She leans across Claire and stage whispers: "Mal och, huh?" She is testing my knowledge.

"Of course." Grace reaches behind Claire and pats firmly the flesh of my thigh.

"That's okay," she says. "How old are you?"

I smile. She winks at her friend.

The tea arrives. Grace slips the bag into her pocket, reaches for the cruets of oil and vinegar and blows across the water in the teacup. "Mack says you're Jewish. I got lots of friends, Jewish."

"We talk direct now." I answer her. She glances at me quizzically. She is a church woman. She shakes the oil.

"My Mack he misses his father. He says you and Robert are like parents to him." She passes her hands over the water slowly. "What he needs is to settle down. What he needs, he says, is a girl like you, a nice girl. A good cook. Enough of this running." She is speaking to me.

I reach and pinch Claire nastily on her buttock.

Grace shakes a drop from the stopper of the cruet into the teacup. The oil drops stay together. "He is a nice boy. Hey, chickie, a clean knife."

"Have you seen Jesus?" I ask Grace. "Are you waiting for Jesus?"

"Me? I got no time to wait. Why should he come to me?" She looks at her friend and they pass a secret about me. She cuts the knife into the water of the teacup, drawing a circle around the spots of oil and then cuts the circle into quarters with a cross. "Five, ten minutes, it'll be gone, your headache," she promises Claire, and reaches for the check. "Maybe Mack looks at you, chickie. Maybe you should clean up. He likes clean girls." So shall it be Claire?

Is this the best I can do with the new woman? Is this the first child who shall carry forth my powers? Already, I am sick. I taught her only a few simple unimportant things and she has misused them when it suited her purposes. She betrayed me and my secrets. What will happen when I tell her the big ones?

What will she do if she knows that all heavenly events repeat themselves in the psyche, passing first through biology and history? Ontology, I should inform her, recapitulates cosmology? That as above, below?

That magnetic events in the heavens change the minds of men? But that the minds of men can affect the magnetic events?

What will she do, go on Dick Cavett and giggle?

What will she do if she knows that magnetism is both a cure and a cause of disease and damage? Will she become a wan scholar and co-ordinate the plagues to the events in the heavens above Egypt as recorded? Claire, I want you to study the Ten Plagues of the Passover, which was actually when I, Venus, passed over and destroyed Egypt among other unnamed places and please do a neat graph on the relationship of the Angel of Death and the Fire of Heaven to the plagues. Yes, that's correct. I am also the Angel of Death and the seder is the night of watching and praying that I don't return in that costume. I should tell her this? I can see her now. "DEAR MACK, STAY CLEAR OF ISHTAR. SHE'S THE ANGEL OF DEATH AND SHE CAN GIVE YOU CANCER AND WIPE OUT YOUR MIND. COME TO ME, INSTEAD. LOVE, CLAIRE."

Will she find a way to use magnetism and the electric properties of metals to cure disease? Will she find a way to avoid illness by injecting microwaves before certain planetary movements? What will she do if I tell her that evolution exists slowly only for the animals and then rather capriciously? That consciousness is given? And that knowledge, electricity, levitation, magnetic controls, nuclear fires, are all antique and yet to be recovered. Will she study the Celts if I tell her they spread knowledge of the powers and learning into the Fertile Crescent, not from the Fertile Crescent upward to Europe. That Hebrew read from left to right is Gaelic?

And that all antique words, Tara, Isis, Vladivostok come from the word Ishtar?

And that the Star of Bethlehem and of David and of Solomon and of Bar Kochba who left his coins in Georgia, U.S.A. . . . that Star is me? And that I intended woman to be the sponsor and spinner of new life and that woman is by nature superior? What will she do, spit in my eye? There is so much. And I tell this child, who is powerful and is worthy and has the imagination to know large things and can laugh in the face of the waves, I tell her to pick me some mushrooms and she uses them herself on the one man I want. Aah, her jealousy and her one-ness are like mine. But they are not tempered with responsibility. The Angel of Death, the Whore of Babylon, the Mother of the World, we must be all of these things, Claire, all at once. That woman you have on your coins with the balanced scales? She is not Justice. She is woman balancing her roles. Standing on one foot, blindfolded. Half queen, half whore, half goddess, half kitchen help. "Cunt, my dear fornicating child," I tell Claire as we drive to Rochester, with Grace and her friend behind us in their aprons under their pastel mink-collared coats and their Dynel wigs.

"Cunt, my sweet child, is from the Sumerian word cunnus. It means burden. It is not something to be treated lightly. Nor is any of this."

I shall tell it first to Mack. He, after all, understands transistors and electronics. If then Mack will explain the simple technical facts about electronics to Claire, she, I know, will be able to grasp the relationships between heaven and earth. That is what a woman can do best.

As we leave, I see Grace patting Claire's behind and hear her say, "Good. Solid." The mothers begin to crochet as soon as we are in the car. Their booted feet rest on the five gallon cans of honey from Grace's beehives. Grace has brought with her a serrated edge pizza cutter. All is well. I turn on the speed control and curl my feet beneath me. The honey under their feet is truly powerful and growing more so. I prepared it myself in the quiet of the rotting chicken coop behind Mack's house. Mack stood outside in the dark guarding the door as I lay my hands on rhythmically, transmitting powers. Birds sang in a mimosa bush growing along the split rock foundation of the coop.

His mother was sleeping in the house above the fields. I whispered to her son, who smiled down at me. "Honey. I brought you a dab." I touched my sticky finger to his forehead, his eyes, his earlobes. "Hindu brides anoint their grooms with honey. And then the bridegroom says to his bride, "Honey, this is honey."

"Hindus should go far with that kind of smarts."

I continued, ignoring his levity. "And then the bridegroom says, 'The speech of thy tongue is honey. In my mouth lives the honey of the bee; in my teeth lives peace.' I say to you, Mack, may your teeth have peace."

"My teeth?"

"Yes." I poked a finger into his mouth, exploring his palate. He licked the honey off and bit my finger, nibbling softer. "In Egypt the word to kiss is the same word as the word to eat."

He kissed my forehead politely. It was all he could do.

"I'm sorry you won't come tomorrow night, Mack. I need your strength."

"Listen, Ishtar," he said very softly. "What have I got for you?" He ran his hands over his body demarcating his limits. I did not know if it were an offer or an apology. I went inside the chicken coop to finish my work.

Much later, when the honey was pure, I stood with him again.

"I got a tough date tomorrow night. That's why I can't go. See this cross?" He pulled a cheap cross from under his jacket. His gesture had been an apology.

"It's ugly."

"I've got this whole fan club in Utica . . . stewardesses. She gave me one . . . I gave her one. So she'll be safe when she flies and I'll be safe when I drive. Wild chick. Hey, Ishtar, you probably know . . . is there anything to having your period that makes chicks come harder?"

"Ugly. What you must go through to become a man. And it is so troublesome waiting for you. Go now."

"Jealous. Wow? Well, may *your* teeth have peace. Don't think I'm . . . are you really jealous?"

I walked away into the fields then. Yes, bitter and jealous. I tore the black nylon of my underslip into strips and tied the strips to the beehives. The birds slept in the mimosa. The night was lonely. I found the familiar luminescence of the mandrakes by the rhubarbs. I covered my head with a coat, knelt and spread my legs over the family, anointing the cluster with menses and urine. Mack's car was gone when I drove up the farm road past his house. At dawn, with flour to sprinkle on the ground from which I had torn them, I would choose my mandrakes.

"Mandrakes," I advise Claire, who is sitting with her magnificent profile next to me, "are female and male. They shriek when they are plucked. One must use an animal to root them out. Often, the animal dies. You are to twist the tiny apples from the female mandrakes and the genital roots from the male plants, liquefy them in a Sunbeam, preferably, and keep the male juices and female juices in separate protected containers. See?" I point to the bottles in my pockets. The bottles glow in the dark, warm through their heavy wrappings of cloth and tin.

We whisper. The tapping of the crochet hook stops. We are overheard. We speak of music. "Almost there, Mothers," I assure them. They begin to work their beads as I pull into the neon strip of motels and used car lots. "Get ready please."

We hear them stretch and shift heavily over the springs and clear their throats. Beyond the unmarked railroad tracks, surrounded by dirty banks of old snow, stands the Wonder Hostess Bakery, square and solid in the night, crowned with red letters. Floodlights cast the letters on the snow, exaggerating their shapes.

"My headache's gone," Claire whispers to me.

"Evil eye. Would you like a mother-in-law with an evil eye?"

"I'm ready to make sacrifices."

"I'm not." I bring the car to a stop under its delivery ramp. "There are only these few perfect moments for the mixing and the baking, Claire. Venus will cross its heliacal arc and appear on the horizon of Lake Ontario at dawn, moving eastward as we have driven westward to Rochester."

"I'll try to remember."

"That's not good enough."

"I'll remember."

"And you'll shorten that coat."

"Yes, ma'am."

I smile at her while the mothers lift themselves from the car. "I will make him a man for you. But I will have the first fruits. I'll show you what it means to sacrifice. Furthermore, my behind is much lovelier and my breasts are even. Is that clear?"

"Yes."

"And the words," I continue as I cut the wires to the front door and allow the mothers to pass in, "matter terribly."

The mothers hang up their coats on walnut racks, remove their shoes from needlepoint shoebags and line their boots up nicely on the draining plastic. I point to Claire's hiking shoes. She bends to remove them. We tie our aprons in double knots and ride the elevators down to the bakery. At the swinging doors of the baking room a green blackboard holds the next day's baking orders in yellow chalk. Profile, Molnar Rye, hams, franks. I draw concentric eyes and flowing spirals around the frame, erasing the day's orders. We enter. There are only two bakers working this night shift.

The bakers shout at the mothers and Claire. I stand beyond the doors. The women brandish whip creme cans as if they are guns inside the deep muslin pockets of their aprons. Claire, within, is tying their sleeves behind them while they laugh at her.

I listen.

"You want some free Cupcakes?"

"Look, we don't wanna be rough with you ladies . . ."

"We're on schedule."

"For Godsake, ladies, what do you want?"

"Hey, maybe they ain't ladies. That one has a mustache."

I enter as Grace's friend with the dark lipline pirouettes before a baker and kicks him at the knees. "Next time, son of a gun, higher."

"Wow, that one . . ." one says as he sees me emerging from the double doors. "That one definitely ain't got no balls."

"You got any respect?" Grace's friend kicked him again, higher.

With a red lever, speechlessly, I halt the conveyor belts. The room is quiet. I wave the bakers out. Claire leads them away. She returns with a load of honey and passes it as planned to the mothers. The mothers climb the running boards near the mixing vats.

As Claire and I bring in the tins of honey, the mothers take turns pouring and stirring the viscous amber into the vats. The cake mix thickens and is difficult to stir. Their faces flush with their effort. While they are busy, I stand near the creme injectors and nibble on a pinch of yellow powder from an umbre can printed in Spanish. I no longer remember the translation. The can is much used and stained. I open my bodice and press a nipple between thumb and forefinger, pumping a thin stream of clear milk into the creme injector. When my left breast is emptied, I demonstrate without words to Claire, who watches with an astonished mien, I press my right breast. Now, into the injector I pour the female mandragora juice.

"Cupcakes?" she inquires. She is quick-witted, knowing the left is the female side.

"And Twinkies," I advise, pouring the male juice into the second injector. I raise my hands over the machinery and move my lips in prayer. I am not quite ready to divulge the magic cadences to her. I sense Grace and her friend watching me. I button my bodice hurriedly, licking the remainder of my milk with my forefinger.

"Hey, Ishtar, what's the powder?" Grace approaches me. "You got a new kid? My daughter-in-law got a new kid. You don't have a new kid." She thinks as she walks to me and then buttons on my bodice a button I missed.

"Claire," I call as I walk away with Grace where no one can hear us, "tell me when the creme shines." Grace walks around me and looks at me from many angles. I stand proudly.

"Would you like this powder for your daughter-in-law?" I ask, offering her my stained umbre can. "It is afterbirth. It will help her love her new child longer. That is the difficulty with modern mothers now. They never eat the afterbirth and they despise their children."

"It's natural to love your kids." She continues to walk around me and I turn.

"It is as natural to eat them." She stops. I continue. "Afterbirth begins the instinctual love which animals have for their offspring and humans do not."

Grace pockets the can with her teabag.

"Dilute it, otherwise she'll get mother's milk."

"You help Mack. Keep him away from Nino?"

I smile although my lips tremble. She pats my marble smooth cheek with her sandpaper hand. "I'll help you, Ishtar, if you help my Mack."

"Yes," I answer, and I believe she knows my intent.

"Cooks of the Week, we stick together, huh?" She nudges me sharply below the ribs and I elbow her back nearer her shoulder since she is short.

"Good food," I say, quite together now, "makes good children."

"Look at that! Look at that!" Claire screams. The creme she points to is resplendent as the living mandrakes had been in the night field. The women circle around the creme.

"Cupcakes, first," Grace calls.

The machinery, flashing blue with my furca, begins it motion. An aura of ultraviolet frames the oven and I examine the blood tapering into my fingers through the light. The mothers' faces gleam as they stand before the glass windows and watch the cakes pop and rise and pass out to the cooling and wrapping systems. The molds turn on their sides, wax paper enfolds the cakes, cardboard bases support them and at last the cakes are pressed with my own labels. It is dawn by the time the final Twinkies are produced and packaged and then we are finished. We are wet with perspiration and fatigue but the baking is completed and well.

Claire brings in the bakers and the mothers push the two men against the wall. They are cold, for having been on the platform these long hours, and I am sorry for them. Nevertheless, I stomp on their hats, which are the hats of priests and not deserved, and I serrate their tongues with the pizza cutter so we will be unknown for a while. "We are the ovens," I tell them as they sink to the floor, their aprons to their mouths. "We kindle and we bake. You are unclean to trifle with the Cupcakes of the Hostess." They blink at me. They do not understand. "I leave you honey to lay upon your tongues that they may heal. I am satisfied," I tell them and I tell the mothers and I tell Claire. "Ishtar is satisfied."

Outside on the loading platform, my hair blows across my face. The sky above Lake Ontario is pink. Over the flat roof of Shakey's Pizza, Venus rises faintly as the morning star. "Wonder Bread," I call out. "Miracle Mix," I call out. "Hostess," I call out. "You will be mine again." And I toss the letters on the roof, crashing them into their footlights and burying them in the snow.

In the Country Squire with their tired heads tucked into their mink collars, the mothers sleep already. I recite the recipes again and again to Claire, committing them to her memory. They will be hers.

13

Ishtar lay in her king-size bed, lilies of semen-crusted Kleenex scattered on the olive turf floor beneath her as she languidly twisted the globe of her Spitz Junior Planetarium, weaving summer heavens into winter heavens, night by night on the darkened plaster of the ceiling. She plunged Ursa Major over a green fly flattened the last summer.

"Ennui," she pronounced, and the Great Bear dipped before her. "I myself, even I, the Lady of the Southern Sycamore. I who fashion all things. I who bring to life. I who am sharp of tooth. I who am unsparing of fang. I who am both cunning and lingual. I need a dentist."

The seven sisters appeared in the East over a pair of two-dimensional mosquitoes and the hairline profile crack of George Washington. Ishtar sighed heavily. There was much to do. The layer of ice was shrinking from the canal. Easter was approaching. The children in three cites had annihilated dance halls and schools. Club owners from distant cities called day and night booking ahead for summer jobs. The crowds came, hoping for the mother and her magic, in passion over the music, but Ishtar had not appeared. She had agreed with herself to leave at Easter, which was of course somewhat traditional. She was not ready to leave. Grace fretted over the shortage of Cupcakes, the factories were not organized and the boys, with their silver and inlaid instruments and clothes of suedes and leathers and cars of terrible beauty, wanted still more money. And Mack was sullen, passing in large curves around her and shifting his blackened eyes from her questioning smiles.

Ishtar trailed Cassiopeia closer to the windowsill. And her teeth were rotting. Which meant it was time to go.

Pumpernickel seeds were caught between her teeth, dull and threatening, like shark fins in clean waters. The gums of her mouth were swollen and painful. She would have to see a dentist if she were to remain after Easter. And she hated dentists and loved Mack and wanted to remain. Clouds of glory have never satisfied the hunger of great women.

Lazily exploring among the stiff lilies Robert had left so joyously in his wake, after having been seduced with cocoa and cookies, Ishtar found a damp one and daubed her heel for good measure.

She could stay, she considered, as the southern November sky passed from view, and the demands would be enormous. Her name and their name on a thousand lips, a thousand times a thousand lips, and then, she sighed, it would be, according to the old plan, the time to die and return, nailing in her godship. With rotting teeth. Shit.

Ishtar turned on her tensor light and danced in among the stars freely, without orbit, as she had so long ago, zigzagging wildly across the heavens, until that terrible day when Paradise ended, when the apple orchard was closed and ugly Mars stood between her and her children with his flaming sword of war turning forever. And her children began to fight then, with Mars above them, sending his terrible metallic heat and hatred into their veins. She couldn't tolerate her children fighting.

Sirius climbed up the bathroom door. Ishtar rubbed a nub of Kleenex between thumb and forefinger and jammed it into the eye of Mars on the Bakelite globe. Without Mars, December and January, February and March passed and it was spring. Preparing herself for the pain and ignominy with a fingernail measure of spruce bark and mandrake root, Ishtar dialed the dentist.

The dentist, one nylon sole loafer on the stool, stands above Ishtar reprimanding her for her lateness, genitals pressing insistently into her funny bone as he sucks his own teeth clean from the inside and examines her mouth. He pronounces her plagues: silver birch bark, mandrake root, pastrami, pumpernickel seeds. His belly rests against her cheek meat. He levitates the labiodental throne. Ishtar watches his lips, brisket pink, slime quivering on the ends of the cilia in his nose as she rises in his seat to meet the needle.
And the worm, she reminds him in silent incantation against toothache, *went weeping to Shamash, the sungod, for food and Shamash offered him a fig and an apricot. No, lift me up and among the teeth and in the gums cause me to dwell. The blood of the tooth I will suck and of the gum I will gnaw its roots and I will grow wise.* Oh, DK, Ishtar offered her help, fix the pin and seize its foot. Because thou hast said this, O worm, may you be smitten with the might of his hands.
The dentist heard her not. "Now lie back and relax and turn your head toward me.
"YOU WILL FEEL ONE SMALL PRICK."
He is the Tooth Pharaoh, this latent Jewish dentist, wearing his catpaw soles and cockaleekie Arnold Palmer golf pants under his clean butcher apron, out of Egypt into the desert, weighing her heart and shoving a needle of novocaine into the sanctity of her gums. A small prick, she condemns him silently, and you are such a good golfer but then I measured your soul from the sound of your caterpillar tread sucking on the urethane floor beneath us. I understand that you need no organ of regeneration in this business for your offices are death, your poison is in my mouth and your name is decay, DK. Suck, she whispers as the novocaine seeps into her

sinuses toward her brain erasing the boundaries of time and memory.

"You won't feel a thing in a minute."

And when Tiamat opened her mouth to consume Marduk, he drove in the evil wind that she close not her lips and tightened the screws until her mouth was open wide. The moon he caused to shine, this Marduk, the night to him entrusting. My moon, Ishtar whispered, my night, and he vanquished me, unbridled in his arrogance, he constructed stations for the gods, fixing their astral likenesses as constellations and took the Tablets of Fate and hung them from his breast and split Tiamat, the Mother, in two.

"A little wider, honey."

Suck.

"That's better." He tightens the clamps. He raises a silver claw to her cavity. "I'm really disappointed when you are late. I could have arranged to have another patient before you, honey."

Suck. There is no one before me. I am one and my name is one. But forgive me, DK, be gentle with me and forgive me for being late and charge me not double as you so often do, for Robert Moses will then know my fear.

"Just a little more, honey. I have to scrape away the excesses before I begin. I'll have to charge you, you know, for being late. I lose money waiting while I could fill in with other patients."

Reckon not my fear on your monthly statement. Her head swims, a rock, heavy, cascading wildly through rapids of thought and dream while he scrapes. She opens her eyes, ringed now with tears and strangely glazed. Forgive me, DK, and don't tell, oh Tooth Pharaoh. Let my funny bone go and I'll go down to Egypt on your diamond tipped tool and touch with sin your sterility as you faradize me and I will watch your soul dancing its farandole sextuple on the single pedal of this Muzak chair, tiptoeing to the two lips of the speaker in the ceiling and I'll sigh deeply from my depths because I want not your pink hands furrowing and plowing in my gardens, I want my love's hands, lettuce/letos farmer hands, rock garden hands, thick and libidinal and raw. Hands that stretch and pound and pump his polyphonic organ with flue stops, labial and polypedals and tinkling harpychords and drumming passion flower pedals, the sweet hammering in of many sons, and hair that falls to his shoulders and you, all you have, Pharaoh of another age, is one tread pedal that sucks, this sad but brave sterile flute at my funny bone and I, even I, Mother, shall take an oral fixation on you while you excoriate my teeth if you will not reckon my fear on my monthly statement. Besides I have nothing else to do, having left my macramé at home.

"Do you feel anything yet?" Who said that, I or you?

She spreads her hands in emptiness. I am depressed, Tooth Pharaoh, down in the mouth, because my love loves a candle-eyed, splay-fingered child and can not yet love me. My love, he sings also, as the head of Osiris, while his manhood is in the mouths of the letos fish. But it will be found. It will be found. She twists a Kleenex into knots, sealing the strands of fate. And verily, someday, she speaks to his astonished and grateful eyes as she fumbles under the butcher apron for his tongue depressor, you will die at the fourth hole of your cunt tree club under the sycamore rolling agonized in the mud trying to pass through a sclerodermatic urethra one large pumpernickel seed from a pastrami sandwich. Which I loved so well. You are, DK, because my hair stands on end and I sit here among your gasses in the bellybutton of the world surrounded by Lily cups and I myself am pythic, phythogenic, pyorrheic and pythenic and I say unto you they will carry you away in a fold up golf cart and all the members, black stripes on their Arny Palmy pants, will wail against the wall of the pro shop and bury you then in your two-toned Bonneville on the green for removing the excesses of the Mother . . . I who am still known, absurdly, as the Mother of God.

The tears slip over her cheeks to her mouth. How am I to tell you? I can say neither Lilith nor Lollipop as I blow you. Why all this pain, why crosses and nails and double axes and diamond drills and Bolivian bullets and childhood diseases? Why must I die for them? Let *them* die for me. I know. Let *them* learn by dying. I should die for their sins? Let them die for *my* sins.

Aah, Osiris, for all your sweet singing, for all your pain, they know you only as Humpty Dumpty. And Jesus, did you teach them anything . . . even to fold their clothes in neat sanctimonious piles as you did in the crypt? And Moses, you were brilliant to insist they all come with you into the desert, if you had to be a sufferer for them, they'd suffer too. Smart. But you weren't gentle with me, were you? And I zigzagged that cloud for forty years, Moses, that was my price for the roll by the riverbank. And I led you not to oil and when you returned, did anyone but your desert band honor you? And Quetzalcoatl, burning on your fiery raft at sea, who remembers you? A lone dirt picker finds the Star of David in Tikal or some ended place and thinks perhaps Moses had been there. And Bar Kochba, son of the Star, leaves coins in Georgia and no one understands. They don't know any of you; they don't know my Star. They find it in Mexico, in Auschwitz, in Anatolia, in Brittany and they don't know it is my Star. So then, how am I to do it, this resurrection of my own? Is there a safe crypt somewhere, a pryamid still perfect after the magnetic reversals, where my body will stay whole? Shall I die to return in pedal pushers on a Little League diamond? Even if I could cross the Arab-Israeli border as a gentile, Cheops is no longer a perfect pyramid. And the Czechs, the Czechs who know the secret of Cheops with their cardboard pyramids to keep liverwurst fresh and resharpen razor blades, could I ask them to fit me out in a cardboard crypt? It is unseemly to resurrect from cardboard. And is there myrrh and frankincense from Ethiopia to sprinkle on my form to preserve me while my Great Soul travels in the spheres? Is there even a trade agree-

ment between the Czechs and the Ethiopians? The diamond digs deeper into her roots.
"Just a little deeper here, honey."
You were fools to die. They just went on sinning, your people. They weren't your people. You were their god. Big difference. Oh! Her jaws shiver with pain, blinding her. Oh, farther, farther. Go down, she cries, go down to the fourth hole, your promised land, for this execration is upon you and you shall return my Tablets of Fate and my Snake Banner and all which is rightfully mine. Melt no more the golden calf, throw no longer your mother's bones behind you. It is I who sow and I who reap. Raise that pedal, roll those balls, open that petcock, pet. Tote that barge with your nile on souls and we'll sail down my Pharaohnyx to the Eerie Canal because I am also Lilith the Witch who roams in desolate letos fields attacking children and golfers and you are going to die on the fourth hole, DK, with your wattles turning as red as your waterpicked gums. You'll die for me as it used to be; I'll stick around. To be mortal and have bad teeth and unhappy loves is enough. To hell with resurrection.
He offers her a fresh Kleenex. She refuses, preferring Robert's. He drills with a diamond. His knees shake. She works to bring him to abundance. He isn't abundant. He rolls scarab beetle balls of silver and mercury between his Norman Vivisection Peeled Fingers. With clay he fills his fingers, with goodly clay, his fingers creating life for my decay and he's going to fill my mohole. Oh, Mack, if you could be here to help with the pain, to ease me while this Ra does his Ra Bit in Ra Dio land with Muzak filling his head, with the red eyes and pale nostrils and hairs waving wildly in his Moses nose under his putt putt breath and his toes curling in the catpaw treadmill of his dental floss soul as his blood rushes to its appointment.
"Just a wee bit longer and I'll have this all cleaned out."
We agree. Tears catapult from her eyelashes.

"Tell me if it hurts."

Oh, Mack, be here with me. Hold me against this pain. All I have is my anger and this poor man who sincerely wishes me no harm is to suffer for the sins of his forefathers and his foreskin. Oh, farther. Farther. Let this be done. And you too, DK, shall come to pass, so consider your cockaleekie pants and my fine raiment and my flesh. My flesh, she warns him with a basilisk stare, as the shoulder of the drill pinches her lip.

"Filled." He places carbon impression paper between her teeth. "That's better. Just a little more and we'll be finished." Muzak plays don't sit under the apple tree with anyone else but me and Ishtar agrees with the Ra Dio and the Ra Bit and mouths the gentle percussion of ten trombones and two guitars as she brings him to abundance and curses him in an ancient manner as his eyes rise to the ceiling.

And I write your name on clean parchment or blue carbon and I place it in my mouth and I spit on you four times in the course of each day and I wipe you out with my left foot and throw you in the flames and I will be triumphant over you.

Ishtar presses her sandal on his loafer, suggesting a rhythm for his soul.

"Very good. Bite down and gnash your teeth."

Bite down? she inquires with her periwinkle blue dazed eyes and bites down sharply on the little league diamond depressor and the carbon impression paper and releases him and there is a hot molten trill on the organ as an untold multitude of homunculi candystore owners, unregistered pharmacists and vivisectionists die foaming in the flaming pink of the Lavoris rinse. And your children's children after that. Your egg shall be lost. Your seed shall not knit. I am triumphant over you and you didn't get any on me.

His eggshell fingernails quiver as he offers her the Tablets encased in silver foil. A pale stain spreads across his butcher apron. "Take these for pain. There isn't any charge."

Ishtar agrees.

She nods, wiping her eyes with the knotted Kleenex, clutching the Tablets in her hand. I'll be down to meat you, fourth hole, DK. DK waterpicks behind her and she weaves into the office and wraps herseif in a trench mouth coat, smiling at the jackass-eared receptionist. "There is no charge," they reassure each other.

Ishtar speeds along the glissando back of a seaserpent along Hiawatha Boulevard, around Lake Gitche Gumee, to Mack, to ease her pain. The novocaine slips out slowly from a fracture in the rock of her head, hissing. The boulevard arches and dips in her coming and Gitche Gumee rises with her tears. To be mortal is enough.

14

Ahasuerus was a boor.

I, as Vashti, had extended his reign from India to Ethiopia. I was a good queen with goodly limbs and justice in my heart. I had chosen Ahasuerus. I make errors often because I am tempted by juicy and aggressive bull-like men. But although their inconsummate appetites for rapacious lovemaking are appealing to me, I find their beer swilling and machismo prancing utterly intolerable. You know some of this story. It is recorded, although by prejudiced patriarchs, as the Book of Esther. Although it is not allowed into the Bible since it gives away the story of the overthrow of the matriarchy and doesn't mention God, who really wasn't terribly on the scene then, it is quite important. The holiday, Purim, is still celebrated for the children each year. It is a gay holiday. The Megillah is unrolled and Esther, once again for the children's ears, saves the Jews and has Haman killed and everyone lives happily ever after and punch and hamantashen are served in the social hall after the announcements of the next bas and bar mitzvahs. I grind my teeth. Esther was a decoy of the Hebrews: a false queen. Actually Ahasuerus deserved her with all her cute fainting tricks and deceits.

At any rate, it was time for Haman to become my god-king and Ahasuerus was to step down. Most kings welcome Paradise and a glorious death. But impure A., even though I assured him of beer parties in the afterworld if he so wished, did not want to step down. Haman, who may also be remembered as Amen of the Egyptians, and the ends of all your prayers, reasoned with the king about cycles, rebirths and the necessity of bringing one thing to an end to begin the next. Proudly, A. laughed and invited all the princes and kings to a party for days on end. Pig. He, drunk as a beast, insisted that I come down and let him show me off. I refused. I do not like to be paraded as a possession and that is what my husband was on to. A. blew sky high that I would not obey him. Others have tried to stop the tides and fared as poorly. I would not appear. Well, he and all of his drunken male friends decided that my offense against him was an offense against all men and they issued a royal decree that not only would he transfer my position to another more deserving than I, but that from then on all wives would show proper respect to their husbands, whether of high or low birth. I laughed in my quarters when I heard and simply began the temple preparation for his death and the initiation of Haman as elect. I had not figured the bestial arrogance of Ahasuerus and the other men we had chosen from the fields and the plains for civilization. I was locked in the temple, my priests bought off.

In the streets, thousands of young beauties paraded in rich gowns and caravans, dangled by their fathers, incestrual uncles (Mordecai was such a one) and pimps. My Playboy of the Eastern World invited each to his chambers, one by one, until he found one more deserving than I. That was easy enough. I was hardly deserving of that pig in his purple gowns. Much of this is written and only bears reinterpretation. You realize, the Book of Esther marks the end of the matriarchy. A.'s decrees were that a man would forevermore be master in his house and that his native language shall be followed by all in his household. No longer does the Goddess choose the king, no longer do the queens continue the line, no longer is civilization directed by woman. It really was an ending.

And along comes Mordecai of the Jewish men, with his

delicious decoy Esther, who must have been really good in bed, for A. was a dirty old man. Mordecai was a diviner of dreams, self-fancied, and an eavesdropper. Esther was from nowhere, no class, no bearing. But she was beautiful. Haman and I, realizing the momentous mischief A. was causing, plotted to get rid of A. and continue the cycle of killing the year's king as must be. Mordecai fingered Haman. We were in trouble. The matriarchy would be overthrown by Mordecai and the Jews . . . who really had no one important yet as a God. And Esther was pleasing A. right and left and in between. Haman finally convinced A. to reason and A. agreed not to sleep with Esther for a month while he considered what he had done, dethroning, after all, the Queen of Heaven. I am still amazed he managed this far.

Esther was ignored in her chambers. A. understood that he had committed a monumental sin, an act of intolerable disrespect for the workings of the world, an act of pride. He considered. He decided, for he was still aggressive and needed to be king, that he could save himself by killing all the Jews and blaming the entire scheme on them . . . which is nothing new. But this time the Jews *were* responsible. Which is why the Rabbis wanted to leave Esther from the Bible.

A month passed. Esther, covered with unguents of mare spoor, adorned in robes of white linens (mine), appeared before him. She came in fainting and carrying on and passing out. You know the tricks. A., who kills anyone entering unbidden into his rooms, was overcome by the spoor and his pent-up desires . . . which, believe me, were considerable . . . rushed from his throne to her and held her in his arms as she faked the faint and asked him, fluttering her eyelids in innocent wonderment, to save her people. "Kill Haman," she said. It isn't enough she has my first husband and my mare spoor and my robes. "Kill Haman. He did this to you." A. didn't know what Haman did to him except keep him celibate for a month, but it would get that king-elect out of the way. So A. agreed to kill Haman, save the Jews and give

Mordecai a seat of importance. He dragged Esther off to the chambers. Good-by, Esther. Enjoy yourself.

Good-by, Vashti. I am not stupid. And if the times are against me, I do not stand around waiting to be hung on crosses. I pack and leave for the cliffs of Mohr, where the good O'Briens have a pleasant castle, albeit covered with guano, and I leave Persia, Medea, Israel, Ethiopia . . . all of it . . . to the masculine apes and their fainting deceitful women whom they think are obedient. And from Ireland I hear that A. had a very grand celebration. Haman was killed and the Jews were allowed to kill others and they, according to the Megillah, smote their enemies with blows of death and devastation, three hundred here, five hundred there, seventy-five thousand there and Shushan, the city of A., was glad and rejoiced and they ate Haman. Ahasuerus got the thigh meat; Esther, the cheek meat; and I, cursing the rain and the guano, traveled across this new island planting palm trees. There is a great festival in the Sunday Schools even today, this Purim. All the children eat the hamantashen, the cookies of Haman, all those little God-eaters in their Florence Eiseman and Piccolino, nosh on the hamantashen for strength, joy, fertility, fecundity, new ten-speeders and anything else one might acquire by eating divine flesh of the god-king. It is equivalent, nowadays, with my recipes, to a Twinkie, but their reasons for eating it are impure, and hamantashen will never help them. Amen.

From now on, gentle men with delicate ankles.

There is a problem at home. It is not pleasant. I sit awake in the bed. I hear Robert scratching himself in the dark next to me under the Hudson Bay. There is a red tower signal blinking over the airport through the trees. I whisper, "Are you awake?" Because I am lonely. He does not answer. I do not know if he is awake. I watch the red point pulsing against the black of the sky and I feel the pulsing within myself.

I have had my spiral removed. I have given up that delightful spiral which had eased my mind all these loving nights. I do not wish another child of this nature. "Too long," my gynecologist said. "It must come out and be replaced." I know about these things, seven lean years, world ages, and so on and I do not argue with him. "Don't worry," he assured me with his simian hands, "I'll give you an abortion if you need one."

It is not a particularly divine thing to do, an abortion. I do not disagree with the principle of free will. But an abortion is simply not in my style. I want my spiral back and I may not have it for three months. I am not happy with this. A spiral is a happy thing. I have had it traced and etched on all of my temples. It is the basis of the chain of life, and the staircase to heaven. I can close my eyes and see, in the sunlight filtering through my fluttering eyelids, spirals and spirals and spirals. And they have taken mine. When I have time to be scholarly, I shall do something scholarly and abominable about why men become gynecologists. I believe, sincerely, it is out of fear of the organ.

Robert, in a false spirit of generosity, seeing my great unhappiness, suggests that we do not make love for the three months. This is not a nice suggestion of Robert's. I shake my head, no. I am speechless. "There are devices, foams, procedures," I tell him.

"Oh," he says lightly, ignoring my eyes which fill with tears, "this will be easier." I suppose he has been waiting for an out like this since his fear of me has increased in these last months. I believe he is relieved.

I do not like seducing men. It is a cheap act of love. It is Claire's mistake, to trick them into displaying their needs and weaknesses. I will have to seduce my own husband. That is what he wants, to be tricked into weakness. Suicidal, Black Widow, weakness. "Just come to me, Robert," I whisper at his back under the Hudson Bay. "And I'll come to you." It has only been a week. I do not sleep well without his warmth. He is so afraid of the succubus in his remote unconscious that he sleeps on top of the top sheet with his own Hudson Bay knotted under his chin. I am underneath the blankets and I am cold. I cannot touch him. I understand this. I understand it all. It would never have happened if the spiral had not been torn from my womb. Yes, it might have. I no longer prepare his breakfasts. This would be the next step.

"Hear this now," Isaiah warned me, cursing so long ago. "Thou who art given to pleasures, that dwellest carelessly, that sayest in thine heart, I am and no one else beside me. I shall not sit as a widow neither shall I know the loss of children. But these two things," Isaiah warned, "will come to thee in a moment one day. The loss of children and widowhood."

I laughed at him and said, "I will be a lady forever."

"Sit thou silent and get thee into darkness, O Daughter of the Chaldeans, for thou shalt no more be called tender and delicate. Sit thou silent and get thee into darkness, O Virgin, Daughter of Babylon, sit on the ground. There is no throne. Thou shalt no more be called the Lady of Kingdoms." I turn on my bed lamp and examine Robert's face. He is faking.

I refuse. I categorically refuse an abortion. I categorically refuse coitus interruptus. I categorically refuse to be left alone like this.

There is no other woman. He is an ethical man. I shall laugh if he sheds his seed in his sleep and warn him that no Jewish man should sleep in a house alone, for the succubus shall descend and produce demons from his seed. And I shall laugh. But I am not happy. I do not wish vengeance. I want to screw. "Robert, wake up."

I turn off the lamp. He mumbles and flatulates. Beast. As for adultery, Moses forbade it entirely, as esteeming it a happy thing that men should be wise in the affairs of wedlock; and that it was profitable both to cities and families that children should be known to be genuine. He also abhorred men's lying with their mothers as one of the great abominations. Robert is also having difficulty with his teeth. His gums need cutting. I do not wish to be blamed for the connection. I will only be kind to him in our household affairs and continue to support him. He knows, however, my strengths and is beginning to suspect my powers and I shall not deceive him into thinking I am weak and silly. I abhor that in women.

"Aah, Robert." I tuck his blanket in against his shoulder. It is rather a difficult job, this being a man, wresting money from a cold world. I understand. I am here to help. But I can not help Robert. I hope to help others. Robert's laws and fears are too entrenched. Robert, whose body I adore, whose bulges I contain, who can dance gracefully and kick both ankles together in the air and uphold me, I do not wish to lose. I also need him to direct the production of my Cupcakes. He will not allow me to help him.

"Robert," I whisper loudly. "Are you awake?" I touch his ankles with my toes. He has been awake, lying there, trying to keep still and breathe regularly. He is very very big. His bones are sharp, like sacrificial flints. I want him to smooth my hair and hold my hand. I want to play with the hairs of his sideburns, which will be red in the morning sunlight. I tear off his covers, leaping onto him. His knees go up in self-defense. Part of him doesn't want to push me off. I am now well attached. At last we work together. But it is not tender. Fields and fields of dead men, all erected in the abominable ecstasy of battle lying heel to mouth, I have done this to them in my dark days and mandrakes have sprung up where they lay. I can not see his face. He can not see mine. I am finished first. Then he is. We go tripping over shoes and the velvet forms of dogs and cats to separate bathrooms to cleanse ourselves. When I return to our bed, his shoulders are turned in on himself under the blanket, knotted tightly under his chin, and he is, I suppose, asleep.

I scratch my own back. Dawn is coming. The tower signal fades. I hear him flatulate under the Hudson Bay. Again. Involuntary acts to relieve the organs. I am sorry.

In the morning I wait for him to mention this strange act of mine. He does not. He strews the eggshells and orange rinds on the black countertops, albumenlike slug marks along my Woodmode, and leaves, the station wagon throwing up gravel as it roars, a mad bull elephant tusking the earth, up the driveway to the road and toward the office. Later I will call him at the office and he will have to be kind because his secretary may be listening.

"Mommy," I hear my son calling from his bed. "Did Daddy go yet?"

"Yes," I answer, wishing things to be easier.

My son is now ready to get up. I wash the dishes and make the beds haphazardly. The dog has eaten the last of the cats' food, leaving her own. I kick her. We both regret our acts. I am not good today. I do not even wish vengeance.

My young son climbs onto my lap at the kitchen table. "I want to be a baby today. I don't want to go to school."

"Do you pull out your teeth," I ask him, "because you want to be a baby?"

It is a mistake on my part to ask him.

"No," he answers. "Do I have to go to school?"

"Yes, of course. It is your job right now."

"I have to be a man before I can be a baby again."

This is strange. He watches "Space Trek" too often. "Do you pull out your teeth because you have to be a man?"

"Is it nice to be a man?"

"It isn't easy."

He climbs from my lap and eats the pancakes I prepared. "How will you be a baby again?" What secrets has he seen on "Sesame Street" or "The Doctors"?

"My spirit," he says with syrup slipping from the corners of his mouth, "will go out of me when I die and get born

again. I'll be a baby from a tiny egg. Maybe I'll be a baby man. Maybe I'll be a baby lion."
"You mean eggs like we have in the refrigerator?"
"No, purple eggs."
"You watch too much TV." He doesn't comment on this. He has told me a shape-changing man in a striped polo shirt sits on the edge of his bed and changes shapes at night. "He isn't real, but he is real in my head. I'm scared of him even though he isn't real." If I watched TV myself I might be able to cast judgments on all of this.
"Can I go to community swim Sunday?"
"You have Sunday School."
"Do I have to go to school today?"
"I'll talk to Daddy about swimming. You finish up and get ready for school." At dinner I talk to Daddy. "I think I'd rather send him swimming than to Sunday School anyway. If he starts to drown, he can pray while he's swimming to shore."
"I don't know, Ishtar. He should have divinities in some way whether you believe in it or not. What does he have anyway?" We had a box of egg matzoh on Passover. How can I make Passover when I know that the matzoh which does not rise is in celebration of my end. I should wait for Elijah?
"I don't need a conscience." The boy has been listening. I don't know where he picks up these concepts. "I don't want a conscience."
Robert's eyes meet mine. It is the first time this week. I feel a thrill.
"What's a conscience, Buddy?" Robert asks him.
I am smiling into the sink.
"A little voice that tells you right from wrong. But mine always breaks in half."
I turn. Our eyes meet. I love this man. Why must this child's disaster bring us together? Is this what the child knows? Is that his sacrifice?

"It breaks in half?" Robert asks, incredulous at this infantile wisdom.

"Yeah, it doesn't always work. So then I can do what I want."

I swell with pride. I pour Joy over my hands.

"Well, take a day off from Sunday School, Buddy. I'll take you swimming."

As they leave I call softly, "Why don't you stop and buy some rubbers?"

"I have rubbers in the car."

And then Robert realizes what I am asking and grins, toothy, at me. "They don't make them big enough for me."

The boy says, "I'm in a size five men's already."

"Hate, hate, hate," I say, trying to keep it light.

"I'm taking him swimming. Why don't you pick them up when you get the *Times*?"

My face grows radiant with shame. I kick the dog again. She understands. She's been spayed.

This can not go on. I am prepared halfheartedly to accept a compromise with the gynecologist. If he cuts the time to a month, I'll allow him to write me up in the Medical Journal. No pictures though. He has, by the way, become very religious and prays even while examining me. He used to giggle as he searched my breasts for cancerous nodules. Now he prays. Loudly. The feathers trouble his soul.

15

"Better than a half year has passed," I read in Robert's Making Progress brochure, "since the government for the first time other than in all-out war imposed direct controls on sources of income." It is a neat and intelligent white and blue folder from Shearson Hammill & Co., Inc. It lay next to Robert's bed in front of his luminous dial clock, which I will neither have on my side of the bed nor touch to dust. I do not like man-made luminous objects. I continue reading. "In spite of the inherent risk that such massive tinkering with economic forces could be counter productive, the stock market has been taking the anti-inflationary controls in stride. The outlook for equities indeed continues to be bright, probably for the rest of this year at least." I have spent the morning sorting out pennies with old backs from the receipts of last night's gig at the Lake Forest Hotel for Robert's penny collection. It pleases him. The language in the brochure is wonderful, is it not? "The general expectation is that the real growth in Gross National Product this year will run about 5–6 percent, roughly double the percentage of 1970, after filtering out an inflationary factor of 3–4 percent. In the meantime the new economic controls have been effective to some extent in blunting the former excessive rate of inflation." At Delphi we never used such close figures.

But this language becomes boring. Worse than his pennies. I do the pennies because we ran out of napkins this morning, and when he shrunk his lips in displeasure, I offered him a pretty flowered cocktail napkin which he threw to the floor. Of course, I realize this is only a manifestation of his great and growing fear and he took the cocktail napkin offer as an effrontery and a proof, further, of his unworthiness. I hope the pennies please him. The task is becoming, as they say above, counter productive. Do you know that we, when pleased with a well-membered man, spoke in delight of his boring love? Isn't that funny? I have much on my mind. I do not wish to read the economic report. However, the language is blindly convincing with its neverthelesses and its by slowing the momentums of inflations and its given furthers. Would it impress you? I do have something rather oracular to tell you. I shall attempt it.

"Better than a half year has passed since the electronic industry for the first time other than in all-out war, imposed direct controls on the electromagnetic field of the planet. In spite of the inherent risk that such massive tinkering with life forces could be counter productive, the industry has been taking anti-universal balance controls in stride. The outlook for cancer, mutant births and species extinction continues to be bright, probably for the rest of the year at least.

"In the meantime, although labor is not yet aware of the fact that the human cell is a semiconductor and receives in great part its directions for basic functions from this electronic magnetic field"—am I doing well?—"the new rebalancing of the electromagnetic field has taken some of the wind out of the sails of the species. Ironically, existence of the new imbalance of controls has given rise to the hope and expectation that as and when the Fed begins laying on a new round of restrictive policy it will be insulated from having to revert to quite as drastic a regimen of "stop" and "go" policy as has frequently been the case in the past; some observers believe a policy change is already under way."

Hah, hah, Making Progress. *I* call it magnetic pole reversal.

"As to the effectiveness of the controls themselves, the government lately has evinced some disatisfaction with the way things have been progressing. Yet, short of fundamental overhaul, the system remains spongy at best. It remains sufficiently porous [he spelled dissatisfaction wrong, didn't he?] to permit corporate management for the most part to pursue their respective objectives without great sacrifice, under the program. In other words, labor and management can have their cake and eat it. This is a prescription for a cyclical upswing which in turn can be expected to benefit . . ."

I am lost. I turn the clockface to the wall and stick a penny in a socket. People read this little book and obey it. For instance, it recommends purchase of Fibreboard Corporation stock and states that Leeds and Northrup is an attractive stock for investors seeking longer term capital gains.

This must be the way to direct Mr. America's thoughts. A stock report. Buy this. We can expect solid growth, often erratic, but extensive in this field. Even with an unstable monetary picture on the international front, or with an all-out war, electronic equipment will . . .

No, that is not clear. The production of electronic equipment is on an up cycle and investments made in these companies will be, up to a point, productive. The introduction of electronic activity into the electromagnetic force field of our planet will naturally upset the cyclic balance of these forces which we understand control such processes as birth, growth, healing and aging. It has been recognized statistically that the human cell, a product which has been in the past a fine investment with many multiples, escalations, built-in obsolescences and market splits, is actually a semi-conductor. This fact therefore relates the work of the cell to the increase of the electronic industry's capacity to change the electronic-magnetic environment, thereby influencing mammalian reproduction, regeneration, cyclic patterns in the earth's field, the central nervous system and the possibility of induction of behavioral or cognitive disorders of a basic nature. Since this information is not known popularly, the time is ripe for a good buying opportunity of electronic equipment and installation corporations and the further expectation of rapidly increasing sales in the electronic line with regard to hospitals and the health industry. Although, eventually, in all probability, humanitarians will force the Fed to effect controls on the injection of electrical energy into the universal system, until that unpropitious event, we can look forward to a happy state of increasing cancerous growth, scrambled nervous systems, mutant births and an active market.

We wish in particular to bring your attention to the manufacture of a small box by Pfitter Labs with electrode probes that can dedifferentiate the human cell into erratic growth patterns simply by increasing the electric activity around the cell. It is of inestimable interest to amputees, who wish new limbs, heart patients who wish to replace damaged tissue, farmers and defense industries. Enormous preliminary sales prior again to the possibility of Fed controls can be anticipated.

Well, then, would a form letter impress you at all?

To Whom It May Concern:
The human cell is a semiconductor. You are surrounded by a vast electromagnetic force field. That field regulates the clocks of your body systems. Electronic waves regulate cell functions. Electronic waves begin growth, initiate healing, stop growth, replace damaged parts with new parts, you name it. All of this has been arranged above. Your engineers, however, are sending up vast quantities of electronic disturbances into my system and I am having great difficulty keeping all the systems in balance up here. Because, down there, your cells are receiving messages from

me, you follow normal cycles of birth, growth and healing.
With the incidence of the man-made erratic electronic
activity in my force field, the normal cycles of birth and
growth and healing have been severely interrupted. There is
at present great trouble in Booneville, New York. Many
mutants are coming from Booneville. There is at present a
severe and shocking relationship between terminal cancer
deaths and electronic centers. I do not know offhand what
is happening in Booneville except that there is a great deal
of radiation in the Watertown area. City dwellers who live
in highly disturbed areas with complex computer systems,
etc., should be advised to take great caution. If enough of
these electronic devices are fed into my system, I will have
no alternative other than reversing the magnetic poles once
again and re-establishing foundations and forms. Microwave
ovens, television sets, computer banks should be avoided
with diligence. It has been called to my attention that
bedsores are being healed with a low intensity electromagnetic
force field . . . DC 1–3 or something (I didn't hear the fellow well) in small black boxes in major hospitals. Please
advise your associates that, since they do not yet know what
the effect of microwave injection into cells might be, they
would do well to keep the bedsores and avoid other cell
behavior of a more drastic nature. The triggering of cancerous
growth is a direct result of electronic messages from the
atmosphere. I do not know what the imbalance does to
potency and sterility. It is, in conclusion, my sincere hope
that you and your associates learn to accomplish healing
and regrowth with electronic energies. However, allow me to
remind you that since the commissions that use, test and
distribute much of the power are self-regulating, the safety
levels set, for instance by the Atomic Energy Commission
on the amount of radiation which is safe for human beings,
or the safety level of television leakage . . . these safety
levels are equivalent to a rotten child setting his own
bedtime. The regulations and levels of safety are established

by the commissions in order that they may operate as they wish. The smallest electronic activity is residual (and it is in the small frequencies where the danger lies). You may expect, as the electronic industry advances, more cancer, more mutation and more cellular disturbances within the next fiscal year.

I do not know what fiscal means.

Very sincerely yours,

The Queen of Heaven

Does that make sense? The electronic forces we surround ourselves with directly affect the basic biologic activity of our cells. This has been done in laboratories. But it has been done also in your cities and you are in great and immediate danger.

Does that make sense?

I will try again. Don't stand behind television sets. Don't buy microwave ovens. Don't live in areas where there is an intensification of electronic equipment.

Does that make sense?

Does this make sense: Don't fuck with Mother Nature. You keep messing up my timing system and I may just pull the plug on the big clock up here.

I really don't know how to make you listen.

We, the undersigned, find that since the electromagnetic field has vast and terrible and positive effects on our biological functions, anything which is of a radioactive and/or electronic nature which might change or imbalance the original intention of the force field of this planet, is needful of careful, immediate and far-reaching controls.

Maybe if I tell Mack. He understands transistors and he in many senses has knowledge of me. Perhaps he can explain it to you.

On the steppe she created Enkidu.
Offspring of the moon that fell down from heaven.
Shaggy with hair is his whole body.
He is endowed with head hair like a woman.
With the gazelles he feeds on grass.
With the wild beasts he jostles at the watering-place.
With the wild beasts he drinks at the watering-place.
With the creeping creatures his heart delights in water.
"There he is, O Lass! Free thy breasts.
Bare thy bosom that he may possess thy ripeness.
Be not bashful. Welcome his ardor!
As soon as he sees thee, he will draw near to thee.
Lay aside thy cloth that he may rest upon thee.
Treat him, the savage, to a woman's task!
Enkidu sits before the Harlot. Sits the two of them. Enkidu forgot where he was born. For six days and seven nights was Enkidu come forth mating with the Lass. Then the Harlot opened her mouth saying to Enkidu, As I look at thee, Enkidu, thou art become like a god. Wherefore with the wild creatures dost thou range over the steppe? Up, I will lead thee to broad marted Uruk, to the holy temple. Enkidu, arise. He hearkened to her words, accepted her speech. The Woman's counsel fell upon his heart. She pulled off clothing. With one piece she clothed him. With the other garment she clothed herself. Holding on to his hands, she leads him like a mother.

16

I have been requested by the boys not to watch this small television set while they play their music and I receive admittance monies at the Lake Oneida Amusement Park. However, just as I am drawn to that manner of auto accidents at which onlookers lift the eyelids of the car occupants, I wish to watch this current moon walk. It is, as you know, a female attribute to blame oneself for death. Many of us, at a distance, take pleasure in war for that reason. Which is a perverted use of our instincts. I take no pleasure in a moon walk. The moon after all, had been, in better times, my son, and I cry his death each month with my own bleeding. Blind he was and torn from my thigh. His life was short. They do not know this. His bones are his mother's bones. And they, unknowing and unfeeling, walk on his grave now, tampering, and I am not happy. But I watch.

I sit with the set here in the back dining porch of this abandoned summer hotel with its unmatched chairs and linoleum capped tables. It is open now for its bar and its rock and roll dance hall. I had walked proudly through the bar, holding the set far from the reaches of my functions for it is, although informative, poisonous, and I walked to this slope-floored dining room. Alone I sit now, watching and waiting for Mack, who will finish his music soon and find me. The set is unclear. As I near it, it clears. As I back away it becomes misty. Beyond the plastic covered windows is the parking lot, beyond that the row of elms and a small stone seawall, more like a farmer's fencing, and the choppy lake with dots of boat lights and jetty lights. And beyond the lake are vast flatlands of onion fields, and as I sniff I draw in, through the plastic, the onions, a multitudinous mixture of dead fish, the fresh bottom land of the fields, vinegar, strange meats of the runway stands and the cheap perfumes and tonics of the hundreds of children beyond this room.

I have sat patiently without Robert this night for his business again calls him away. He has a new patent on a machine for gossamer threads and I have received handfuls of dollar bills from children who do not even count their change but crane to see beyond into the crowded room. I, of course, give them proper change. I cannot, however, trust the hotelkeeper's loose-panted phlegmy friend who carries hundred dollar bills and wears a belt engraved with a horse on its buckle. Now he will take the monies and assumably there will be less than expected but as usual more than deserved and Robert, when I give him his dollar bills and the old pennies for his collection, will be pleased I came here with the band. I am not pleased. I attempt to adjust the television, holding a magazine over my private parts, but the action on the screen slips further into invisibility. Soon Mack will come and adjust it for me. He is more neutral.

I am, as you know, more interested in Mack than the moon. He kissed me last night. Mack stands above me. My skin tingles. There is excitation in me. He kissed me last night in the parking lot of the Port Byron Savarin on the Thruway. We sat waiting for each other for long intolerable moments in the dark early morning. I would not attack. Finally he brushed my lips with his. He swallowed afterward with such terrible tension I could hear the seas retreating in the constriction of his tongue and throat muscles. Now he is above me. There is a fallen, sunken look about his mouth.

"I gotta talk to you."

"You are very attractive tonight, Mack. Blue as in your shirt is a fine color for you."

"Yeah. I washed my hair." He runs his hands through his long hair.

"I noticed. It shines." I had not noticed. I had noticed his smoothly fitting bulging pants, the macrame belt of love knots with a snake buckle I wove for him, the transparent blouse through which I could see his body hair. He sits before the set. He crosses and uncrosses his legs, rubbing the inside of his shoe with his palm. He constructs another triangle and shines the other shoe with his other palm. I measure the triangle formed by his upper legs. I would enjoy stroking within this triangle, all the square roots and the shortest distances between two points. But I sit here. When one approaches frightened carnivores, one remains still and allows the animal to smell and hear. With bear, who are nominally powerful and attack out of fear, one, even if omnivorous, must sing to allay the bear's fear. I wear little perfume and have not patience to sing. Also I remember with a modicum of shame that he called me old lady. But early in the evening as I held the cashbox and he tested runs on the Hammond he said, "I gotta talk to you." And now we are together, I with a twitching triangle, he with a changing triangle and the plastic sheets flapping over the windows. He stands to fix the television. He carries a mirror. I offer him a Twinkie. It is the seventh night that I have offered him a Twinkie. He has come to expect them. I watch the moon through the windows. He eats his Twinkie and holds his mirror before the set. I think about his mouth with its fallen edges. His Twinkie finished, his crumbs picked off his see-through shirt, he adjusts dials and tubes, working in opposite directions to the image in the mirror.

"It is a lovely thing, that mirror with its snap and leatherette case. Do you always carry a mirror?"

He is surprised. "I told you I used to repair TV sets. I told you I got this whole video setup. We're gonna video tape the screwing tonight."

I say nothing.

"You want me to pick you up a mirror like this?"

"Yes." There is pain in his mouth. The picture scrambles. "I want you to kiss me again." The picture goes blank. He becomes busy with dials.

"How's the horizontal?"

I am the prime force in human advancement. I sigh. "Not good."

"Godalmighty, Houston," I hear. "I dropped it."

"Anything now?" Mack asks.

"No." It is a nuclear instrument this man drops on the moon. Atlas, he drops it.

"Sorry as hell, Houston. I think nothing is damaged."

A girl walks behind us to the stairs. There are bedrooms above, unused. She returns, walking toward Mack. "Hey." He grabs at her. "Where'd you get the french fries?"

"Want some?" She stands at the stairs. "They got vinegar on them."

"Come back and give me some."

"Come get 'em." She runs lightly up the stairs.

"I'll see you later."

He spreads his hands to me and shrugs. "Part of the game. Gotta line up my meat for tonight."

"Of course."

The bartender comes from the kitchen, wiping glasses on an apron. "They doing all right?"

We shake our heads yes and no. He leaves.

"You have a problem, Mack?"

"Yeah." He sits beside me now once again. There is a muscle twitching along his thigh. "Claire." This boy is able to collapse the hope in the lining of my stomach. I pale with jealousy.

"I got a reputation. I can't get it up with her."

"Goddamn, Houston, I guess I broke the cable."

"I've been balling all week . . . except for last night . . ." I hear him swallow with difficulty. "No sweat. But with Claire . . ."

"You are afraid of her. Men fear the organs of birth. You cringe at menstrual napkins as we cringe at guns. We are superior."

"C'mon, get serious." He laughs, easier now. "Can you change a goddamn tire? Can you design a transistor like I can? Can you put in wiring? You can't adjust a TV for God's sakes."

"The intent of nature is woman. We are superior." I am jealous and unkind. I am also correct. "You fear Claire. She is not one of those." I wave to another oddly clad young child walking up the stairs.

"What can I say? You're wrong."

"I still got the farts, Charley." I hear a voice from the clouded set.

"Then come here and touch my breast and put your hand between my legs and kiss me." My voice is cruel. I can not help the impatience and anger I experience.

"How they doing?" The bartender who thinks the clowns on my moon are the New York Yankees comes out. He has flour now on his hands and apron. "I got pizza going for later, Mrs." I smile. He leaves.

"To begin with, don't stand behind televisions. It will make you impotent. Come."

"Knock it off, Ishtar. You've always been a lady." Mack pulls at his sideburns.

"Come, Mack. Let me see you unafraid."

"Forget it! I got enough going upstairs."

The moon god fell down from heaven. But no one saw him. The storm god sent rain after him; he sent rainstorms after him so that fear seized him and fright seized him. What art thou going to do?

"I am the primary force in human advancement." I put my hands on his square roots. He knocks them off. His hands are iced with fear. I laugh.

"Jesus, Ishtar, you've always been a lady. I'm going to get

some fucking french fries." It is too late for french fries. He has already had seven Twinkies. I laugh again.

"Go!" I say, and wave him off. He goes. The bartender brings in a small metal cashbox. The dollar bills are not new ones and Ishtar feels a repugnance. Nevertheless she counts the singles deliberately and stacks the coins into their ocher bankrolls and passes dollars to the bartender for the pizza and the gambler for taking the monies and writes up the tallies for Robert, after having separated his pennies with the different backs from the bags of coins. As she counts, the springs of whatever it is rolling on the floor above her rasp against the cracked linoleum and she knows it is the communal bed to which she has not been invited. "Tie their legs together," she says to the television. "Keep them from my son. Get off," she mutters. "You are sticking pennies in sockets. Get off my moon." And then she does battle with the tables and with the chairs and flies, furious, into the kitchen. She does not laugh.

Patience has never been one of my greater attributes. Nevertheless I adore your geologic timetables. They are so believing and hopeful. To even consider, though, anything short of cataclysm in my stop and go procedures is foolhardy. I follow the noise to the stairs. I do not know if I am being compulsive or impulsive. When once one follows universal rhythms, the categories of behavior do not matter.

The hallways here are peeling in large green scales and the Wilton carpet strip, unbound, arches its muddy flowered back down the crevicular, cervicular hallway. I love it. I follow the smell of apple vinegar and french fries. I find the room. The pressed glass handle of the door, once painted white, is now chipped and jewel-like with striations of paint on its facets. I stand beyond it and breathe deeply and open the door. There is a giggle but it is hushed by a hand. The linoleum, interestingly enough is a 9×12 patterned Congoleum rug with a red, white and blue border of ships on chipped seas. I have examined the linoleum. Around the bed on the floor, clothes are strewn like offerings. Though I admittedly obey the tugs of the universe, I still am human. On the bare bed, where there is a wild tumble of parts and limbs, the activity has stopped in a rather end of Pompeian scene, strangled positions caught by death.

There is another giggle, muffled once again.

"I am not Death, today," I assure them with the deepest grandeur I can derive under the circumstances. My fingers perspire around the seam ripper and the ※1 golf club sock I clutch. I find it difficult to remain calmly superior. Actually I feel left out. They are frightened for I have powdered my face white with flour from the kitchen and wrapped the fringed tablecloth over my shoulders. It is likely also that my eyes burn. I am blushing under the powder. I walk steadily over the cracked blue sea and find Mack's face. There seem to be four female faces and five male faces. I am not certain though of their limbs and it is possible, with the slope-browed mien of the female faces, that each of them has more or less than the normal amount of parts. Television babies most likely. They continued to stare. The bed shakes as someone hidden underneath is racked with laughter. "I am not Death, but I wish one of you." I find Mack's shoulder. I tap it. He asks with his eyes what I wish.

There is a game we played as children with our hands piling one atop the other and then extricating the bottom hand. On ugly days we would pinch the thin top skin of the hand and hold it away from the bone. I watch these children trying to find their parts, pulling out limbs from the levels of the now writhing mass. There is something anti-structural about this. I do not like it. It is frightening. At last all of Mack has emerged. His body is very pretty. He has large parts that fit neatly between narrow hips and lovely tufts of body hair. I try to keep my face deathlike. He stands up and approaches me.

"What do you want, Ishtar?" He finds black undershirt and shorts on the floor.

I say nothing but beckon with one finger to lead him from the room.

"What do you want, Ishtar?"

He takes his pants from the floor. I throw his pants back onto the floor. He follows me from the room. The noise begins behind us as I close the door. I carry my furca openly now. It is, as you may remember, a large cursive *e* which glows with blue flames when I am needful of its energies. I direct Mack with it down the dark halls, trying doors as I follow him.

"Why me?"

"You are gentle and beautiful."

"You saying I'm a fag, Ishtar? Is that what you're saying?"

"Special men," I answer softly to the lovely fur tuft of body hair at the small of his back, "special men have joy and gentleness. Special men who have allowed to live that which is the profoundly feminine in themselves, and still remain men, they are beautiful to me." I wish to imagine the tuft is a tail. "I would get you in the bathtub." The bathroom is at the end of the black hall.

He laughs without assurance. He opens the door. We step inside.

I close the door to the bathroom. I swing the furca and its blue light is cosmic in the darkness. What I can glimpse of Mack's face is solemn and tense. There is great beauty in his body. Outwardly he is calm. I am not. My hand quivers as I drop three drops of Durkee's Food Color, blue, edible, in plastic squeeze bottles, into the tub. The tub is streaked from its faucet with acid green and blue. I turn on the faucets. They fight me and then, with agony and coughing through the pipes, down into the bowels of the old hotel, the water rises, spitting, into the tub. I hang the furca, which spits also now, on the shower faucet above us. I remove the cotton balls from

Mack's ears. I tear from top to bottom his black shirt and the black shorts and I say:

"I am now taking away from Mack darkness and stiffness caused by the matter of uncleanness on account of which matter of uncleanness he became dark and stiff; I am taking away sin."

He is somewhat amused. I believe he welcomes the delay.

I hand him his mirror and my seam ripper in his hand and I beckon to him to crawl between my legs. He laughs and obeys. As he stands behind me I take away from him the mirror and the seam ripper and give him the ※1 golf club sock and I say: "Behold, I have taken away from you womanhood and have given you back manhood; you have cast away the manners of woman and you have taken up the manners of man." He allows me to kiss his feet, which have brought him to me.

He is likely not convinced. It doesn't matter. They need ritual.

"When do we fuck, Ishtar? I mean, I have a lot going back there." He waves to the bedroom of snake babies writhing without consciousness on the bare nest bed. He passes me the mirror and the seam ripper. I place the golf sock on the tub's rim. The water is ready. Mack is grinning but he is docile in his actions. He allows me to kiss his knees, which have knelt already to me. He allows me to kiss his organ of generation, which shall bring him pleasure. He allows me to kiss his breast, formed in beauty and strength. He allows me, at last, to kiss his lips, which shall utter the sacred names.

"Come on, Ishtar."

As I slip the tablecloth from my bare shoulders, I beckon to him to descend into the tub. He steps in and I clip the tendon of his heel with my seam ripper. The blood flows beautifully into the blue water. It is blue enough to be Aegean. I cut a small incision into my breast, which spurts blood. I too climb into the tub. He is in horror. He sits on the edge of the tub grasping the back of his heel. He takes the seam ripper from me, thinking that he has disarmed me. I watch in the waters the bloods mingling. I point above to the furca. It spits and heals our wounds. He shivers. "Heal," I say loudly, and he bites my ankle. My cats bite my feet and reach often for my neck. I understand.

"Why me?" he asks again in a strangled voice. I put my finger to my lips. I take his hand and pull him to me. We kiss, standing. We sit. His eyes are large and soft. He shuts them closed as I hold his head under water. When I release him he jerks up angrily, but I smile and, standing over him, pull him toward my feathers.

I hear him exhale sharply, his breathing still uneven. He sinks himself into me and I, standing above him, blessing his head and his shoulders with fruitfulness and everlasting grace, am, at last, eaten. Around us the blue arcs leap from the sweating steel faucets to the toilet handle and along the shower curtain rack. I feel a floating ecstasy, my legs without gravity, only magnetism. He works magnificently, carefully, assuredly. I sink down to him. He begins to enter me. I push him away for a moment for a donation into the ※1 golf club sock. I pull the string closed tightly and he takes me finally. Ishtar is satisfied. His eyes are closed. This man, this God eater, knowing fully who and what I am, is also satisfied. I offer him a feather which has been adrift on his shoulder. He opens his eyes. They are bright with the brightness of clairvoyants and seers. "I know. I know," he whispers often as I hold him and dry him with the tablecloth. He is sleepy and soft. "Feathers?" he asks tranquilly.

I kiss his forehead, his cheeks, his lips. "When you are awake, you will go to Claire."

"No," he murmurs. "You."

"Claire." I do not like doing this.

"Wasn't I good enough?" He kisses my shoulder blade and turns in my arms.

"Perfect."

"Want you only. Ever."

I slap his feet to waken him. "Claire."
His eyes are large and filled with mysteries. I love him.
"Do you love me, Ishtar?"
"Completely."
"Then how come you send me away?"
"You must be fruitful; you must multiply; you must teach." I shine the furca into the waters of our love and he looks with me at the reflection of my face. My cheeks are round and flushed. "Claire is I. With you, she will be much more than she is now. Neither of us is anything alone. Help her, for you have been chosen and you are a good man." I am very beautiful after I have been loved well.
"I don't want to give you up, Ishtar."
I wink at him in the water. It is all I can promise.
"Do you really think I'm good, Ishtar?" We look now at his reflection. I point to the waters. I point to himself.
"All of you. All of you. Go now."
I watch him walking, limping, down the hallway out of the darkness of the hotel corridor. He will do well. His chin is a little too soft. But he will do well. His ankles are lovely. I would like also to be Claire.
"Don't stand behind any TV sets. Don't fly your kite near wires," I call to him down the hall. It is not an ordinary way to end these initiations, but then times have changed and new dangers stalk the dark halls of these worlds. "Don't play with electrical appliances near water. Call your power company if you see a broken line." My heart is tangled as the thorns as he goes to his young bride. The tear is on my cheek. Who shall comfort me? The rug at my feet is covered with hot tears. I am void. I am empty. I am waste. My heart melteth. My knees smite together. "Never use anything wire or anything metallic in your kite," I call down the emptiness. "Never fly your kite on rainy days." Much pain is in my loins, and darkness gathers. Remember, electricity is energy looking for a place to go." The hallway is empty. There is no one to comfort me. There is no man to hold me and under-

stand. There is no man to rub my back and breathe into my hair and be mine forever. There is no man to hold me and say, "I understand." There is no man.

I dress, nailing with pegs my tablecloth into the old floor of the dining room. There is a Seven-Eleven grocery store where I will pick up napkins just above Chittenango. I throw the ⚹1 golf sock into the lake and pray that the seed of Mike and the egg of Claire have form, joy and continuation. I have done this well. The seam ripper I throw also and pour out the remainder of the food coloring. The lake gleams cobalt and well under the moon. I keep the mirror. I wish, halfheartedly, that I could be Claire and she could be me and do my work. I weep into the chest of an old elm. Who shall comfort me?

    He wasn't *that* good.
    He will ask me, before going to Claire, to run away with him. Where can you go, I shall ask him, with a woman with feathers?
    Altoona, he will answer.
    And where is Altoona? I shall ask.
    Anyplace. Altoona anyplace. Let's just go.
    Where can one go with a crotchful of feathers? With a boy who is just knowing his manhood? For a night perhaps two nights and he would make love once, twice, somewhat competently, and then sit up with his naked knees and beauty-spotted shoulders and say, "I'm scared."
    And if I were also to eat the pomegranate of this rock star's fruits, would I too have to dwell in his underground. Once, in Sunday School, I was allowed to read a prayer to the congregation. I approached the pulpit too quickly and had to wait, standing before the people who watched me, for the rabbi to finish his discoursing. I waited, with pre-pubic impatience, resting an elbow on the pulpit and my chin upon my hand. My mother hissed from below, "Remember who you are."
    They always remind me. "How can I become King, Ish-

tar?" they ask as they roll over, still quaking with my postpubic rhythm. "Do you know the best way to demolish the most Phoenicians with the fewest Etruscans?" "I've been to the moon because I think I'm a god. Maybe because I've been to the moon, I therefore think I must be a god. Which do you think comes first? As a god, I can have any woman I want but I keep screwing up with my wife, who I really love, and she always catches me and I think I want her to catch me and tell me I'm not a god so I can relax. What do you think?" "Would you write a set of laws up for me, Ishtar? For my people?" "And whose name shall I sign, Lipit?" I ask as I daub my feathers clean. "Well, if you don't mind, uh, Ishtar, just sign mine." "I think when I grow up," he said as he sniffed my bicycle seat, "I'll be a ladies' doctor. What do you think?" "I'm worried about that eclipse. Would it be a good time to plant the grapes?" "Hey, I think I'd like to have a studio and record music. What do you think? I always dug building things."

And flying kites near power lines and sticking pennies into sockets and shoving your glorified gonads into the wellsprings of life and wondering why you are burned alive and eaten whole. You are ascending into the source of life, the universal power, with your little kite, darling, and that is why, rightfully so, you are afraid. Don't hurt us; we won't hurt you. Okay?

"If you could be as accomplished a man as you are an astronaut, love, you might at least not get caught." "Why?" he asks under his crew cut and heterochlorophened smile, "wasn't I any good? I thought you enjoyed that." He shoves his ringed pinky into my bellybutton and I squeal. None of them have been that good.

I'm waiting. And so is Robert. A month has passed.

Do you ever listen to Paul Harvey?

He spoke this winter of a woman's body found in a frozen grave between Turkey and Russia. A ram's foot was perfectly grafted to her ankle. The foot was grafted on by electricity. There could have been no other way. Let them speak of medicine men and shaman magic, and Lickety shick split razor blades. The foot was grafted on by electricity. That, as a modern miracle, is being discovered. Jewish students were warned not to study those parts of the Texts which dealt with the power. Already, ancient battery cells have been found in a Baghdad museum. The girl was a high rank priestess. The men who limped, Jacob, David, Achilles, Baldur—and the men who wore golden high heels, and the men who had shortened heels or shortened thighs—they were ritually lamed to show their divinity as I had chosen them above others. I asked only a simple shortening. Some played at being divine and chosen by mincing around the Senate floor, but I had long stopped that ritual by Roman times. In Spain, I have seen matted dirty black sheep in the fields above the beaches with their back legs tied together. They were bad sheep, I was told. Tied, they found no mischief, and did not jump the fences. It was precisely this way in which we began the laming of those first men whom we chose to be civilized and to dwell within the walls of our cities. Just as today, we must wear wedding rings, they wore buskins, their slippers, their golden sandals as a sign of their chosenness. There was an old woman who lived in a shoe. My posts were buckled, my temple floors the scene of sacred limping dances, the coffins of my people slipper shaped. You have forgotten why you drink from my shoe, haven't you?

I am sure you know that the Queen of Sheba had a donkey's foot.

Guiding kohl on her eyes from an alabaster frog palette, Ishtar stirred from her golden stool and viewed Set, the dark year's king, in her hand mirror.

"Lady Mother, One who Sits, Isis, all my horses and all my men can not restore Osiris."

"Aah, no, Set. Restoration is guaranteed, granted, promised after dismemberment. You must not shirk this or Osiris will treat you equally at the year's end when you are dismembered and tossed to the waters. I have spoken, my pretty king."

Set prostrated himself at her heels. "The river people tell me that his organ of regeneration has been devoured by the letos fish. It is that which we can not find."

Ishtar turned, under the circumstances, quite calmly. "Set, my lover, my son, although I can tolerate your dark ways and your heavy-handed love-making for the year of your reign, it would be utterly impossible for me to retain you as king. I could not bear your sullen morbidity the next year without the lightness and sweetness of my King of Light."

"He's a fool. He sings his head off. He is impractical."

"Yes, his singing grows cloying. Too much perfection, too much harmony can be dull, and often during the year while you lie fallow, I confess to yearning for your passion and your thrusting, for the thickness of your body and the boring of your member. I am charmed but tired of the smoothness of his boy's love. I am needful of you both. I can have neither of your without the other and, Set, without kingship, humankind would stray off balance. You must take all of your horses and all of your men and scour the river until Osiris is back together again. Before the seasons change."

Set kissed her feet and Ishtar smiled. "Ah, then, Lady who Sits, am I a more pleasing lover than Osiris, the World Egg?"

"You are both divine. It would be so nice, Set, if without the priests knowing, I could have both of you perhaps only for a mad, rolling, tumbling night, the totality of light and dark, boy and man, lover and non-lover at once. But it would raise such total havoc among the stars and the crops."

Ishtar touched his shoulder with the mirror of her soul. "Come, Set, dark builder, my architect of the lower regions, take me as I sit and then go to seek your brother." Ishtar watched the curves of his back and the tuft of hair at his tailbone for a few moments with her mirror. A man with the qualities of both brothers would be delightful.

Later, when Set withdrew himself from the lap of the Mother, she spoke wisdom to him breathlessly. "No longer shall dismemberment occur in my lands. It is too good, this act, and it is too dangerous this remembering. Fashion for me, Set, a building with its four corners precisely at each wind and its center reaching to the polestar. Let the mathematicians and the astrologers construct it so that my heroes and my kings may perfectly leave their bodies waiting while they project astrally and that when they return from my gardens of Paradise in Venus, whether a day or a year has passed, the body will be as fresh and the weapons as sharp."

"And after a year?"

"Bodies will not matter if they choose to remain in my gardens, under my apple trees. Nor weapons." Ishtar-Isis blessed him and kissed his mouth. "Go now, search the river and its banks, search the wadis and the runs, search the highwalls and highways and the White House Lawn and if you find him not, you and your children and your children's children and their children after them shall seek him ever, crawling over the world on my day. Go."

17

"She's dirty, she don't put one foot in my kitchen. I don't cook all this for dirt. You hear me? And make her take those damn boots off. The floor's clean. You hear me?"
    I am in Grace's basement. I sit on a crate and listen. I hear Mack. He slams the door. His engine flatulates. Since daybreak I have listened to Grace's Enna Jetticks snapping angrily on the kitchen Congoleum. Grace has thought for days of sauces and Claire, who shall arrive soon, has thought of blow jobs. I, of course, balanced in my desires and my abilities, think simultaneously of these and other exotic items. Grace, bless her, is too old and Claire has much to learn.
    It is pleasant, albeit lonely, in this moist penetralia, where stalks of strange roots are tied into sacred bundles and piled on wooden tables, where seeds germinate in flat beds under taut cheesecloths and slatted boxes of mushrooms trap moonlight from an open coal shaft. There is a wonderful, perceptive clicking at my shoulder and below my feet. Two black boxes with red dials measure time and energy and below my feet, I hear either a sump pump or a quark detector.
    I am not certain and so I divine, lifting my sardonyx, and my sardonyx lights up with cosmic brilliance in my presence and lifts the dark from the room as a torch. I test the sound below the concrete. Seeds burst their shells prematurely and I am sorry. The machine, grinding and pulsing, responds eagerly to my rays. The stones of the foundations sing in chords.

It may very well be then a quark. With Grace, all things are conceivable. Write that down, somebody.

With Grace, all things are conceivable. I should not be surprised if, upon lifting the stretched corner of cheesecloth, I should find nestling planaria or seeds of infants. There is a synthesis here. Time is Energy. Time, more than a measuring, is a form of energy and like the knots on Grace's crochet work, time maintains life, connecting events yet keeping them apart. It is this energy, I shall tell Claire, which keeps things from skittering off into low places and lumping up in Cornwallian peat bogs and Californian tar pits. If, for instance, Claire, I tip these timetables, life, whole populations, would slide to tangled chaos, planaria buried in the rutabagas. But no, all is well, for the most part, and today I shall tell Claire, who needs so much knowledge, "Claire, Time is Energy."

Bitch.

While we are waiting for the roar of the chariot, I would without being shameless, indicate to those of you who are interested, that the horseshoe, the signature of Lady Luck, is significant of the magical female parts. Pudenda. Pudenda were in the basket of Delphi, the holy basket. A tisket a tasket. Only afterward did such trash as the phony fabled smelly foreskins of the Christ become sacral objets, venerated and stored in jeweled arks. However, all such information being lost, as well as the basket, green and yellow, I was pleased to find in Woolworth's today, the rhinestone stars, palms and horseshoes of another age there in the wire basket and I drew my perfect hand through their sharp five and ten contours nostalgically. Much has passed. But much is to come. They in the basket began to glow, my symbols, impregnated as they were with my sensuous cosmic touch, with the soft and tender mother hands, with . . . you realize I'm simply jealous and it is why I am bragging so. I am tragically envious of Claire of the Unmatched Breasts now entering above as the Sabbath Bride rather than myself. Let us then go above and witness this scene.

Bear witness, then, with me, in this rear bathroom with a

view of the hallway and the kitchen. I am burdened with hatred and motherhood. I feel old as I perch on the curved rod, the phantom of the shower curtain, my wings tucked beneath, and I watch Claire of the Unmatched Breasts enter the dingy but spotless hall. She wears a dreadful pink plush jumper under the dark cape and stands, bends, removes an encrusted hiking boot. Its sole shatters mud on the Congoleum. One-legged, still, her face burning flamingo pink, she watches Grace wipe the floor with a sheet of newsprint. There is yet another boot with which to deal and I am enjoying this. With extended teacup finger, Grace accepts the dirty cape. Mack, who removed it from Claire's shoulders, is ashen pale. At last, Claire puts down her foot, bravely removes the second encrusted boot and smiles shyly at Mack. Cunt.

I perch. I hate. I brood. I rip the corners from my cue cards.

Grace enters the bathroom with the cape and tosses it over my curtain rod. I squawk in indignation. She washes her hands many times in hissing waters and Lava soap.

"Grace," I call. "Up here." I present her with the three sardonyxes in the goldfish container. "Each of you must wear these at your shoulder. They will by their beams indicate my presence even at the most remote of distances. Tell the children." And then, seeing the perspiration on her forehead and the blood of a dozen sauces on her terry cloth Vera apron, I cackle loudly at her.

She drops the cape in the tub and turns on steaming water. "It ain't easy to give up my son to this weirdo."

"Ahh, do you mean to poison her then with all of the sauces?" I tip my wing to the palette of smears on her apron.

"Listen, Ishtar, I don't have to tell you dirt is poison. I'm cleaning her up." Grace pours Axion, Pine Sol and a quart of milk over the cape.

"Milk?"

"Removes the fishy smell."

"Oh, thank you." I lift my skirt in a measure of respect for the basic intelligence of this woman and from my height, display my fine and feathered pudenda. She lifts the towel attachment on her Vera, a female Mason, to her eyes. It was once, this gesture, a form of recognition among those who worshiped the Goddess. "In my basket was just such a pudendum as mine which men rubbed across their bodies to be born again."

"Say." She has dropped her apron. "Is that right?"

"Of course," I answer, easing into the dialogue. "Same as a horseshoe."

"But feathers."

"Oh yes, particularly."

"That's something. They all worshiped *that?*"

"It's been so long ago, Grace, I don't remember clearly myself."

"I know what you mean."

We shrug, two old women trying to forget our glories. Grace leaves me. She passes by again with a cat wrapped in a sheet of newspaper and tosses the package to the outside porch, explaining as she returns to the kitchen: "Hair. Gets in the food."

For as to these stones, which we told you before the high-priest bare on his shoulders, which were sardonyxes (and I think it needless to describe their nature, they being known to everybody) the one of them shined out when God was present at their sacrifices; I mean that which was in the nature of a button on his right shoulder, bright rays darting out thence had been seen even by those that were most remote; which splendour yet was not before natural to the stone. For God declared beforehand, by those twelve stones which the high-priest bare on his shoulder and which were inserted into his breastplate when they should be victorious in battle; for so great a splendour shone forth from them before the army began to march, that all the people were sensible of God's being present for their assistance. Now this breastplate, and this sardonyx, left off shining two hundred years before I composed this book, God having been displeased at the transgression of his laws. Of which things we shall further discourse on a fitter opportunity; but I will now go on with my proposed narration.

                                        Josephus, *History of the Jews*

    They are preparing to eat now. She calls to me. "You want some food?"

    "No, thank you. I will hang here and suffer."

    "You don't have to, Ishtar. You could eat with us."

    "I prefer hanging here," I answer haughtily. "This is my hanging time. There is a time for planting, a time for reaping, a time for . . ."

    Grace shrugs and melts butter in a double boiler. As it melts she sprays Lysol into the corners of the kitchen, behind the refrigerator, and then, stealthily, opening wide their mouths, into Claire's hiking boots.

    The kitchen is small. Grace, without moving her chair, can serve from the stove, empty food onto platters and deposit pots into the sink to hiss. She serves generously. Claire, stupidly, accepts all that Grace offers, often asking for more. The tablecloth is black and white check, strewn with linoleum daisies of yellow. Fringe surrounds the field, and under the fringe the dear young couple hold hands. In the center of the table sits a swan napkin holder and three unmatched salt shakers. I need not remind you but I shall, for I wish to draw comparison between style and necessity, of the munificent welcome Solomon afforded me when I arrived as his bride to his palaces. Actually the events bear no comparison.

    I hear Claire sucking, a Kali on the lobster tails. Mack is silent and suffering. Claire shall be grossly unhappy in her bowels. I sit here unhappy in my heart above the steaming and soaking cape. I watch as another tiger kitten laps up the hot milky water. The kitten will die from the Pine Sol, an offering, I suppose, for the sacrament of marriage. I had untold numbers of white oxen offered, but then times were different and meat is expensive now. I am bored by this and find it an effort to pass the kitten on gracefully with proper benediction.

"You play the big violin, huh?" Grace asks of Claire while the kitten climbs the shower curtain in agony.

There is no answer. She may have shook her head, her mouth full.

"You want some more gnocchi?" Plates move. Claire sucks. "You know Lara's theme? I have a jewelry box. I open it, it plays Lara's theme."

"I could try, sometime." Claire's mouth is full.

"Oh, you mean you're gonna be around here, again, huh?" Grace wins.

There is no response. Claire shovels food onto her plate. I hear the scraping of spoon against china. Grace has been too harsh.

At last she speaks to Mack. "Marry this one. No more clap."

I think that Grace is super.

The cat passes on, slipping silently from the shower curtain into the caldron of the cape. Claire approaches. She does not walk straight.

I sing at her pain. I warble at her illness. "Here comes Claire. Here comes Claire. Bent over double, her stomach in trouble. Here comes Claire."

"Go to hell," Claire mutters. I don't know if she is addressing Grace or myself.

I sing.

"Oh, God!"

"Claire, Time is the energy of the female principle. It may be said, verily, Time is Woman. How about *that*?"

Claire groans. She bends over in pain. "Hey, Claire," I call from the curving section of the acetate shower curtain. "If you screw too much, you'll walk crooked."

She attempts to ignore me as she strains to defecate the poisons she has stuffed her uppers and lowers with.
"I've had him and he's only fair. Only fair."
"Shut up, Ishtar."
I am quiet as she strains. I cackle, however, and hum my ditty from time to time.
"Oh, God."
"Actually," I continue, having been thusly addressed, "he isn't half bad."
"I don't like you, Ishtar."
"That's no big deal, Claire." She groans. I seek my cue cards. They are rubberbanded. I refer to them and read.
"Half good as a matter of fact, with his tellurian testicles and his antediluvian terror of what to do with it, where to put it, that drives him drumming into nightmare alleys and dismal swamps, a lizard sac, red and pulsing and no place to go. Where to put it, dear, oh, dear. Ask Claire."
"Shut up. I don't want to think about that."
"That, in a way, is progress. Now hearken and remember. You must be patient. You have millions of years on him. His poor lonely privates are simply a gross exaggeration, a quirk of nature, of the finely tuned and far more civilized clitoris."
"Oh, God."
"Just remember, the bigger the penis, the worse the constipation. Jams you all up."
"Ishtar, lay off."
"My final words: don't be impressed, delightful as it may be at times, it is simply a mutated extended clitoris fashioned for our amusement. It is also his own particular albatross. Don't, whatever you do, let it be your albatross."
"I don't believe you."
"That's all right, darling daughter, hang your clothes on a hickory sticky but don't bite off myrrh than you can chew." I tuck my cue cards away. "Furthermore, Time is Energy."
She pauses to write, with a purple Flair, my axiom, on her forearm.

"Claire, you okay in there?" Mack is back.
She is too busy to answer.
"Learn also that one can neither deliver a child while panting nor speak while defecating."
"Claire, you okay?" The bridegroom knocks.
I unbend, slipping a graceful hand through the curtain while I hang slothlike by my fine narrow feet and punch her in her blocked bowels. "Last tag!" I cackle wildly. They bang on the door. "She is not ready, you people. A moment, please."
"Darling daughter," I continue as she eases quite suddenly her plight, "although the bowels of the earth open and he takes you into his underworld in his flaming chariot, no matter. You will have a young and tormented soul to cure, adjust and balance so that he may evolve into a whole man. What you, Claire, do is fearfully important. Others shall follow you. What you become together will be the joy and nourishment of mankind forever after. It shall be written of you and Mack and your children and your children's children. So don't fuck up."
"Why should I?"
You bring them up to be independent and they are independent and it hurts. A little.
"Hey, Claire, hurry up."
"I'll be ready soon, Mack."
"Wash your hands," I admonish Claire, who is more interested in the smoothness of her cheeks. "Shame."
She washes and I bless. I fill her pockets with marjoram and cakes of many navels, fennel stalks and balls of salt and sesame cakes, my holy things, fig branches I lay in her lap and whisper, "You do not need to marry him, this serpent of the underworld. You are my daughter and therefore holy." But I am burdened with ambiguity and I, although I truly love her as a daughter, sorta, I despise her for her young cheeks and the joy she will have from the serpent and her firstness, this kore. "Don't eat the pomegranate." But truly,

deeply, I wish to be gone, to find a god to lie with across the night sky and loose the bonds that tie me, divine as we all are, to the tedia of mortality. Let her stay. A daughter is a doctor—the words are disarmingly close—and she, this child, must heal and cure and teach the torn and troubled soul and bring him to wholeness as must her sisters. Round cakes and poppies, ivy leaves and the woman's comb to be worn atop the man's cock. Ah, and these are my symbols among others and I display with a wink my pudenda to Grace and Mack, who have forced the door, "And it shall be as a sign between your legs that you are a mother and worship the great Demeter, da mutter," I mutter and utter the benediction. "I bless the mushrooms of your cellars and the seedlings of your flatbeds and the hairs on your chinny chin chin and I leave you to each other, the rays on your shoulder sardonyxes fading as I depart the family scene."

"She's clean," I pronounce to Grace over my shoulder. "Guaranteed clean."

18

The seven musicians were dressed alike for the bar mitzvah gig, having been offered fine suits for the appearance at the Temple. They wore tightly fitted plaid yellow bellbottoms. They wore navy linen jackets with golden buttons, pale yellow wide collared shirts and full cravats of navy and yellow stripes. Ishtar kissed each of them on their clean-shaved cheeks as she twisted boutonnieres into their lapels. Two, who were mechanics, had fingernails so short they were hooded by a drop of skin. One had monkey body hair which stuck out of his cuffs and above his collar. Nevertheless, nails cleaned, sideburns flattened, they were ready for the bar mitzvah.

As the equipment truck pulled into the elm-lined parking lot, the seven Demons and Ishtar arrived in a rented limousine. Children waited for them on the broad steps. Mack and Nino circled around to the organ loft; Ishtar sat in a rear pew and trembled with excitement. She dug her fingernails into her palms. It had been a long time since she had been in a temple. She wore a gown of finely woven white linen and a coat of the same rich cloth. The ark opened. Ishtar bit her lips.

The rabbi and cantor, both exceedingly short, stood on tiptoes to remove the Torah. They stripped it of its silver dress and jewelry and unrolled its two scrolls on the pulpit. Ishtar leaned back in her pew and coughed loudly. The rabbi introduced the quaking bar mitzvah boy and he began, in a faltering manner, his speech.

"Today I stand here. This is where my father stood as a bar mitzvah boy before me and my grandfather stood here before him. Just as the rabbi teaches us, Judaism is a link between father and son. And so today . . ."

"Wait." Ishtar bellowed from the back. "You have forgotten your mother!" As her words rang through the temple and people turned to her, she walked, a majestic bride, down the center aisle. Nino shook his sistrum in the choir room above the altar. Behind her the door opened and the remainder of her band and their friends streamed in, arranging themselves in two lines under the stained glass memorial windows on either side of the hall.

I pass the boy's mother. She recognizes me as a Mah-Jongg partner years before the supermarket change. I watch as she beats upon her husband's chest and her mother beats upon her husband's chest accusing them of inviting strangers. The men attempt to catch the flying wrists. Beverly, the mother, wears a magnificent pin and turquoise watered silk with tiny covered buttons from neck to hem. Her head is absolutely clouded with matching bird of paradise feathers and her face covered with a lustrous pink pearl foundation. Behind me, a flank of ushers is massed at the rear. They are surrounded by the children I have invited. The rabbi and cantor are subdued as is the plan. Mack plays "Go Down, Moses," from above and I, lifting my skirts, step onto the pavilion. From my shopping bag, I withdraw two cans of Three-in-One oil. I anoint the forehead of the holy men and chant quickly. The rabbi's eyes are dreadful. They are predatory fish eyes, thyroidic and clear. They oscillate, involuntarily, in nystagmic horror. "Wait, I would speak," I tell the congregation. There are polite coughs. They respect the richness of my clothes and my inherent manner. Beverly is not impressed. She screams, however, in an impressive high note. Sonny, the trumpeter, sits upon her. She continues to scream from beneath her feathers and the trumpeter's Buddha bulk. Soon her pitch becomes involved with Mack's chords and they are together. The lights gleam on the ringlets of hair on my white back.

"Boy, what is your name?"

"David."

"Is it all right with you, David, if I speak for a few minutes with your congregation? I am the Star of David."

The boy leans on the pulpit. His father calls to him. My own band, formidable and elegant, carrying fold-up croziers, tomp them as bishops. They walk and form a phalanx at the altar.

"David," the father screams as he clutches his heart. "Don't speak to her!"

"Ten minutes, David. We'll play for free . . . no charge for the music."

"Okay." He is in conflict. He does not know what is right. He just saved his father nine hundred dollars.

My band, who collect money, begin to signal me. I ignore them. David raises his eyebrows at his bar mitzvah class in the side aisles.

"David, you are being initiated into manhood today. How exactly will this happen that you will become a man?"

The boy shuffles his feet. I am not pleased. "Speak!" I call loudly. Beverly screams in a different note.

"I, uh, read from the Torah and then I'm blessed and I get a Bible. And of course presents, you know. And . . ."

"How will you know, then, David, when you are a man?"

Politely, his face scarlet, he bends and whispers to me. I nod.

"And when do you expect this to happen?"

He shrugs.

I turn with disdain to Beverly. "Beverly, have you arranged for this? Do you know who and where? Or are you satisfied with an unclean person on the back seat of your Bonneville?" Dear Mack adds subtly to the variations of her response.

"David." I turn to him. "I, the Queen of Heaven, am here to make you a man today."

He rubs his smooth chin. "I mean, couldn't we do it someplace else?"

"No, that won't do. This is a ceremony dedicated to your manhood. It is to be done correctly, properly under the eye of your friends, parents and congregation." Beverly watches the equipment truck setting up mikes and speakers in the parking lot beyond the memorial windows. "Beverly," I call. "Woman is the connection between father and son. She is the connection. You also could be."

She speaks. "I didn't invite you. Or your low-class friends. And you look stupid in your long gown. No one's wearing that length. Rabbi, do something." There is a shaking and rocking of the wonderfully carved high back chair in which the rabbi is imprisoned.

"If there is mayonnaise in your chicken livers, it won't freeze. There will be no bar mitzvah if you continue to stop me. Your liver, your baby orchids, the boiled salmon, the watermelon baskets will all rot." Beverly's head disappears. She is a practical woman.

"Bring me the rabbi." I rub my hands together. The rabbi's face is apoplectically red and pastry-puffed as my two musicians bring him to me and stand him, on his weak bandylegs, before me. With a rubber blackboard pointer from the Sunday School Wing I snap the band of the rabbi's Patek Philippe watch.

"Witch," he hisses. I have heard that before.

One arm behind me, I lunge and shout and lift the hem of his robes. He wears saddle shoes and maroon socks woven with gray clocks. A few children giggle. For their further amusement, I place the rubber tip between the rabbi's eyes and cross them. They laugh. I reward them with a smile. "He leads you to God in golf shoes."

"Crazy woman!" he parries thunderously. "You desecrate my pulpit."

"See, children. Your rabbi wears a dress." I cross my arms over my chest as saltiers. My voice raises in thunder better than the rabbi's. "Give ear, O ye heavens, and I will speak, and hear, O earth, the words of my mouth. I am Ishtar, the Lady of the Book of the Hidden Temple. I am the Lilith of your folk tales and the Queen of Sheba. I am the Ashtoreth that your Solomon, as they say, went up after. Wow. I'm wisdom. I'm the bride in his song. I am the Shekina, the succubus. You name it. I'm it."

"You weren't invited, Ishtar. I didn't invite you." Beverly is weeping. I am sorry.

"Your grandmothers braided their bread for me, the Weaver of Fate. They baked a tiny cake for the Sabbath bride each time. Remember?"

Someone begins to clap. I find a wizened face in a powder blue suit. "My secrets have been churned into the sea and ignited in the rocks but I live still. You, grandfather," I call to a distant liverspotted face. He pauses in his ritual prayer. "Grandfather, do you know why you daven in such a way, rocking on your feet?"

"Always." He answers and continues to rock.

"Your grandfather copulates until his spirit passes into mine. Your ancestors baked cakes in my form to send their children into the arms of my ecstasy. We gave you mushrooms and manna, honey and mead. You have Sara Lee. What does she do for you? Any more than the rabbi? She saves you a little time. I offer you eternity."

I drink from the water glass on the pulpit and pour the remainder over the altar.

"I raise the cake and I raise the penis. To heaven. And this man . . ." I flourish at the rabbi. "He raises your pledges and offers you flat matzohs. Now figure out why that bread was unleavened. It was, when I was denied for a piece of real estate, a sin to raise the bread. Right?"

No one agrees. They only stare. I lift the rabbi to a coathook and he hangs trophied by his cuffs. His twenty-five year diamond cuff links glitter under the eternal light. His little legs dangle among the rich velvet pelts hanging from the walls around him. He wriggles, enmeshing himself further. The ushers attempt a storm. They fail. Mack plays "Go Down, Moses," from above. Nino shakes the sistrum. The rabbi spits and misses me. I point to him and I begin to teach slowly. "His dress is a woman's, in honor of the woman he once served. His hat is that of a baker for it was his role, as priest, to attend the baking of ceremonial bread." I run the pointer, head to toe, prodding ungently. "His body is sheathed also as a penis, his hat, the glans . . . shit, Rabbi, stop wriggling. You become blue. His hat the glans, purple, dyed by the menses of my virgins and his body was anointed with the semen of my devotees and he raised himself upward into the Holy of Holies and entered me, penetrating the vulva of heaven. And no one got in with socks on." I squirt Three-in-One on his forehead and robes. "And his tephillin? Once a shoe, the box of my secret. The sperm was within it, wrapped in parchment with my many names, wrapped in the sinews of the cow. What else then should be a sign between your eyes if not your manhood and its dedication to me? The pelt on the altar: from the Ram, my husband. The fringes on your shawl, from the goat hairs tufted thirteen times on the sacred trees where men dedicated their semen. Right, I gave at the grove. The eternal light is my Star."

"Knock it off, Ishtar, that's enough," Mack calls from above.

"You have denied woman. You have denied time and you live half-lives in terror of death, joyless and lost. Today, here, someone prayed for a gross order of maple rockers."

There is a distant gasp.

"Filth. Witch!" The rabbi has loosened himself slightly.

A hand is raised from the bar mitzvah class. "Does that mean that the, uh, dresses and wigs that the English judges wear . . . is that from you too?"

"Yes, the law was in my house."

"Oh." He is satisfied with the answer. I am pleased with the question. I would like to remain at the pulpit and teach them. I can not. David is restless. Mack is awry and Beverly will not last much longer and she is needed as a witness.

"Okay, my people. We will reopen Paradise. No Moses in between. No astronaut swinging golf clubs, flaming or un, to keep us out. Come. Raise yourselves." The congregation stands at the lifting of my hands. The grandfather, finished praying, waggles his happy fingers at me. "Come. Bring me your torn souls and your broken hearts. Join your mother and join heaven again to earth." I think I am crying. I am very good at dramatic scenes. I pour the remaining Three-in-One oil on the altar and light it with a wooden match. The congregation howls with terror. The fire, naturally, does not consume. "Come," I call over their shouts. "Come sit in my vulva and I will heal thee. Come, David. You will be a man."

Isn't that well spoken? They are not convinced. But they are impressed. I sit on the pavilion carpet below the smoking altar and speak softly to David. I hold him steadily by his thin shoulders with his back to the congregation. His mother has lost all her rhythm. She flaps and contorts beneath Sonny, who seems to be enjoying himself. An elderly aunt from Cleveland gasps for air. I have forgotten much of the original ceremony, but I never lose track of the ultimate. "This is my body, David. A temple for your worship. These are my thighs, David, a Torah for your knowledge. This is my vulva, David, as is the word between the thighs of the Torah: the big secret. You shall know me."

He trembles. I pause as the aunt collapses along the length of a pew and others slide down to accommodate her prostrate bulk. The grandfather waves again in recognition.

You recall the ceremony. "Blessed be thy feet that have brought thee in these holy ways. Blessed be thy knees, which I kiss that shall kneel at the holy altar. Blessed be thy organ of generation, which I kiss without which we would not be. Blessed be thy breast, which I kiss formed in beauty and strength. Blessed be thy lips, which I kiss that shall utter the sacred names."

Droplets, like dew, of perspiration are on David's forehead. His face is pale and he bites his lower lip.

"My thighs are friendly," I assure him. Among other sensory areas, his eyes are engorged with fear. I put his mouth to my breast to quiet him and gently I open his golden Farah slacks, keeping his back to his parents so they can not witness his sweet erection and great discomfiture. The father, I notice, although I am also busy, lunges forward to stop us but he is rather excessively tripped with a crozier. Other croziers jam into the tasseled shoes of the band of ushers. "Disgrace! Abomination!"

"Enjoy," the grandfather adds.

"Molesting a minor," someone with a legal background protests.

I continue, swinging my legs out from the pavilion around David's lithe body and wrapping my hands about his back, much like a honey bear climbing a delicate succulent tree, carefully and hungrily. The grandfather has assumed David's new rhythm. He is with me too. I watch him, holding David as I watch. They sway in long forgotten ecstasies, eyes closed, sputum running lazily from a corner of their mouths. The bar mitzvah class beneath the stained glass memorial windows giggles and sighs alternately. All else is quiet now. Except for the Cleveland aunt and the strangling rabbi, no one in the entire congregation misses a shiver of David's glen plaid jacket and his golden Farah slacks as he looks into the eyes of heaven and, as is a boy's way, dammit, completes his momentary, sudden, initiation. My thighs, although friendly, are abysmally lonely. I touch the damp edge of his prayer shawl on my heel. I drop my skirts elegantly and lead him to the altar now, where the Torah lies ready for him. He places my shoe on the pulpit. Shocked into a profound silence and the inherent respect for the open ark, box, coffin, shoe, holy of holies et cetera, you understand now the relations of these containers, the people are still.

If you don't know the relationships, be assured that electricity is only energy looking for a place to go and I am the place to go and am so represented by the above-mentioned.

"Whore!" They wave their fists at me. They shout to gain courage. My heroes did this.

"Witch!" On ramparts and hills before battle, begging for my strength and power.

Beverly's eyes are schistoid, pure quartz. Her pearly makeup is mica flaked now, dry with rage. The spines of her feathers are cracked. I am sorry for her but she is useless, having sold herself.

"Go now, David, as a man, for you are truly, in the sight of all, a man. Go now and read the Torah to your people. Someday, for your sons, there will be new laws."

"I love you," David tells me quietly. "But you ruined my bar mitzvah."

I laugh at him so that others may not hear. "You are too too practical, David. May you go down in history."

David chants now, opening the deep secrets between the lovely scrolls. His cheeks are flushed and his tongue nervous. He shifts back and forth across his forehead with his free hand and sings over ropy saliva. At his pauses, I curse the dying rabbi. I move to the background ready to slip out unseen. I leave, parting curtains, I whisper further curses to the rabbi.

I am stopped. A boy catches my arm. "Come to my bar mitzvah."

"No, darling," I whisper, terribly anxious to leave before the spell is uncast. "Ask your mother. Who else but a mother?" He smiles crookedly at me. I present him with my other shoe and walk barefoot out the side door after burning my name just once in the blue and gilt dome of the Temple. When the congregation is in the Social Hall eating boiled salmon and picking fruits from watermelon baskets and all the children are dancing in the parking lot, I burn with my furca the doors of the Temple, sealing them and the rabbi forever. The people have already forgotten him. Actually they haven't and there will be a lot of trouble a little later. By itself, truthfully, the electric organ in the organ loft explodes and its pipes, as they burst, plotzing in pleasure, howl maniacally and go sailing, like golden spaceships, through the memorial windows, stained. I see through the broken windows that the doors to the ark are split asunder. That's really a nice touch, a little overdone, though. I go quickly down the sidewalk. I hum "Go Down, Moses." It was a good day. Isn't there anybody around, I ask discreetly, who would like to make me a woman? Above me, a telephone pole crackles, but that is ridiculous. Let my people go, but hold on to me.

I circle around the parking lot and watch for a while from the neighbor's garage. Claire sits in a booth in the parking lot healing a line of old members from the congregation and handing out mimeographed secrets to the young. There are occasional silly shouts of "I'm healed." "It's a miracle." She refuses payment from the grandfather but a musician, watching also, puts out his hand. It is Nino. I do not like him. I am beginning to like Claire. Kind of. She gives everyone slips of cardboard printed with their fortunes. Still, she smiles lasciviously at Mack. I do not like her. Often.

The music is good and I dance, twisting and turning, by myself, behind the garage. I would like someone to dance with.

19

Many moons ago when animals and people married each other, Bear fell in love with a chief's daughter. He pined for her. His heart cried for her. Woodpecker, who wanted to have Bear's teeth on a necklace, saw Bear pining.

"Bear, why do you cry?"

"I love a beautiful maiden. I don't know how to tell her."

Woodpecker stood on one foot on Bear's shoulder. "Give her your tail. She will rub it softly on her cheek or scratch her back with it. She will soon want to rub her cheek on all of you and scratch her back on all of you. And she will love you."

Bear tied his tail to a tree, ran around and around the tree and then ran away from the tree. He cried. The tail wore off. He wrapped it up in fresh tobacco leaves and brought it that night to the tent of the Indian maiden. The Indian maiden was standing under the moon. Bear danced toward her and dropped the tail at her moccasins. She screamed. Her father ran out of the tepee with a shotgun and shot Bear in the shoulder. He screamed. Bear ran back to the forest to Woodpecker.

Woodpecker said, "Oh, Bear. I have made a grave error. She screamed because you frightened her. Did you smile at her?"

"Yes," Bear answered, his head hanging down.

"That's why. That's why." Woodpecker jumped from shoulder to shoulder on Bear's great back. "Those teeth! You frightened her with those teeth. Next time go without your teeth. Smile at her and she will say, 'I love Bear.'"

"Take out my teeth?"

"It will hurt, but think how she will love you."

Bear tied vines to his teeth and Woodpecker bound the vines to sky high branches in his tree. Woodpecker shouted, "Run, Bear, run!"

Bear ran until he had no teeth left in his head. Woodpecker and his wife and his woodpecker children gathered up the teeth.

"Now, Bear, go and dance and smile for the beautiful maiden you love."

Bear, his gums bleeding, ran through the forest to the camp. There he hid in the bushes until the moon rose and the maiden came out of her tepee. Bear smiled, although it hurt, and danced into the enclosure. The maiden screamed. Her father ran out with his shotgun and shot Bear. Bear did not scream. He died. But he heard the maiden say before he died, " 'I love Bear. We will eat Bear tomorrow.' "

Woodpecker and his wife and children strung the teeth on a beautiful necklace for Woodpecker and from that day on Woodpecker was very wise and had many many children.

The moral of the story is: Save your teeth because if everyone in the world has a woodpecker, which I am beginning to suspect, you're going to be glad you kept them.

My son is learning to waterpick from Robert. It is weakening his gums. I do not like this. I must already replace two permanent teeth and I am not quite certain, with the air polluted and the force field out of balance, if I shall be able to do that particular material reproduction. The waterpick also soaks his clothes.

Robert comes in for breakfast. I play with the cats while he prepares his eggs. I am sorry for him. I love him. Truly. I would like to love him. He is miserable and beaten. He eats his eggs without pleasure. "I can't replace them." He speaks to no one. "I can't replace them."

I offer him a steaming platter of blueberry muffins. Thoughtlessly he accepts. He opens one. The butter melts

over the parchment within. He licks it off. The parchment reads Cupcakes. He says nothing. He eats the muffin.
I wait.
"I'm insured. The band's making plenty of money."
My son enters the kitchen. There is blood on his Snoopy sweatshirt. The waterpick is dangerous. Robert reads to both of us from the dentist's publication. He has warned us to care for our teeth. "What I will attempt first is to remove the tartar or calculus within the pocket that has accumulated on the root surface of the tooth. This is called subgingival scaling or therapeutic root planing. As we continue with these weekly sittings of root planing, we will also scrape the lining, the infected lining of the pocket. This is called intra-crevicular curettage." Robert sits at the table, considering the damage to his machines, and cleans his teeth with a round-edged toothpick. My son stares at his movements.
Robert stares at me. I begin to rub my gums obediently.
I destroyed twice last night. Ordinarily, in order to create, I destroy. Of course, in order to destroy, I create. Cyclical. This night I destroyed not only to create but to satisfy a certain vindictiveness. My first act was minor and resulted directly from boredom, sexual frustration and feminine caprice. Robert and I, assuming serious faces and moderate clothing, attended an Independent Parent-Teacher's Organization meeting. It was a long and dull meeting, made duller by the fatuous suggestions offered to raise money for the purchase of a combination washer-dryer needed by the physical education teachers. I deride the title. The children learn nothing of importance physically from them. The parents of this Country Squire crowd suggested bake sales, box lunches (I giggled at this point and Robert pinched my arm), an after school movie, a roller skating party or newspaper collections. I had sat patiently through the foolishness, my arm smarting, tying braids in the prayer shawl Robert had agreed to wear for my amusement under his Harris Tweeds. I, of course, as a baking mother have earned a modicum of success and recogni-

tion at this school. I am known. I have been recognized for my Santa Claus cakes in molds which I decorate with colored sugars and icings. They have, on occasion, unfrosted, resembled the vast serene face of an Olmec god. I fill in his ancient cracks with icing and repair him with toothpicks and carry him to the children on Holy Days. None of the children want to tear the face apart, but then, as the cake sits, beckoning and appetizing on the teacher's precisely laid out desk, they, atavistic, descend upon the god cake and I remember. I deliver gingerbread men that often bear close resemblance to the Kens and Barbies of other households. I deliver these forms as often as I can find an occasion. Another mother, a good Catholic, supplies the Hi-C and the napkins. I was actually offered the position of Grade Mother as a reflection of their gratitude for my fine baking, but graciously reneged, not wishing to limit my effectiveness. In apology, I sent in shirt boxes stacked with raisin-nippled double-breasted hot cross buns without the cross. At any rate, I am respected here and I raise my hand. Others are speaking heatedly.

For his school birthday party, my son receives vulva shaped cupcakes, which I arrange with a heavy imprimatur and a generous filling of Ready Whip. The children are not ready for knowledge yet and Ready Whip lasts up to two weeks in the refrigerator. And my Armenian gorabia, which are shaped interestingly like halfmoons, which of course is an organic form, become, when the children study Greece, koulouria. When they study Italy, I coat the cookies with sesame and when they study Ireland, I coat them with green sugars and when they study Alaska, I coat them with poppy seeds and confectionary sugar. They get them, whatever reason, depending on what they are studying in social studies. There is nothing more social than a vulva shaped cookie. If you think that language is cognate, consider the cookie. I must tell Claire: the Continental Drift Theory and its functional and dysfunctional effect on cookies. Perhaps she'll be interested. I take the stage. They had expected only a question from the floor. I rarely refuse a stage. And I suggest that at one time to raise funds for the building of a wall (I do not mention time or place and make the building of the walls of Ur sound rather like a garden club incident than a time-honored procedure) the ladies of the city removed their bodices . . . I have to stop and explain a bodice . . . and threw them, I continue to the politely attentive parents and teachers and the Fifth Grade Jazz Band, we threw them, checked with a number, into a pile and the men pulled out in exchange for the properly numbered ticket, the bodice, and then, for a sum of money which can be set by the organization, mated with the proprietress of the bodice. The monies earned, I assure them, are considerable and particularly since this type of event is rather innovative and will attract a great many Country Squires and Mercedes-Benzes . . . I see Robert waving his prayer shawl over his head in calf-roping motions. I continue. The faces below me are not entirely visible because of the stage lights. I hear some sharply drawn breathing. To reassure them and show my good faith I unlatch my bodice, slip it through the sleeves of my dress without disrobing, over one elbow and in and then all of it out one cuff, like the magician's pigeon. I toss it over the lights into the audience. They shrink back from it. I do not know why. It is a pretty thing, a Bali bra with a tiny inset ribbon and lace. Actually, they more than shrink; they leap in horror and Robert, somehow, is behind me, pulling me back inside the curtains by the hems of my dress, his prayer shawl about my neck.

My cheek meat blazes red. I will not go there again. Nor will I contribute to the washer-dryer combination fund.

"The Hanging Gardens, the Lion Gate . . . we built the cities with coinage thus collected, Robert," I argue on the way home to his stiffness. It is useless. He remains stiff. Soon, again, he will suggest a marriage counselor.

"I think, Ishtar, you should rest a little. Stay away from the band. Relax."

"Would you like to pause at the drugstore"—I tug with affection on his prayer shawl—"and purchase some contraceptive devices?"

"No, I want you to get plenty of rest."

Perhaps he wishes me dead. I listen that night to the trains coupling beyond my house. At midnight, I burn pure linen parchments over green compelling incense manufactured and distributed by E. Davis, Brooklyn, New York, and repeat my desires simply and fervently seventeen times into the grinding of the machines on their tracks and fervently I pray from a great distance and with great energies, my cheek meat still ablaze, fed by the utter consummation of pure mandragora juice, that the machines in Robert's limited factory mate.

"An enormous crack, like a cake," the foreman tells him in the morning. "And the machines are wrecked. Totaled."

The shell of the building will be soon outfitted for Cupcake production. Prophetic abilities aren't all lucky guesses. There is also something for Claire to think through about ancient knowledge wrapped up in the center of the Chinese cookies. I have also been called Lady Fortune. Claire has much to do. Grace will help.

Robert's teeth are giving him great pain. I offer him Cupcakes to help his teeth. He refuses the Cupcakes. "No," he says to me at the door to the bathroom, where he is waterpicking his gums. "They're bad for my teeth." He is correct. Not only are the Cupcakes bad for his teeth, but soon he will notice a sanitary napkin afloat in the toilet. I have done this monstrous menstrous thing to test him. If he is more alarmed at the danger to the septic tank, then I have not progressed as I wish.

He will begin to shout and the waterpick will wave, wildly spurting its vinegar and warmth around the small room. It is worth the entertainment to wipe up.

There goes the waterpick. Here are the shouts. Ah, he flushes the toilet. I am making progress. His shouts are ugly and deafening. He is particularly alarmed. Isn't that funny? "Ladies don't do things like that," he screams.

"Your idea of a lady and my idea of a lady are years apart," I say with deliberate punctuation. "I am a lady. God knows where you got your definition."

He leaves soon after, having nicked himself numerous times on his smooth cheeks. There are spots of toilet paper on the nicks. Some of them still bleed. His teeth are giving him pain and he is going to have them examined by a tooth surgeon. I prepare dinner, which shall be corn, cookies and crisply fried chicken. "The tank's backing up again in the garage," I hear my cleaning woman calling to me. Robert does not like this woman in his home. She is not his and her commitment to his clean shirts lacks purity.

THOU SHALT LOVE, HONOR, OBEY, FEED, WASH SHIRTS, SQUEEZE BLACKHEADS, CLEAN CLOSETS, PICK UP TOE-NAIL PARINGS, NEVER RUN OUT OF MALLOMARS, DENTAL FLOSS, TOILET PAPER, Q-TIPS OR MATCHED SOCKS.

It is my contract, and I will try harder— Perhaps then he will find in our bed the solution he now is ready to seek with The Marriage Counselor.

20

I am in the attic. I have acquired somehow a spider web. The web wafts from my shoulder to an attic beam. I wear only a perky patchwork apron. I sit on a pile of *Life* magazines with June Allyson on the topmost cover. You have seen the small statue of Isis on a pig, her legs spread as All-Giver, All-Receiver, sidesaddle. It is as I now sit. I have not been here terribly long. Robert and I had a mutual understanding following breakfast this morning. He told me, as I was boiling my son's clothes and shoes, driving out disspiritedness, that I had a messy attic.

Actually, because I do understand Robert so well, so terribly, banally well, I chose this time not to understand him.

"Messy attic," he repeated with gleaming tooth.

"Vision," I added to clarify my position and confuse his. He chose in turn not to understand me. In some ways we are well matched.

"Try climbing the stairs and see. You won't be able to get up."

In the oven my feather pillows, stuck onto the rotisserie were turning heavily, passing at the apogee of their rotation and then dropping, plummeting like twist-neck pigeons to their nadir near the consuming element of the oven only to be caught up again, saved from burning. I have been, in a housewifely effort, reading Heloise. It is she who recommends cooking pillows to regenerate the life of the feathers. It is a curious hint. We did once set children upon hearth fires to give them immortality, but never pillows. Heloise has some astonishing ideas which I shall take with me where and whenever I wander. When my son has chewing gum in his hair, I have learned to rub in a handful of peanut butter and the chewing gum lifts out at once. I have to read further to find out about removing the peanut butter. I have learned to cook, with an ordinary household iron, foil-wrapped cheese sandwiches. I am consummately impressed with the pre-sifted flour Heloise mentions. When my grains needed preparation for the sacramental bread making I would advise a nearby king to send his churls, knaves, captive nations, etc., etc., to thrash and sift the fine grains in return for the friendship of my thighs. It was, in those days, easier to get help. My greatest political error, however, stemmed from my fame as breadmaker, which is actually what the word lady means. "Mother," he called from the marketplace. "I need bread." I ignored him, this upstart. "Please, Mother." A few loaves did not pacify him. He'd been warned not to refer to me as Mother in public, giving away my age and all kinds of things to those rapacious crowds. Simply to shut him up, and annoyed with his begging, I dropped another load of ba-bread. That was the last I heard from him or the rapacious crowds. Not so much as a note.

Meanwhile in the attic. It is Robert's idea that I be here atop the magazines. But it is good for one must always ascend before beginning a major task. For instance, when a newborn is taken from the first room of his/her life, the one who carries him/her must not step down over the threshold but up. Up onto a stool or chair placed before the threshold. Ascend.

Ascend.

So it is well I have climbed these stairs. I hope Robert, who after all has demanded me here, no matter how fortuitous that I be here, remembers to turn off my son's boiling clothes and take the knife out of the center of the kitchen table. The Redball Jets must be fair overdone by now.

Robert attacked my care of the attic because I was boiling the clothes and the Redball Jets and also curing the cat's cataracts by a tried and true method which I have written on a three by five card and mailed to Heloise's publisher in return for her excellent hints. Blue, my wonderful male cat with whom I am in love, is tied to a ladder in the basement, spread-legged. Of newborn feces, cummin seed and my own saliva, I have applied a paste to his poor failing eyes. He will remain on the ladder for three days. At the end of three days his vision will be restored. Do you think Heloise will like this hint? Robert did not. He became upset this morning when he found Blue thusly.

"I have been feeding him," I assured Robert, who had unceremoniously dropped a bag of garbage, spilling coffee grains, egg shells and newborn feces on the basement floor. "For I dearly love my cat, Blue. I have also been feeding the ladder."

"What will people say?"

"They will not know. That is why"—I indicate the large pot of bread sops soaked in milk—"that is why I feed the ladder and the furniture in the immediate vicinity so all will be well and the furniture won't tell tales. I know, darling." I walk close to him, stepping over the debris of the garbage at his feet, attempting to caress him as I speak. "I don't want the neighbors to talk. This sort of thing embarrasses you. No one will know. It is spring and I am making things right, darling."

He jumps back in a nervous tango step, quite precise and graceful. I smooth my perky patchwork apron, not to be disappointed. The marriage counselor assured me that if I accept willingly my housewifely tasks this man will once more, quickly, take me on again as a wife. Make love, in other words.

After sweeping up the debris and refilling the garbage bag, I served up breakfast to Robert on the sunporch since the new and large kitchen knife was struck into the exact center of the kitchen table. Which is prerequisite for boiling clothes. Robert did not eat but sent me to the attic. I am sure he has not turned off the clothes. And the pillows must be well done by now also. I hope he does not forget to turn off the oven. I am prepared to arrange the attic alphabetically. I believe that is a most perfect idea. I need not be around to give directions as to the location of the boots, the old diaper pail or the few relics/antiquities and parchment scrolls I carry with me at all times. Anyone can find anything once an attic is done alphabetically. The Marriage Counselor had suggested I stay at home and care for Robert and work my role as a woman. I asked him politely to define that role at our first and only meeting. He mumbled, this M.C., about staying at home and taking care of things. Certainly, willing, curing the cat's failing eyes and my son's sad disspirit and regenerating the feathers are excellent and housewifely tasks especially when I wear this perky patchwork apron over my naked body. Nevertheless, Robert, totally unimpressed, suggested I clean the attic and I shall. The M.C. seemed quite impressed with me and assured Robert, after expensive consultation, that our minor marital problems could be worked out, at home, together. I had a sense that our definitions of womanhood probably differed in certain aspects but since I had just purchased this wonderful Heloise book I was more than happy to stay at home and doubly hopeful that I would be taken to bed passionately thereafter but I sit here, with my wonderful tasks proceeding in the house below me, ignored, alone and sitting with my friendly and aching thighs on June Allyson's face.

    I admire the M.C. He believes in free choice. I understand from a friend who attends him regularly that he so believes in freedom of choice, when his own wife chose to commit suicide he allowed her this freedom. He, actually, is more interesting than Heloise and it is why from up here I listen attentively as Robert calls him and describes my curing of the cat, feeding of the furniture, boiling of the troubled son's Redball Jets, the rubbing of a pizza cutter across my stomach and my split personality.

"Get dressed, darling," he calls up to me. I roll the spider web and blow it over the beam in safety. I peel June from my thighs and descend. The house smells terribly of burned feathers.

"What's up?" I ask jokingly.

"I think," he says rather abjectly as he leads me to the bedroom, "it would be a good idea to see the Marriage Counselor again."

I look at him seriously now. He does know the law, his law, better than I.

"And did you turn off the oven, Robert?"

His shoulders bow in guilt as we enter the car.

"And did you turn off the clothes?"

"Of course."

"Good."

I am beginning to understand this man even more. He is treacherous in his organizational capacities. The M.C. is smiling as we enter. He will speak with both of us and then alone with me. He is a nice man, small, with a lean face, dark gypsy lean, city sallow. His neck is chicken thin from out of his loose and starched shirt collar. His pants billow and there are no bulges to entertain myself with as he scribbles mysteriously on a yellow legal pad. The thin wrist rubs along the legal sheet like the legs of a calculating fly. I do not like the sound. He looks up, from me to Robert. From Robert to me. There is a carbon sheet under his top sheet. There is a connection somehow with this man and Robert Moses. The connection is on the pad. "I understand, dear, you are having a bad day."

"On the contrary." I remove my Heloise from my shopping

bag and lay it ostentatiously on my lap. "But I do not like the attic."

"Aah." He writes. "Why do you think you don't like the attic?"

"I am willing to please Robert but I can see no sense in straightening up the attic. The suggestion being that cleanliness is next to Godliness. It is not. He has not"—I point to Robert—"even caressed me once. He doesn't wish to be next to me at all. I do not know if boots should go under Army or Navy. There seem to be regulation Air Force boots and Navy boots and I don't know if they are A's or B's and frankly, I can't understand how a clean attic will feed my cunt."

He writes. Robert clears his throat. Both men smooth their socks over their ankles. I wave my Heloise at them. The M.C. follows my movements. He speaks.

"Work is healthy, you know. Especially when you are . . . uh . . . not at peace."

I laugh. I review for him my accomplishments of the day. He is not impressed. I describe for him the roach egg hunt Heloise has planned for Easter. I outline the cleaning of beetles from the shelves and boll weevils from the pre-sifted flour bags. I speak of the primacy of Baker's Chocolate Chip cooky recipe over the Nestle's Tollhouse cooky recipe. I tell him how I care; I tell him about my perky patchwork apron and my lonely thighs and I tell him with tears in my periwinkle eyes that I would sincerely like to be a good housewife if just to get laid. He pulls at his socks. I have offended him, this small listening man.

"Robert." At last he speaks, his writing done once again. "Robert, perhaps you should allow this woman to choose the tasks she wants to do. Give her a sense of her own freedom."

"Hello," I say to him. "Tell me about your wife."

They both begin looking at their watches. "And beef ribs are cheaper than spareribs and make marvelous b.b.q. for twenty-nine cents a pound, which is unheard of in today's supermarket. I am quite pleased to do these tasks and have great joy in them. I was not having a bad day at all. Robert, in his judgment, was having a bad day and when he is wretched and I can not help him, it is best to give him territory. Would either of you like a Cupcake?"

They of the smooth socks have not been listening. They don't care. "Well," Robert says in a sad voice, kissing my cheek lightly, "you sit here and talk all you want. I'm off to work." He kisses my other cheek. Judas.

I reach to hold him but he slips away and I am left with the sweet smell of his aftershave on my fingertips. I love this man. He does not glance over his shoulder. He closes the door quite silently but I hear him checking it to see if it clicked in.

"Actually. M.C., it would help if he made love to me. Can't you talk to him?"

"Yes, that can be very disturbing." He pulls at his socks. "Do you masturbate?"

"No," I answer. "Do you?"

His socks begin to breathe hard. He folds his hands in his lap. I wink at him. He writes. His sleeve rubs. He underlines something and numbers other things. He is outlining me.

"What is this," he asks, "about boiling Redball Jets? What is a Redball Jet?"

I explain it to him.

"And the cat on the ladder?"

"I do not know yet. He has another day to go on the ladder."

"The pillows?"

I offer him the book. He shakes his head no. I offer him a Cupcake. "Eat of this roll. It is sweet. It will give you knowledge."

"Where did you hear about boiling clothes?"

"It's something I've known a long time."

"And the pizza cutter?" he asks, underlining and labeling capital *A*, capital *B*.

"That's a secret. Robert should not have told you my secret."

"Dear . . . we have no secrets between us if I am to help you." He smiles.

"Do you masturbate?"

"No." He is lying. An elastic thread snaps on his sock in sheer frustration.

"From a Chinese acupuncturist." I do not lie. He thinks I do.

"A pizza cutter?"

"You killed your wife with your freedom of choice. Here, please take a Cupcake. It will help. You ought to do something for your socks. It isn't fair to just leave them. Let not the testimony of a woman be admitted on account of the levity and boldness of her sex. Moses. He said that."

"You see"—he puts his hands together in prayer and swivels—"part of this mmm malady is that at times you are perfectly rational."

I kiss his forehead and take my seat again, adding, "And at other times, irrational but always perfectly. Tell me, M.C., what you recommend."

He looks at the ceiling and lectures about being a good wife. I borrow his pencil and legal pad to take notes. He doesn't mention the roles of mother, maiden and harlot. You didn't think he would, did you?

"Tell me now, dear, what you want." I give him back his pad and pencil.

"Well, as you know, aside from the fact I am Robert's wife and the mother of my son and most attractive to other men, I am the Queen of Heaven. You know that, do you not?"

"Uh, no, Robert never mentioned that."

"Yes, public image: Queen of Heaven. Privately, I am other things. What I am doing, M.C., is co-ordinating full and well both my divine and mortal roles as a woman. And I am doing very well at it."

He pushes a button on his cassette. I speak of Erich Neumann, pronouncing the Neu as Noy correctly. I speak pedantically and slowly for the recording. "Some of Neumann is accurate. He acknowledges my pre-existence. Lady of the Beasts, Lady of the Southern Sycamore, Lady of the Plants, etc., etc."

"Do you ever feel you want to harm people?"

"There have been times when it is necessary. You are contemplating my commitment to a psychiatric unit. Perhaps I should harm you." I stand to full glory and kick out the plug on his cassette. He presses an intercom and describes my affliction for an outsider as I roll my tongue, smile at him and stretch out one eye until it reaches my hairline and shrink the other into a Gog slit, terribly. He fumbles for a button. I take his hand. "Would you like a Cupcake. Believe me, it would help."

He shakes his head. I am stepping on his hand.

"Do you like eclipses?" I produce, without fanfare, a total eclipse. He strains to turn on a light. Shaking his head he presses a button kneewise beneath his desk. I have seen enough movies to understand his action. I offer him a view of my feathers. "Do you like feathers?" I ask.

"Put down your skirt."

"Do you like feathers? Do you like my eclipse? You're so negative." He is very negative.

"Yes. I like feathers. Please put down your skirt." His face is ashen now.

"Shall I boil your socks and shoes? It will help you." I drop my skirt. He hands me his socks and shoes. His socks are damp. I receive his garters, his belt, his shirt. I stop him at his wristwatch and prepare a neat bundle (that was I in my son's tomb wrapping the clothes), bless him and leave, pausing, however, to display once again my feathery finery to the receptionist and an unhappily married couple in the waiting room.

I think maybe it's time to start packing.

21

"Lady, we gotta put you under arrest."
"The charges, sirs?" Ishtar asked politely.
"Indecent exposure?" the policeman answered, shrugging his shoulders.
Ishtar watched the flight of a pigeon above her head and walked, following the arresting officer, toward a patrol car. It would be unfitting, she felt, if this were indeed a final scene, to walk in humiliation or even in humility, which was hardly her style, whining that her father had forsaken her. As others had done. They had cried for their fathers because they knew full well it was their mother leading them to their ends, usually irrevocably and with justification. The men at the golden oak booking desk asked Ishtar if she wished to call her lawyer and her husband.
"They are the same."
"Is your husband a lawyer?"
"In the strictest sense."
"Don't book her yet. Wait until he shows," the arresting officer advised a clerk who seemed to be fascinated by Ishtar's hem. The police were exceedingly embarrassed. She had wished them to be impressed.
"I'll stay. Really. Please write my name, Ishtar, Queen of Heaven, in the book. The charges, bail and all that. As I have seen it on television."
She had hoped also for something if not dramatic at least melodramatic, something cruel and heartless that would

make for good text and legend when the police records would be demanded by the populace and would be iconized in small golden houses to be carried into whatever wilderness was left.

"No, we'll wait for your husband. We'd rather he took the responsibility."

Ishtar grew powerfully angry and twisted the knob from a golden oak chair, until, unable to remain still, she stood on the chair and addressed the startled group, arms raised above her head to the large fan on the ceiling. "I, even I, Queen of Heaven, take the responsibility for the bursting of the factory, for the disorganization of your schools, for the death of a rabbi, hanging quite strangled in his cloakroom, for the organ at the Temple, which has burst its pipes and caused considerable damage, for the radical activities within your churches, for the ecstatic states of your children. All of it. Furthermore, my own husband, Robert, has grown impotent from fear of my power. That also, which I regret, I have done."

"Lady, is this a confession? Come down. Do you want this to be a confession?" The clerk lifted his pen.

Ishtar beat upon her chest. "I confess to no one. It is truth I speak." They shifted on their feet. "I am responsible. I would like a record made at what time I came in and at what time I went out. I want it on your blotter."

"You're not responsible for anything you say unless your lawyer is here," the arresting officer advised her, his teeth grinding behind his cheek meat. Something shorted in the electric overhead fans, which began to whine fearfully from their stations in the ceiling.

"I, even I, Queen of Heaven, am responsible. Utterly. You do not believe me." Angry amber tears coursed over her cheeks. "You do not believe me. Here, I will show you."

It was just as Robert pushed open the double doors, his rep tie sailing behind him in the wind and behind that a small friend-of-the-family judge, that Ishtar lifted her skirts and, howling, displayed her feathers. But the men had looked away at the doors and the clerk hid his face and she went unnoticed. She stomped her foot in the chair and aimed two golden acorn knobs through a windowpane. It shattered convincingly.

"Are you all right, baby?" Robert, his hands shaking to his shoulders, questioned her, and gently, albeit palsied, guided her to sit. She allowed him to guide her.

"I'm well. I have done all of these things. Do not call me baby."

The night before, when the starter broke on her small car, Ishtar had attempted to push it with Robert's many horsed station wagon and had shattered the rear end of the small car twice, while Robert, his face incredibly contorted in the rearview mirror, held the wheel of the small car. They had not succeeded in starting the small car, although Robert had succeeded in sitting quite still as she drove the large car into the small car many times. They argued on the road about Ishtar's incredible mechanical incompetence. He knew her as incapable. But she could see in his eyes, in the courthouse, above the neatly striped tie, the gray flecks of his supernatural rising toward the centers of his sharp black pupils. He blinked. Between his blinks she saw everything of his nightmares and visions that he remembered from high school *Macbeth* and he removed his glasses to cleanse the lenses on a navy blue handkerchief which was torn. Ishtar dismissed the touch of guilt she felt for the torn handkerchief. She was pleased, however, with the disintegration of his rationality.

"I'm a notary public." Robert turned to the judge, seated now before the golden oak desk. "If that helps."

"If you take her home in your custody, we won't have to take further action tonight."

"Robert, I wish them to write my name in the book. When I came in and when I went out."

"In the morning," the judge murmured. "Women, Robert, often want to take the responsibility for major events. They come in here and confess to every murder, fire, theft. Even suicides. I've had three women at once confessing to the same suicide. Your good wife wishes to confess to many things. Her charge is indecent exposure. She may have been suffering from a temporary instability. Come here, dear." The family friend judge addressed Ishtar.

"I chose to expose myself." Ishtar fought the petulancy in her voice. She was frightened that she would, in some grotesque turn of justice, be saved.

And denied.

She stood before the small judge, passing her hands over his head and withdrawing a sack full of ashes and three large acorns. "We'll get this straightened out. As soon as the excitement dies down." He leaned across his desk to pat her head. "I've known your husband since he was a boy." She sprayed Easy-Off into the eyes of the judge.

Ishtar spat the three acorns, one after the other, at his shining forehead and, squinting at him, laughed low, deeply and crookedly within herself. The judge gestured for a cloth for his eyes. To the arresting officer, Ishtar solemnly, as Robert led her out, awarded the screws from the fans, the large oak chair and a particularly manic grin. Claire stood outside with a zoom lens camera, photographing the event. Ishtar threw her a kiss and an acorn. Behind her the fans were blowing ashes into the courthouse, filling the rooms and covering the faces of the people. There would be no Youth for Christ this time to clean up after this exposure, which, although not indecent, was real.

Snow covered Robert's lenses. Ishtar and he walked toward the car. He wiped his lenses with trembling hands. They did not speak to each other in the car. Ishtar nodded her head to the beat of the windshield wipers. Robert's eyes were totally gray now, the flecks floating to the surface as he blinked. Along the highway, the fields were covered thinly with snow and the late afternoon sun, in pale streaks, lay across the snow. Ishtar asked to stop at Carrol's for her son's dinner. They stopped.

"I don't think you're crazy, honey." Robert returned with the red and white striped bags. The red light of an approaching snowplow flashed on his sugarcube false front tooth. Ishtar did not speak. She was considering the giving of the breath of life to cars.

"But the lawyers, bail bonds, psychiatric examinations. Do you know what this means, honey, what it's going to cost me?"

"When the back seat breathes heavily, Robert, the windshield wiper is having an orgasm. When good food turns you on, turn into Carrol's."

"Can't you take anything seriously?"

"Oh, yes." She touched his sleeve. "People who can't take jokes."

"This isn't a joke, Ishtar. You have a child to consider."

"Robert, it will cost me something too, won't it?"

"I'm sorry, baby, I didn't think of that just now."

"Perhaps, Robert, you are mad. Perhaps you are crazy. Listen to the back seat."

"No one in their right mind would do what you did, Ishtar."

"Then I did it?"

He didn't answer her. She traced dot to dot the freckles on his trembling hands.

"Come now, Robert. Did I do it?" His flesh danced under her touch.

"I guess . . . I guess so."

Ishtar leaned over and kissed his damp cheek. "Thank you, Robert. Thank you." She began to hum, murmuring. "Out of the East I come, unsparing of fang and sharp of tooth. Out of the dark behind the moon and I see my lover on the Argive plain and I bare my breast, exposing my thigh and I greet him . . . and I greet him. Aaah, stop here!" The brakes of the rosewood metal Plymouth station wagon screeched at the road's shoulder. And, as Robert expected her to, from all the terror of his childhood and his Halloweens, Ishtar jumped, laughing fantastically, as closely as she could enacting the Wicked Witch of the West. She flung her arms up against the graying sky. "I did it, Robert/Moses. I, even I, did it! Recognize all of me!" Then she dropped her voice, shoved the red and white striped bags across the car and whispered: "Feed the boy. The cats get their wormings on Tuesday at four-thirty." And she raced across the fields. Robert pulled away into the traffic without waiting. Without looking behind him.

22

Covertly, from my coffin as I lie in my living room, I watch Robert. On the day of my funeral he is reading the morning newspaper. Claire's cello and stand are in position near the piano. She will play later.

Too long or long enough I had lain in the snow in the field by the Thruway just beneath the Crowley Cottage Cheese Light as a Breeze billboard and the Volkswagen We Grow Better with Age sign and was discovered by Robert, along with the usual winter's morning bag of split cats and flattened raccoons, with a fine dusting of snow over my body, quite at peace, a tiny smirk across my lips. My obituary reads that I have died of overexposure and I consider their choice of terms amusing although I am grateful that they included my recipes in the column.

I have at last solved this problem of exposure. It may be, much later when everyone understands and the bobby pins in my underwear drawer become relics, that I have done a number on a Mao-Lenin-Marxist religious quasi-metaphysical something or other. I am quite inept at these definitions. But taken in the light of the twentieth century and its great revolutionary tics, I have distributed my divine wealth in such a way that all people have the secrets. No priests, rabbis, pastors in between us. No teachers, lawyers, policemen with their secret sets of rules. The people will have seen enough of me to believe in themselves and recognize their own divinity and, of course, each other's. What passes from one person to another person is divine, if only the principle that afforded the passage is recognized. Robert has already come to suspect that I am multiple. Anyone now can bake my Twinkies. Anyone can bake my Cupcakes. As above, below. Nothing says loving like something in the oven, right? All things will rise in joy and the heavens too will be joyous. I am quite certain that things will be better for all of us once I have been recognized and I am looking forward to a nice juicy retirement. I am regretful that I leave still hungry. Men who hold me sacred are frightened to hold me but I am so available. I am God and I am Woman and so are all of you. I *was* available. My juices have been taken, quite temporarily, but definitively, and I must wait.

Robert, of course, is functioning perfectly. Although he does not now and never will have an understanding of death, I appreciate today his great capacity to face my death with his usual blind power. I sense that he is truly relieved. I was a little much. I have always been. I have always been a source of inestimable confusion, growing composite as I have. He reads the morning paper, waiting for the baked goods and the extra folding chairs to be delivered. The chairs arrive and I watch him lining them up in precise rows, so that the old gold printing PROPERTY OF APPLEBAUM'S FUNERAL HOME, BEECH STREET, SYRACUSE, NEW YORK, is in perfect alignment with my rosewood fireplace wall. I do not admire the carnations filling the corners of the room. I want roses. Robert's body moves in graceful bends and dips. I see his pants stretching over his lovely rear end and I wish he were less ethical and had learned from the Egyptians not only monotheism but the beauty of necrophilia.

Hungry.

As usual he closes his eyes to my hunger, which for some reason has always threatened him. Recently though he has been peeking at his own supernatural. This is not easy but it is a beginning. I am not asking him to be totally irrational.

The world needs people to plug things in, but I am asking him to understand his own multiplicity. Perhaps, I consider, he could bring me back to life. That would give him something to write home about. I could do the choke on the apple and kiss me bit and wake up. Watching his back and strong hands, I consider masturbating here but it would be really dreadful at the moment to heave and be seen. Muscle spasms? No, it is really in bad taste. And I do not wish to be accused of bad taste. Did I remember to tell you that Snow White's glass coffin and the tephillin are directly connected in meaning? That girls who carry dolls are the inheritors of women who carried my sacred image?

The boxes of schnecken arrive, dripping with honey. The community, suspecting my death a suicide, may not turn up in great number and Robert has ordered too many Schnecken. I would have preferred Hostess goods, of course, but production has not quite begun. Soon, if I have done well, Robert will think of nothing but the supply and demand of baked goods. Glory. Under my coffin dress . . . a cheap Celanese construction purchased for the occasion after a discussion Robert conducted with a telephone order clerk, convincing himself that I'll only wear it once and it doesn't have to last so he needn't spend much money on it . . . under this rag I hide a zebra black striped notebook with matching pen. I shall record names and remarks. My friends are terrified and ecstatic and better dressed than I am in their Anne Klein outfits. I can not forgive Robert for this. My friends have prepared, in their ecstasy over my end, great mounds of tuna and chicken salad pyred in Lucite and silver bowls with matching servers. Betty's chicken salad, as usual, has the capers and Eileen's the green grapes. Someone has used Empress Tuna, waterpacked, and disguised it as chicken. I know because Blue is busy at the Jensen bowl it came in and Blue isn't allowed to eat chickens because of the eggs. I am leaving Blue, although I love him. Someone has been going through my jewelry, which I consider fairly poor taste also, but I have stuck her in the palms with pins, from this, my distance, and she has stopped her rifling. I have already slipped away my son's Teddy Roosevelt pin and the two teeth here in my coffin. The teeth are warm against my cold. I heard my closest friend whispering to Robert last night that she would like to straighten my underwear drawer before anyone goes through my things. I appreciate that sort of consideration.

Robert, however, and wisely, denied her that privilege. Assuredly my Robert has come a long way. For there is chaos in my underwear drawer. Even chaos, you understand, is predetermined. If in the future, the heavens resemble my underwear drawer, you will understand it is my wish. Absurdity is also a pattern. As above, below. In your terms, my underwear drawer is a projection of my unconscious. Recognize it. My underwear drawer recapitulates astronomy and all the stops in between, including phylogeny, ontology, psychology, aging and . . . Claire will explain it to you in time.

> "You must have Chaos within you
> to give birth to a dancing star."
> Nietzsche

She enters now. She is arrayed in a dress of mine. She is clean. Her hair is electric with brushing. She nods gracefully at Robert. She sits in an Applebaum's chair, spreads her legs and enfolds her cello. She plays my "Lamentation to a Raised Penis." It is fine and, in its minor key, touching. Her hiking boots stick out from under my dress. She is sure of herself. I love her. Kind of. She has obviously been laid. Well.

I am thankful in a small way that Robert did not read the financial columns first. As I watched him he turned to the obituaries. He becomes more valuable and respected by the length of my obituary. I am a front page in the *Pennysaver*, a back page in the *Times* and a full quarter page in the *Herald Journal*. My recipes are included. One is for veal cutlet dipped in applesauce, the other for spruce beer of pears and mandrake root. The veal recipe is just a ploy. You know of course how I split *my* dividend. For I have given the secret away and the children shall use it and, with Grace's direction and Robert's productivity and business sense and Mack's love of music and Claire's sense of cosmic rhythm, all will share in my supernatural. As I have become more mortal this time around, you guys have become more divine.

But poor Robert. He is too deeply programmed and he will not be able to play. I am ready to play. Actually we all are. But he can not stop working and that is why he can not come with me. He will be lonely in his desert now but much respected. However, he will not be able to pull off any tricks as he has done before. The people have been re-minded and they know that I, rather than granting him an audience from my lapis lazuli throne or my bed of ferns along the unnamed riverbank in Sinai, I have left him at the cottage cheese sign. Unchosen. I have called him by his name, Moses, and I have left him. I will not always be at his right hand. Grace will though. And she will cook sauces for him.

And Mack, dearest beautiful Mack, comes in, elegantly suited. He kisses Claire on the forehead before Grace, and you know what that means. His new manhood is very very special and the beginning of new things for many people. He has, in the words of one of his songs, looked at things from both sides now, in a Jungian balance, and he will find himself quite a Pied Piper. You wonder why I do not take him with me? I have seen him staring at his own eyes in his poster and listening to his own sound on the radio and I know, we can not share, easily, our destinies. I do not wish to fight. I wish to play. Claire plays circus music. She understands. I must compose myself. I feel deeply for Mack.

I am composed. I am composite. I have gotten it all together.

Grace is wringing her hands. Her eyes are red and sincerely swollen. She has brought with her boxes, shoeboxes, which of course is the original shape and meaning of coffins and the Old Woman in the Shoe (my picture is perfectly painted on the inside of Egyptian coffins), of cannoli, which I know are filled with chocolate cream. She puts one in the coffin. Mack is behind her. He brings in more shoeboxes and I consider asking my son to slip another cake, without ostentation, into my coffin. One for each hand. But it is too dangerous. None of my sons has ever been terribly good at secrets, either keeping them or telling them properly. They have always claimed credit for themselves as the originators of my secrets. No man who would actually be chauvinistic enough to try this again, would brag of his own secret recipes. It is a perfect cross trump. Grace is weeping on Robert's shoulder.

"I don't believe it. I can't believe it. She was so young, so strong. But there she is. I don't believe it. Like a daughter to me."

As usual, Grace's intuition carries her far beyond ordinary knowledge. She shall have fine judgment running things. "I just can't believe it. Look, Mack, isn't she beautiful?" My face is a study in piety and composure.

I can not see Mack's face without moving; I am sorely tempted. By the scent of his hair spray, I know him. I feel Mack touching my cheeks with his fingers and then kissing my forehead. I sigh as softly as if we were making love. "Mack." I touch his fingers with my tongue. He swallows noisily. "A little farther down." His hands tremble over my face again and I bite into his fingertips. I hear him dragging a chair near the coffin. He will sit near me and I am grateful.

Everyone else of course believes I am dead. The others come in, my band, in expensive suits and flowering ties. Everyone sits stiffly in the Applebaum chairs. My Jewish Junior League friends turn casually and whisper hungrily about the men in my band. I have told them my men are demons. They interpret me according to their needs. Under closed eyelids, I feel Nino arranging the two soft curls on my cheeks and because I feel his elbow heavily on my breast, in total disrespect, and because I have reason to terrify him, I wink. A curl drops. He coughs phlegmy and leaves the coffin's side quickly. He leaves in the direction of the kitchen's bathroom.

Now my son leans in, almond scented, chocolate breathed. He takes my cannoli. "I can't find my toothbrush."

"I'm dead," I hiss. "Scram."

"But I can't find . . ."

Relatives and friends are arriving and signing in. Robert is hanging coats, greeting his family, passing bowls of chocolates. I hear hangers scraping.

"Mommy . . ."

"Kitchen cupboard. Go away from me. I'm dead. And give me back my cannoli."

"I ate it . . ."

"Beast."

Someone spills a drink on the tufted arm of my suede sofa and I move as if to rise, but remember. I would like to hold Mack from his trembling. My son is being held and caressed while people whisper around him in great stage whispers: "Poor baby. Poor orphan." He answers in singsong. "She's not really dead. She's not really dead. She's faking." He pokes me to be funny. I am not amused. I know their eyebrows are raised knowledgeably and mawkishly while he continues his singing. I am prepared to strangle him and almost manage to pinch his buttock as he leans in again to complain about the toothbrush. But someone else leans in and kisses me wet and soggily. Unpleasantly. Near me, a familiar voice condemns me: "See what happens to kids when their mothers are such intellectual superiors. He's sick. She couldn't stay home and give him a normal life."

"I can't find the toothbrush. Someone's throwing up in

my bathroom. I don't have enough socks. I want to call Danny. How many pieces of chocolate can I have more? Can't I call Danny and say good-by?"

"Jesus Christ, bug off. Tell them I'm really dead. I'm dead. Look in your sock drawer for your toothbrush."

"She's really dead," I hear him shouting gaily. "She's really dead." His voice trails off as it often does when Robert approaches him.

"Buddy." Robert pulls him out of my hearing. If I do not take the boy away now the balance of his childhood will be spent, without necessity, in analysis. At present, I wish that and more on him for messing up my secrets. Big mouth. Like the rest of them. Any kid with balls like that won't pull any more teeth out.

Robert is above me, whispering furtively. A strange level voice answers him. Figuratively, I hold my breath. "What factories?" Robert asks.

"She has four factories. I have the deeds." Oh, the lawyer. "They're supposed to go to Mack." His voice becomes sanctimonious. "It's what's coming up . . . cupcakes. According to Kiplinger and Dun & Bradstreet, big trend."

"Cupcakes are going big. You got to watch trends. If we act fast, I can destroy the note giving the factories to Mack."

"I don't think I want to give up polyesters."

There is silence above me.

"Think you'll get caught destroying the note?"

I am tense. Robert is about to break a law. I hear him sigh deeply. "Cupcakes." And I know I have changed his destiny.

It wasn't until the first shovelful of soil was thrown on her grave in the crisp winter afternoon that Ishtar made her move. She grabbed the ankle of the funeral director, who, although he had gone through elementary and high school with Robert, had also seen, in an unwarranted fashion, her feathers, and pulled him into her grave, lifting herself out while the attendants and workmen and the funeral party, frozen in terror, watched. With the purple velvet lining she had been very busily tearing from under the brass studs of the coffin she covered her shoulders, threw the Celanese dress at her husband's Hush Puppies, grabbed her son and fled. The boy clutched a toothbrush in his mitten.

Robert stood upright. Behind him the people dropped to their knees mudstaining their Anne Klein's and Barney's, astonished. From the brave way Robert stood, Ishtar knew he had expected her flight. It mattered not whether she rose to heaven or climbed into the Silver Cloud waiting for her. He knew, composite, she was able to take either direction. He had at least recognized her wholeness.

Robert began, 'n his long-legged lope, to follow her, calling, "Please, Ishtar, leave me our son." His voice crackled. She could hear his fear. Ishtar paused momentarily and flung the two teeth before him. A pink granite wall rose from the ground, stopping him.

"No," she howled. "No more of that shit. I give them a few secrets, these sons, and they mess it up. They are bad hash. It is Mother you should eat. Mother! Go, thee, and make Cupcakes."

"I'll miss you," he pleaded from behind the wall, which was rising steadily now. Ishtar caught a sob in her own throat.

"Wait here," she told her son, and skipped back to the wall. "Robert, it was very nice." She managed to kiss his forehead just as the wall rose, groaning, another inch, and then he couldn't see her tears. She passed a handful of amber tears, still soft like Jujubes, over the wall to him. "Darling, go home and mess up your underwear drawer. Think of me. I destroy," she called over the wall. "I destroy so I can love. I love so I can destroy." She felt much gentler, this Time, about it. It had been a good trip.

23

I watch, unseen. At my new Hostess Bakery in Canada, unlimited, the new conveyor belt runs smoothly into the new decoration room. Robert has outdone himself in designing the equipment. Regularly, a machine squiggles my spiral on the Cupcakes, in white, in soft sugar, on the chocolate frosting and plants my star on the Twinkies, in white, in soft sugar, on their bare yellow lengths, unfrosted. Grace has sensibly eliminated production of Suzy Q's and the breads along with other splinter products. The demand for the Cupcakes and Twinkies already is tremendous. The cakes are now wrapped with proper prayers, appropriate incantation and minimum daily requirements for the balancing and fulfilling of sexual roles. Each month the wrappers, which are becoming collectors' items, feature the words to the Demon's newest recording. Their songs of course are as popular as the cakes. There is also enclosed in the biodegradable packages a nice Reuben Donnelley coupon drawing for a trip to Paradise, which I shall soon restore. Actually if enough winners come to expect the restoration, I will then not be able to succumb to laziness and shall get busy planting trees and flowers. That is at least a year away and I'm currently dragging my feet, as the expression goes, until a proper partner comes along. Robert has hit a minor snag in his production also. He has been working on the blueprints of a solid state Easter bunny placement machine. I can not help him, knowing, even after all of this mortality, very little about solid states. And since at Easter, Hostess Bakeries places a white bunny, hard sugar, on each of the Cupcakes and Twinkies, Robert has taken over the Sisyphean task and works by hand.

He is in the decoration room. He wears a pure white linen three button roll suit, Puma sneakers with cobalt blue stripes and a sprig of pussywillow in his lapel. He looks wonderful. I am certain the pussywillow came from Grace. He stands at the conveyor belt. He is surrounded by huge vats of hard sugar bunnies. Grace has fortuitously remembered to note on the Easter labels that pregnant women should not eat the bunnies because of the danger of harelip children. Grace is particularly wise in these things. Robert often eats at her house before coming home.

I am sorry for Robert. His big shoulders are bent in concentration. He works very fast but anxiously. With the thumb and forefinger of his right hand he lifts a hard sugar bunny from the vat, drops it on a passing cake and with his forefinger pushes the bunny into the cake. The sound his fingers make is a heartbeat, tense and overdrawn. The lifting of the bunny with the two fingers produces a light sound, a che; and the pushing of the bunny produces a heavy sound, a chum. Che chum, che chum. But his hands shake and the heartbeat is uneven.

His difficulty is learning to adjust his actions to the tides of other objects. It is not an easy lesson for a Mosaic character who wrestled with the universe for his existences. The conveyor belt is unrelenting. The cakes never stop. He drops a bunny on the floor.

He looks upward in fear. The conveyor belt moves, unbunnied, beyond him. A clanging alarm fills the room and the red emergency lights blink above him. This red alert also is his own design. The conveyor belt grinds and is still. All machinery ceases. He scurries in his Pumas ahead placing the hard sugar bunnies on the unbunnied cakes. He works to the blinking of the red lights, which serve to re-establish the correct rhythm. At last, the Cupcakes are so fecundated and he signals Grace, in the tower above him, to turn off the lights and the terrible clanging of the bell. He bends to his work again, positioning himself by the barrels, legs spread solidly for balance on the concrete floor. He is more rhythmical now. Grace beats lightly a ruler against the Plexiglas window of her supervisor tower. Soon he will learn this rhythm and build it into a new and wonderful machine. That is his capability. He will build new factories and soaring warehouses with loading docks like suckling wolf mothers. In the meantime, there is a loveliness about his personal fecundation of the cakes. Grace will check on the quality of course. The creme, with my sufficient recipes, will be living and perfect, and because it contains the stuff of life, no matter what machine is put to its task, the creme will work its way in perpetuity.

I am satisfied. He is not, my ex-Chairman of Parks and Paradise, but then he has had his Time.

24

His young trees were laid haphazardly in a small gray metal rowboat. The rowboat was tied up among the bulrushes of the canal. The trees had balloon bags of earth at their bottoms. His shoulders were narrow, long and lean in the mudspattered yellow slicker, and his feet, in green rubber pack boots, were covered with gray-white mud. Ishtar stood above him on the berm as he patted and kneaded the rich earth gently around the new trees. She touched the long layers of his fine hair. His head was delicate, much like a bronze now in a cathedral somewhere that had been cast of another favorite of hers, kingly. His ears were pearly and beautiful. Shafts of the winter sun played in the pupils of his wise brown eyes, and bits of dead Queen Anne's lace and bluebells were twisted into each of the buttonholes of his army shirt under his slicker. Ishtar wiped dirt from the oilcloth on his chest and smudged it on her forehead as a sign between her eyes. She watched the muscles of his neck. She watched the muscles of his back working down into the soil. Unbidden, her son helped him by shoveling small piles of chips over the new beds.

When the final tree was planted and the little rowboat was emptied, he stood, stretching his tired knees, and licked his lips. One corner of his mouth twitched and he put a fist up against his mouth, covering the twitch, the smile and his excitement. His eyes were deep and soft. He lifted his arm above his head and pointed down at her with one finger, twice, two little questioning woodpecker taps in the air near her as if testing the wealth under her bark. Twice he pointed at her, a fist still over his mouth. "Do you . . . ?" His eyes were dancing and Ishtar smiled, waiting. "Do you . . . bake?" And he snorted happily at his own question.

"Once, but now I have taught others. I have learned this time to prepare cabbage soup. And have you always worn bluebells in your buttonholes?"

He rocked against an elm tree, holding his fist over his mouth again, while laughter escaped from his eyes. Then he held his hand over his head and pointed twice at her in question and then pointed at himself. Before Ishtar could answer, he leaped up away from his elm, fist off his mouth, and grinned a circus grin at her. "I . . ." He pointed to his chest twice. "I direct traffic around here."

Ishtar clapped her hands. Alone on the stone weir across the abandoned canal, he lifted his yellow slicker arms, elbows straight out, and directed a flow of lengthy safaris, circus parades, Akkadian armies, halting them, leading them forward, allowing them to pass, motioning them to turn aside, bowing to kings and queens and caravans, patting children on the head and camels on the thigh, growing impatient at muddling elephants and angry mules, pleased with the snappy Egyptian barges and salt-laden scows moving regularly and professionally down the canal, and at last, when all the traffic had passed and the canal was abandoned once more, he put his fist against his lips. His eyes danced and he rocked against the elm and watched Ishtar. He finally removed his fist. "Do you . . . ?" And dipped his head, watching her now from beneath his brow. "Do you like my canal?"

Ishtar smiled and waited.

"On cold days you can see to the bottom. When there is ice you can skip stones across it. And there are milkweed pods filled with silk at every turn and wild Concord grapes." He hid his happiness behind his fist again and waited.

Ishtar nodded slowly. "I like your canal."

Then he turned, and scraped one foot behind him in the earth, tapped the air with his two little short taps, then tapped the air near her son, pointing at them both, unmistakably. He swung around before her, spreading both arms in the air. "Is anyone . . . ?" He put his fist against his mouth again. His eyes were filled with laughter. Ishtar noticed his delicate ankles. "Is anyone," he whispered, "waiting for you?" He hid his head against the elm tree and counted to one hundred.

"No," Ishtar answered truthfully. "No one is waiting for me. My job is done. I have given away my very last secret." She showed him her empty hands. "Fresh out."

Then he faced her, thinking, she knew, of treasures in caves and secrets he had left behind the moon, his fist at his mouth, his eyes straining, squinting. She watched the fist move away and toward his lips. His head was bowed solemnly.

"Ah!" He threw both hands high in the air, like a wizard. Ishtar jumped back. The boy hid behind her purple cloak. "I have a new secret for you." He held her elbow lightly. "I have a collection of perfect third year virgin molars. Wisdom teeth."

She climbed, Ishtar, Queen of Heaven, she climbed into the rowboat pulling a milkweed pod apart and trailing the feathery silken seeds along the canal waters. Her son, just as he had learned at Woodcrafters' Camp, pulled at the oars while his mother, the Queen of Heaven, the Mother Goddess, after all, gently removed the fist from her friend's beautiful lips. They kissed for a long time.

And disappeared into the sunset.
And disappeared into the morning.
And disappeared into the night.
And didn't disappear at all.
Check one.

247